BOUND BY LOVE

THE ALLIANCE SERIES BOOK 10

BRENDA K DAVIES

Copyright © 2022 Brenda K. Davies
All rights reserved.

Warning: All rights reserved. The unauthorized reproduction or distribution of this copyrighted work, in whole or part, in any form by any electronic, mechanical, or other means, is illegal and forbidden, without the written permission of the author.

This is a work of fiction. Characters, settings, names, and occurrences are a product of the author's imagination and bear no resemblance to any actual person, living or dead, places or settings, and/or occurrences. Any incidences of resemblance are purely coincidental.

CHAPTER ONE

Knowing he couldn't ignore what he'd seen, and needing answers to the fire he'd glimpsed burning the world, Saber strode over to the bed. Unlike his sister, he didn't get visions of the future, but he was sure he'd just received one.

Saber lifted Caro's phone from the nightstand. He'd left his burner phone in the room she'd given him before going to hunt for the night.

He probably should have called Ronan after he killed the demon in the storm drain, but he'd been too focused on feeding, healing, and trying to get Caro out of his system to think about the Alliance. It was time to remedy that.

He would have called Brie directly for answers, but didn't know her number. Unable to talk to his sister, he punched in Ronan's number.

The only other number he had for someone in the Alliance was Declan's, and he'd never called it before. Part of keeping his distance from others was making sure he had as little contact with them as possible.

Ronan was different. He was the king of vampires and the

only one who knew the truth about Saber's history... before Brie returned to his life.

Now, he was the only one Saber trusted enough to reach out to about this, especially since he had Caro to protect now. He glanced back at where his mate remained sleeping soundly on her bed.

My mate.

His intense attraction to her should have alerted him to what was happening, but he'd never seen it coming. There was no changing it either; they'd bound their lives irrevocably together, and he wouldn't let anything happen to her.

He returned to the glass doors as the phone rang three times before Ronan answered with a gruff, "Hello."

Saber didn't think about the fact he might have woken Ronan. Every member of the Alliance was accustomed to not getting a lot of sleep.

Besides, if he had to be awake, so did everyone else involved in this shit. He needed all the help he could get to protect Caro, find answers, and kill the monsters seeking to destroy the world.

"It's Saber."

"New phone?"

"One of convenience."

"Got it."

"I have to talk to Brie, but I don't have her number. Do you know it or where she is?"

He heard movement coming through the line, but it didn't sound like Ronan was getting out of bed. Instead, he must be outside as stones crunched beneath boots, and the wind whistled across the phone while he moved.

"I know where she is. We've had an interesting development here," Ronan said.

Saber's hand tightened on the phone. Had *they* seen the world burning too? But before he could ask, Ronan continued speaking.

"Elena's back."

It took a few seconds for his words to fully register. When they did, Saber studied the night to ensure the world wasn't burning again before replying. "What do you mean she's back?"

"She's back to her old self again. It's one of the strangest, most amazing things I've ever seen. We have no idea what happened or *how*, but one minute she was one of those things, and the next, she was vomiting black bile all over her cage. And now, she's her old self again, except exhausted and weaker."

At first, Saber couldn't respond, but words gradually formed in his mind. "How is that possible?"

"I have no idea," Ronan replied, "but it happened."

Saber rested his hand against the glass as he tried to process this information. Before Caro, he cared little about Logan and his injected mate.

The only reason this development interested him was because of the new guerrilla warfare tactic the demons had unleashed by creating the injected. In all his years of working with demons and Savages, he'd never seen anything like it.

He wouldn't have believed they could do such a thing until it happened. And once they did, it completely changed the game.

As he glanced at Caro, a twinge of sympathy tugged at him for everything Logan had endured. He could never *truly* commiserate with the man because, while Caro was his mate and he would protect her, he didn't love her like Logan loved Elena.

He never would.

Centuries ago, he stopped being capable of love. Caro had already burrowed deeper under his skin than he would have believed possible for anyone. He'd make sure she didn't get any further. While she'd made him fail in his vow to never care for another again, he couldn't love her.

Saber turned his attention back to the night. The image of the fire blazed back across his mind, but though he could hear its crackle, it didn't materialize. But in his mind's eye, he saw it once again moving across the earth, destroying everything in its path… much like the demons and Savages.

The demons! Or just one *demon. One demon in a storm drain.*

"What time did this happen?" Saber asked.

"Around ten o'clock," Ronan replied.

Saber closed his eyes as he tried to recall all the details of what happened earlier. What time was it when they got back in the car?

And then he saw the numbers on the vehicle's display once more. It was seven minutes after ten when Caro started the car. Elena came back around the same time the demon died.

"Holy shit," he muttered.

The stones stopped crunching as Ronan ceased walking. "What is it?"

CHAPTER TWO

SABER TOOK a minute to compose his thoughts as he tried to hammer out all the details before replying. "My sword is finished. I took it out last night to test it on the Savages. Things went wrong, and Caro was grabbed by some of them and taken into a storm drain."

"Who's Caro?" Ronan inquired.

Saber hadn't realized how much he'd kept from them as he waited for Caro to forge his sword and while he tried to understand the strange effect she had on him. He understood it now; she was his mate, and the demon part of him had recognized it and sought to claim her.

"Caro is the woman who created my sword," Saber said.

"Is she okay?"

"I got her away from them, but not before we also encountered a demon in the tunnels. I killed it... right around ten o'clock. Right around the time Elena came back."

The wind whistled across the other end as Ronan didn't respond for a few seconds. "Why would a demon's death have any effect on Elena?"

Saber pondered this as he stared at the night; he waited for the flames to reappear, but everything remained blessedly normal. An idea was forming in his head, but he'd never heard of anything like it before and wasn't sure how it could be possible.

But, until recently, he'd also never heard of demons injecting hunters and vampires with their blood and turning them into wild-eyed, crazed monsters either. His idea might not be crazy.

"The demon blood," Saber said.

"Yes," Ronan said.

Saber suspected Ronan was already coming to the same crazy conclusion as him.

"The demon I killed must have been the same demon whose blood they used to inject Elena," Saber said.

"When it died, its blood died with it, and that blood also died inside Elena. Have you *ever* heard of, or seen, anything like this before?"

"No. This is all new territory for me. The demons never did or talked about anything like this while I was with them. I didn't know many of their secrets, but *this* wouldn't have stayed hidden. If they'd thought of it while I was still with them, they would have started doing it centuries ago. This is a new development, as is the fact they don't seem to care about the havoc they're wreaking."

He recalled the burning Earth outside the door and realized *that's* what the demons would unleash on them, whether they meant to or not. He didn't think they sought to destroy the whole world; it would be much less fun for them if there was no one to torture and kill.

They probably had no idea they were close to unleashing complete devastation on the planet. However, they were screwing with so many things, it would be easy for them to lose control of it all. They were also far too arrogant to ever think such a thing could happen to them.

"If we don't stop them, it's going to get a lot worse," he said.

"If we kill the demons, we can set the injected, and the rest of the world, free from their insanity," Ronan said.

"Destroying them *has* to be the way to save the injected," Saber agreed. "Unless Logan tried some new experiments on her recently."

"Not in days," Ronan said. "He'd run out of ideas; we all had."

"Killing the demons won't be easy."

"No, it won't," Ronan agreed, "but for the first time since all this injection shit started, we might have a way to save those affected."

"Have you talked to Juan in Arizona? Did anyone there change too?" Saber asked.

"I did, and none of them have changed. Elena's the only one who's come out of it."

"Maybe it wasn't the demon, and the mate bond finally succeeded in pulling her back."

"It could have, but I think it's doubtful after all this time."

"And it would be an awfully big coincidence."

"That it would. If this is true, and the injected will change back when the demon who created them dies, they didn't experience a true change."

"Not yet," Saber said, "but if they somehow get out and start killing, I don't think there will be any way to save them."

"I don't either. We'll have to kill more demons to find out for sure, and hopefully, we'll rescue more of the injected when we do," Ronan said.

"We'll soon have more weapons with stones to help us with that. My sword worked like Willow's on them, and it's an extremely strong blade. Caro can forge the rest of the stones into more swords for us."

"Good. It's time we take these fuckers down."

Saber stared at the quiet night, but in his mind, flames

engulfed the trees while screams resonated across the land. Ronan had no idea what awaited them. "It is."

"I'll find your sister."

Saber glanced at Caro as a door opened and closed on Ronan's end. She remained sleeping soundly with one hand tucked beneath her cheek and an arm above her head on the pillow.

What am I going to do with her?

He couldn't keep her out of this upcoming war; they needed her too badly for that. And if what he'd seen outside came true, there was nowhere for him to hide her.

Destruction and death crept ever closer; no one would escape if the world burned. Not much ever unnerved him, but the idea of losing Caro did. Before letting anyone take her from him, he'd walk through Hell and back.

Muffled voices came across the line a second before his sister said, "Hello."

Saber turned back to the door as her voice caused his heart to jump a little. He'd never thought to hear it again, but there it was, hopeful and a little breathless.

He swiftly buried his excitement and the unexpected rush of emotion following it. He couldn't call it love; he didn't know or understand that emotion anymore, but something was there.

And he didn't like it.

"Brie," he greeted flatly.

CHAPTER THREE

"Hi."

She said nothing more, but her yearning came through with that one word. Saber gritted his teeth as he buried the emotions threatening to rise. This was not the time or place for him to lose control of the feelings he kept so restrained.

"I have to talk to you," he stated.

"Okay," she said.

He listened as she moved away from the happy voices in the background. Judging by the laughter and music, they were having a party.

He didn't blame them; Elena's return and the hope it brought deserved a big celebration. And they hadn't seen what he just did; it would have put a damper on their festivities if they had.

Did I somehow imagine it? But as he asked the question, he knew the answer. What was outside this door wasn't real now, but it would be.

"Did you hear about Elena?" Brie asked when she was away from the voices.

"Yes."

"It's a miracle."

"Or the death of a demon."

"What?"

He filled her in on what he'd discussed with Ronan and the demon he'd killed.

"I'm glad you're both okay," she said.

Saber didn't acknowledge her words; he wasn't here for idle chat and wasn't in the mood to exchange niceties.

"I didn't call because of that," he said.

"Then why did you call?"

He ignored the hurt in her voice. "I saw something. I've never seen anything like it before; it was real, but not real."

"Real but not real?"

"Yes."

"Are you saying you saw something like *I* see something?"

He hesitated before replying. It was too bizarre, but the fire *had* been there. "I think so, yes."

Brie sucked in a breath. "And that's never happened to you before?"

"No."

"What did you see?"

"Fire, so much fire, and I heard screams. I swear I saw the whole world…."

"Burning," she said at the same time as him.

"Yes. Have you seen anything like it?" he asked.

"Yes, last week and again about ten minutes ago."

Unexpected and unreasonable anger boiled up inside him. "Did you somehow suck me into your vision?"

"I've never done anything like that before," she replied with a defensive edge. "I never would have believed it possible, but things are rapidly changing around us. Has something different happened to *you* recently? Something that would make you stronger or more receptive to seeing something you might not have seen before?"

Saber stiffened as her words struck home. Shortly before he

saw the world burning, he completed the mate bond with Caro—a bond that made vamps stronger.

He'd never heard of it creating new powers in vampires, but it could have strengthened him enough to awaken some latent connection to Brie. It was a crazy possibility, but their lives were far from sane lately.

He turned back to Caro to discover she was awake. Her almond-shaped, turquoise eyes latched onto his as she remained on the bed. She studied him with a furrowed brow and a small purse to her full lips.

Her wavy, mahogany hair fell beneath her shoulders and emphasized her square face and slender nose with its slight upturn at the end. Her scent of the ocean, fresh salt air, and the fire of her forge permeated the room.

The place was small but warm and inviting. Hanging from the thick, wood beams running across the ceiling of her apartment, numerous shells, starfish, and other ocean finds decorated her apartment. A blue armchair with a shell pattern sat in the corner.

His eyes dropped to *his* fresh bites on Caro's creamy skin. Something different had definitely happened to him not so long ago.

"Yes," he admitted to Brie.

She sighed. "Are you going to tell me what it was, or am I supposed to guess?"

He decided to ignore her question. The Alliance would soon learn Caro was his mate, but he planned to keep it to himself for a little longer.

It was still so new and unexpected, still so private and *theirs* to share. Not to mention, he had a lot of enemies out there.

The last thing he wanted was word getting around that he'd found his mate. Countless vamps and demons would be more than happy to hunt her down and destroy her once they learned it, and he wasn't ready to paint a giant bullseye on her back.

"We need the stones," he said. "I'll call back tomorrow to tell Ronan how to get them here."

"They're not going anywhere without me."

Saber had suspected this, but he'd hoped she'd stay away. He couldn't avoid her forever, but he had enough to work through between Caro, this strange vision, and the increased presence of the demons. He didn't need Brie traipsing around here on top of it all.

But they had to have the stones, which meant he would be stuck with her. That didn't mean he had to associate with her. He was good at ignoring things he preferred not to acknowledge.

"I'll see you soon then," he said.

"Saber!" she blurted as he pulled the phone away from his ear.

His finger hovered over the red end button before he reluctantly put the phone back to his ear. "What?"

"What you saw tonight wasn't a dream or a hallucination. If we don't do something soon, that *will* be the world."

"I know."

CHAPTER FOUR

HE HUNG up as Caro pushed herself up and leaned against the headboard. When he looked back toward the doors, she glimpsed the sword tattoo on his back and neck. Flames rose around the sword like a phoenix rising from the ashes.

At six foot one, he was two hundred and ten pounds of solid muscle. His short, black hair had grown since arriving here, and his bright, cobalt blue eyes shone in the dark.

His narrow face and hollow cheekbones were so striking that her breath caught as she drank him in. His aura of power and cruelty caused her skin to ripple as the memory of what they'd shared sent a thrill through her.

He was a class one alpha-hole with a *whole* lot of arrogance, but he was *her* asshole. And it was clear something was bothering him.

"Who was that?" she asked.

"My sister."

Caro hid her surprise as she drew the blankets up and tucked them under her arms. He'd already seen everything there was of her, but she suddenly felt self-conscious sitting there naked.

He didn't seem to feel the same way as he stood with his feet braced apart and not a stitch of clothing on him. He drove her crazy, but she couldn't help admiring the view as her eyes ran over his chiseled body.

She hadn't had much time to process what transpired between them earlier, and she still couldn't believe what happened—having him as her mate was the last thing she expected or would have chosen.

He wasn't a bad man, or at least not as horrible as he liked to portray, but he lived a dangerous life and was more closed off than Fort Knox. She would have preferred if fate hadn't chosen him for her, but it was pointless to fight or rail against it.

They would have to find a way to live together... without killing each other.

Besides, she had something else to worry about right now. And that was whatever had caused the tension weighing on his shoulders. "What happened?"

Saber crossed the room and set her phone on the table beside her bed. He glanced back at the doors again as he contemplated walking out of here and returning to the woods to hunt.

He wasn't hungry, her blood had more than satisfied him, and it would for at least the next three days. Plus, he feasted earlier, but he should unleash some of his growing, pent-up energy.

Racing through the woods and tracking his prey would help him forget the demons, Brie, and his strange vision. And he needed a reprieve from all of them.

His fangs throbbed at the idea of hunting, but then Caro shifted. Her blanket dipped enough to reveal the creamy top of a breast; when it did, his hunter instincts focused on her as she awakened another, more demanding hunger.

Caro saw the change in Saber's eyes as passion caused red to flash through them. She sought answers, but her body instinctively reacted to the sudden desire he emanated as his cock hardened.

He was her mate, he needed her, and she wouldn't refuse him. They could discuss whatever happened tomorrow, but for now....

Caro pulled back the sheets, and when she did, the sight of her naked body turned his eyes completely red. His fangs lengthened, and she squirmed a little as she remembered how it felt to have him feeding from her.

Wetness spread between her legs as she opened them. She whimpered when the mattress sank beneath Saber's weight and he crawled over to plant his hands on either side of her.

She sensed his desire, as he remained kneeling between her legs and his eyes held hers. Then, he sat back a little, while his gaze roamed over her. Caro's skin came alive everywhere his eyes touched as anticipation thrummed through her bloodstream.

He didn't touch her, but her nipples hardened beneath a perusal that was as intimate and arousing as his hands would be. It took everything she had not to start squirming again while her body ached for him.

And then his hands rested on the insides of her thighs and slid down. He leaned closer as his fingers skimmed her.

"I want to watch you fuck yourself," he said.

His fangs distorted his voice, but his words caused her heart to jackhammer. She wasn't going to argue with him, especially when she was desperate for release.

Leisurely, she ran her fingers down her stomach to the junction of her legs. His eyes, following her every move, grew redder when her hand slid between her legs.

Caro couldn't suppress a moan when she stroked her clit. Saber's hands tightened on her hips, and his dick stood proudly between them, but he didn't stop her.

As the pressure within her built, her head fell back a little. Saber licked his lips as his eyes remained riveted on her. The hunger radiating from him and the heat of his powerful body was all too much.

"Fuck," he breathed when she came with a loud cry.

She was spiraling down from the height of her orgasm when he pulled her further down on the bed. His low growl rumbled against her throat as he sank his fangs and cock into her.

She'd just come, but she did so again as his body enveloped hers, and the world spiraled away until only they remained.

CHAPTER FIVE

CARO FELT Saber's eyes on her as he stood in the doorway of her forge and watched her melt swords, knives, and statues for more metal. She had some of the rare metal her father taught her to create on hand, but not enough to weld the eight other stones into a sword.

Most of the things she melted were creations she made, but some were her father's. She hated destroying anything he'd created, but it couldn't be helped. Still, her heart ached with every piece that vanished beneath her fire.

She had no choice but to destroy some of them. She required the metal he'd used to forge them.

Saber crossed his arms over his chest while watching Caro work. Despite the sadness she exuded, she didn't hesitate, and her face remained outwardly composed. If he couldn't feel her sorrow, he wouldn't know it was there.

Back in a tank top and leather overalls, she had her hair knotted on top of her head, but some strands had fallen to cling to her face and nape. Her beauty captivated him as sweat glistened on her dirt-streaked skin.

She'd always fascinated him, but now, he couldn't look away

from her. This beautiful, composed, strong-willed woman was inwardly grieving, and no one, other than him, would ever know.

The intimacy of that caused him to shift a little uneasily as his gaze darted to the woods. But he sensed and felt her inside him even when he wasn't looking at her. She was a *part* of him.

After today, he would shut her out, but she needed him right now, and as much as he shouldn't care, he did... a little. However, there was no way he would have this open of a connection to someone for the rest of his life.

Fuck that.

They tried to tremble, but Caro kept her hands steady as she fed more of her and her dad's creations into the fire. Instead of getting easier, each new sacrifice rattled her more and thrust her back into the crushing arms of grief.

It was becoming increasingly difficult to breathe as the flames leapt and danced. She barely felt their heat as the echo of her father's laughter rang in her ears, and she was once again a young girl, standing beside him while he bestowed the knowledge of his craft on her.

Tears burned her eyes, but she didn't move away from the forge. For some reason, even as she was melting down some of his work, she felt closer to her dad at the forge.

She could almost feel him beside her, with his hand on her shoulder, as he guided her onward. He'd understand this and would approve, but she still felt like she was losing little pieces of him all over again.

He was already gone, so none of this made any difference. He'd created these things, but they weren't *him*. They could never be *him*. That part of her life was gone; her *parents* were dead.

She would never again hear their laughter, go for walks through the woods with them, or feel the warmth of their hugs and the strength of their love. There wouldn't be any more Christmas mornings full of music, presents, and snowball fights.

At first, she'd believed the memories were the worst part of losing them. She'd desperately tried to relive *every* detail of the time they spent together, the things they said, and the way they smelled so she wouldn't forget any of it.

The memories tore open wounds that were far from healed, but she forced herself through them. Now, she was beginning to realize the things she would never do again with her parents hurt far more than the memories.

All she had left were memories; she would never see them again. They'd never meet Saber, never get to know her children, if she had them, and never again be there for late nights on the porch while they shared laughs over drinks.

It was all gone. And now she was destroying what little she had left of the two vampires she'd loved most in the world.

Caro was so focused on her misery that she didn't hear Saber approach until his hands rested on her shoulders. "Don't think of it that way," he murmured.

She was so new to the mate bond that she'd forgotten their emotions and thoughts were connected. It was a disconcerting realization; she'd prefer not to have someone else traipsing around in her mind, but at the same time, it was weirdly reassuring.

"How am I supposed to think of it?" she inquired.

"These things he made will go on to save the world."

Caro shuddered at the reminder of what Saber had told her about the fire outside her door. He didn't understand why *he'd* glimpsed such a thing when it was his sister's gift, but the sealing of their mate bond had to have something to do with it. Otherwise, it was a *really* big coincidence.

She didn't think he was clairvoyant like his sister, or at least not as strong of one as Brie, but she suspected something was there—something he'd locked down many years ago.

He claimed he'd never experienced anything like it as a child, and she believed him, but maybe he'd experienced something else in his lifetime and hadn't realized what it was. No matter the answer, something had changed in him, and he caught a glimpse of a future that could be years or hours away.

When a small shiver ran through her, he squeezed her shoulders. With a bit of a shock, she realized he was *comforting* her. Such a thing was probably as foreign to him as Jupiter, but he didn't let her go as he gave her a small hug.

It was strange, but she relaxed against him as his warmth seeped into her bones and eased some of her sadness. She never would have expected the man who walked into her parents' store, all demanding, bossy, and pure jackass, to turn out to be her mate.

Life had a strange way of pulling practical jokes on those riding this big ball of rock around the sun, and it was laughing its ass off right now. She hoped the joke didn't turn into heartbreak.

A loud beeping drew her attention to the video monitor. It hung on the wall in the corner of the shop. Someone had driven over the hidden wire that alerted her to anyone approaching the steel gates.

Saber released her, and she removed her leather gloves before tossing them aside. Together, they walked to the monitor as a black SUV stopped outside the gates and the driver's window went down. A face appeared, and a hand waved at the camera.

"It's Declan," Saber said. "You can let him in."

I can, can I? But she held the question back as resentment churned inside her. She'd known guests were arriving, but she wasn't thrilled about having strangers tromping around *her* home. And she especially didn't like being told who she could let into *her* home.

She was still grieving and craved solace, but Saber's entrance into her life had thrown it into a tailspin, and now, more vampires were invading. The last thing she wanted to do was play hostess to a group of strangers.

If she was going to finish the swords and prevent the coming hell Saber and Brie had witnessed, then this was a necessary inconvenience. It didn't mean she had to like it.

A keypad sat beneath the monitor; Caro punched the code to the gates into it and watched as the gates started to swing open. Declan ducked back into the vehicle, and a second later, the SUV rolled through the gates.

CHAPTER SIX

CARO WATCHED the gates close before turning away from the screen. Saber had already walked over to the doorway of the forge. He leaned against the wall as he waited for the others to arrive.

With nothing else to do, and no way to retreat, she reluctantly joined him. She had no idea what would happen when they arrived.

Saber and his sister should talk. She hoped they'd somehow repair their relationship, but Brie would have to prove as stubborn as her often reluctant and sometimes callous sibling.

And she would have to be persistent, as it wasn't a relationship Saber would pursue. She hoped the woman had it in her, but it would be a *very* tough road to pave.

Saber had said Brie wasn't going to leave those stones unattended and would remain until they were all secured into a sword. Once that happened, they would have to find the rightful owners to fully activate the stone's power.

"Putting all the stones together caused them to react. I don't know what they'll do if we find their rightful possessors and their power is truly activated," Saber muttered.

"Are you in my head?"

He gave her a rueful smile. "No, I was simply pondering something out loud."

"Then we were thinking along the same line of things. Let's hope getting them into the right hands will make them more powerful. Maybe our ancestors used the stones to help push the demons back... or better, destroy them."

"I hope so, because even with those swords, we're going to need all the help we can get to win this."

The crunch of tires on dirt alerted them to the SUV's approach before it came into view. A trickle of unease ran through Caro; she wasn't ready for this.

Every vampire emerging from that vehicle would immediately know what had passed between her and Saber. It was impossible to hide the marks on their necks or the bond forged between them.

It was such a private, life-changing bond they'd created. They could never hide it as it would be apparent to every vampire they encountered.

Declan stopped the vehicle, parked it, and was the first to exit. His auburn hair glistened in the sun as he shaded his eyes against its light. He turned to survey the property before focusing on them.

"Are you ready for this?" Saber asked.

"No," she said honestly. "Are you?"

"No."

But he lifted his sword from where he'd set it beside the door and stepped away as he headed toward the vehicle. Caro followed as doors opened and more passengers emerged from the SUV.

She felt her connection with Saber closing as he worked to shut her out. She wasn't sad it closed, she far preferred having her mind to herself, but the sense of loss following it astonished her a little.

As they approached, Declan started to smile before his eyes widened. He looked from Saber's neck to hers and back again. "It seems there's been another development."

"There has," Saber said and raised his sword to show the others. He wasn't about to get into his personal life with anyone. "Caro has created a magnificent sword."

Declan studied him before nodding and shifting his attention to the weapon Saber held before him.

"It's beautiful," Willow murmured.

"And strong," Saber said.

"Of course it is," Caro stated.

Saber smiled over her unwavering confidence, even if she wasn't thrilled about having vampires she didn't know on her property. Nothing would ever shake her conviction in her work.

"My name is Carolina, but you can call me Caro."

A woman with dark brown hair that had shades of lighter brown interwoven through it approached them. Her ochre-colored eyes shone with warmth as they flitted between her and Saber.

Then they settled on the bite marks on Caro's neck and almost bulged out of her head. She should have taken her hair down before coming out here, but it wouldn't have mattered. They couldn't hide their intermingled scents.

The woman held out her hands to Caro, and after a second of hesitation, Caro clasped them. She knew, without being told, who this woman was and couldn't turn her away.

"It's nice to meet you; I'm Brie."

Caro smiled at Saber's sister. "It's nice to meet you too."

When Brie's attention shifted to Saber, Caro sensed her longing for her brother, but he remained rigid beside her. All signs of the man who comforted her minutes ago were gone.

In his place stood the unrelenting and emotionless man Caro originally encountered and knew so well. She suspected the fleeting glimpses she received of the warmer man below his surface were who he was as a child and young adult.

Years of death and cruelty had molded him into someone who preferred not to feel anything. Caro hoped the warmth she sometimes glimpsed would one day win out over his callousness, but she didn't fool herself into thinking it would be an overnight change... if it happened at all.

For her sanity, and the sake of her heart, she'd do better mated to a man who could care. She couldn't think about being bound to someone incapable of love.

Without realizing she was doing it, she touched Saber's arm as she sought to reconnect with him. Something flickered across Saber's face before his cobalt-colored eyes shifted to her. No warmth shone in their beautiful, blue depths.

CHAPTER SEVEN

"AND I'M ASHER," a man with sandy-blond hair and gold flecks in his brown eyes said.

Caro released Brie's hands to shake her mate's hand. The two other occupants of the vehicle came forward next.

"I'm Declan." His silvery-gray eyes sparkled with amusement as he glanced between her and Saber. "Thanks for helping us with this."

"I'll do whatever it takes to ensure those things die," Caro replied.

"Good." Willow's violet eyes were curious as they surveyed Caro. Her blonde hair hung in a braid over her shoulder. "It's nice to meet you."

"You too."

Willow turned to Saber and held out her hand. "Can I look at your sword?"

With obvious reluctance, he held it out to her. Willow twisted the blade in her hands as she examined the workmanship.

Her mouth parted, and her eyes flitted up to Caro before she handed the sword back to Saber. Then she stretched a hand over her shoulder and removed her sword from its sheath.

She held it out to Caro. "I can see the differences, you have your own unique style, but they're both amazing pieces of art, and there are similarities."

Caro took the sword to examine it. "It is magnificent."

A small smile tugged at the corners of Willow's mouth as Caro's eyes met hers.

"If I'd had more time, I would have added more of my own touches, but unfortunately, I didn't have it," she told Willow.

As she turned Willow's sword in her hand, she saw what the other woman meant. The blades were strikingly similar; the one she held looked like something her father would have created.

"One of my ancestors might have forged it," she murmured. "The making of these swords has been passed down through the generations of my family."

"I agree," Willow said as Caro handed her sword back.

"Interesting," Declan murmured.

"And that ancestor might have been a human," Caro said. "My father was a purebred, but when that sword was forged, his line was one of humans."

"So, the vampires worked with humans back then to destroy the demons," Willow said.

"Weren't they originally demon swords?" Asher asked.

"Maybe, but maybe not," Saber said. "The stones are from the demons, but the swords could be from something or someone else. The truth of it all is lost to history. A *lot* of time has passed since then."

"Maybe the demons built the pyramids." When they all gave Asher a strange look for this statement, he shrugged. "I'm just throwing it out there. Some say it could have been aliens, but maybe it was demons. Who knows?"

Caro laughed, and Brie looked lovingly at him as she smiled.

"Who knows, indeed," Willow said.

"Where are the rest of the stones?" Caro asked. "It will take me a while to get eight more swords done, so I might as well get started."

"How long will it take?" Declan asked.

"At least three weeks, if not a month. I can work on four at a time, but anything more might compromise the quality."

"Understandable," Willow said.

"You'll make as many as you can without exhausting yourself," Saber growled.

Caro rolled her eyes. "After what you saw last night, exhausting myself won't matter if the whole world is on fire."

Declan dipped a hand into his pocket and pulled out a lollipop. He removed the wrapper as he spoke. "Brie told us about the vision you both had on our way here. You've never experienced something like that before?"

"No," Saber said.

"You've never been mated before either," Brie said. "When did that happen?"

Saber shot her a look. She was his sister, but his relationship with Caro was private and something he'd protect with his life.

"Last night," Caro answered. "Before the vision."

"The mate bond makes vampires stronger," Brie said pointedly.

Saber remained straight-faced. He recalled the question he'd pointedly ignored from her last night.

"It's never unlocked visions in vampires who have never received them before," Saber retorted.

"That we know of," Brie said in the same clipped, irritated tone he'd used. "Have you *known* every mated vampire throughout *all* of history?"

Caro had to bite back a smile as the siblings glowered at each other. They weren't as close as when they were children, but Saber and Brie sure had the sibling dynamic down, even if they didn't realize it or preferred not to acknowledge it.

"The vision might be about more than the mating and more

than a vision. You both might have received it because it was so important that you saw what our future could hold for the world," Willow said. "No one else in the Alliance received it, including Kadence. However, Brie's ability to see things is stronger than hers, and you're siblings; there's a bond between you."

Saber didn't look happy to hear this, but he couldn't deny it.

"I'll get the stones," Brie said when no one else spoke.

As she and Asher walked over to the vehicle, Declan leaned against the workshop wall and crossed his arms over his chest. "Most of the stones have been claimed by members of the Alliance. Only two remain unclaimed."

"Who do the other five belong to?" Saber asked.

"Nathan's is the navy blue stone, the blood red one with a yellow center is Ronan's, the pure white one belongs to Kadence, Killean has claimed the yellow one, and the violet one is mine. Before leaving, the others made it clear they weren't happy about being separated from their stones, but you said you didn't want a lot of us here."

That he had. He wasn't ready to share Caro with so many, and he knew she wasn't prepared to have her home invaded by dozens, if not hundreds, of strangers she didn't know.

"When it's getting closer to the time when we face the demons, we can have more come here," Saber said.

Caro hadn't realized he'd told them not to bring a bunch of vamps here; she inwardly smiled. Maybe they'd all be safer with a huge army here, but she didn't think the demons would find them, and she wasn't ready to share her home and her parents' things with so many.

"It's understandable," Declan said as he studied them. "Besides, some had to remain to guard the prisoners, and it's best if we're not all together now. We have to spread out to keep from being ambushed and possibly destroyed if the demons happen to find us again."

Saber watched as his sister and Asher removed the stones from the car. "Which stones remain?" he asked.

"The rose pink one and the citrine-colored one."

"We have to find the rightful owners of those stones. I have a feeling that all those stones together, and in the hands of their rightful owners, will be a lot more powerful and lethal to the demons."

"I have the same feeling," Declan muttered as he stuck the lollipop in his mouth.

No one spoke as Asher approached with a safe securely tucked in his arms.

CHAPTER EIGHT

THE SECOND CARO touched the citrine-colored stone, a flash of color went through it. Her hand clenched around the walnut-sized stone.

"It's mine," she whispered.

The others remained standing in the doorway of her shop, watching as she unloaded the stones. Brie hovered a few feet away as she placed the stones on a workbench ten feet away from Caro's forge.

"What is?" Saber demanded.

"The orange stone; it's mine."

The possessiveness in her voice was undeniable, and when she lifted her head to look at him, fire shone in her eyes. That stone was *hers*, and they would have to pry it from her cold, dead hands.

He knew how she felt about it but *loathed* this new development. Caro was supposed to make the swords and stay out of the rest of it. He'd intended to keep her somewhere safe, even if it meant locking her there.

His teeth clamped down so forcefully that his jaw ached from the pressure. She had to make the swords, but if that stone was *hers*, she would have to march into battle too. Unless she refused, but she was too stubborn and kindhearted for that.

She wouldn't walk away if it meant millions, or more, could perish. She was a fighter and would carry her sword proudly into any battle. Charles had taught her to fight, but she shouldn't have to.

"Shit," he growled.

Declan clapped him on the shoulder and squeezed it before lowering his hand. "I know how you feel."

When Saber scowled at him, Declan smiled in return.

"You should probably show everyone to their rooms," Caro said to Saber. "It's time I got to work."

Unsure of how many would come, they'd prepared the other two rooms in the house, and Saber's, for visitors. She'd loathed the idea of anyone using her parents' room, but it wouldn't be necessary. One couple could stay in Saber's room and the other in her old bedroom. Saber would stay with her.

She wasn't exactly thrilled about having him in her space; with his size and domineering ways, he would be impossible to ignore. Plus, she'd always enjoyed her freedom. However, she *really* disliked the idea of spending a night without her mate.

They would have to get used to sharing space and spending more time with each other... without killing each other. She wasn't sure how easy that would be, but she had plenty to keep her occupied over the coming weeks.

If he annoyed her too much, she had a good excuse to hide here. Plus, the armchair in the corner was comfy; she'd taken a few naps there as a kid and could sleep there again if necessary.

It probably wasn't a good sign that she was already plotting ways to avoid her mate, but this adjustment could be rocky, and options were necessary. Their mate bond was new; they needed time to figure it out. Once they did, everything between them would be good... she hoped.

"I'll be back soon," Saber said.

Caro waved at him but didn't lift her head from the stones as her fingers trailed lovingly across the orange one.

"We brought some clothes for you too," Brie said as they turned away from Caro.

"Thank you," Saber said.

He was beyond sick of wearing the same things and had asked Ronan if someone could pack some things for him. While the others retrieved their stuff from the vehicle, Brie handed him a stuffed duffel bag.

"I'm happy for you," she said. "A mate is a precious discovery, and the love shared between mates—"

"It's not love," he interrupted sharply.

"Maybe not yet—"

"Not ever. I don't love. I'm not capable of it anymore."

He saw sadness settle over her before her gaze fell to the ground. She understood he wasn't just talking about Caro.

"Oh," she murmured.

"Get your things, and I'll show you to your room."

Saber buried the part of himself that felt like a giant asshole as she trudged back to the SUV. It was better that she understood Gabriel was gone; he died centuries ago.

CHAPTER NINE

OVER THE NEXT couple of weeks, Caro spent most of her time in the forge, hammering the swords into place and crafting them into lethal weapons. No matter how tired she was or how much her body ached from standing in the same positions for hours, days, and weeks, she would make sure each sword was perfect.

Often, Saber hovered in the doorway, scowling while she worked late into the night. Sometimes, he would stop frowning long enough to tell her to sleep. Usually, she ignored him, but some nights, she admitted defeat as every part of her yearned for bed.

On those nights, the stubborn, oafish man insisted on carrying her to her apartment. She protested his actions the first couple of times, but those died away when she realized how wonderful it was to snuggle against him. Besides, she didn't have the energy to climb the stairs.

On those nights, once he got her upstairs, he'd help her undress, run a hot bath, and offer her mugs of blood. He'd sit on the bathroom floor beside her with his fingers trailing lazily through the water while she relaxed in the tub.

During those nights, she also learned more about him.

Tonight, as he sat with his hands on the side of the bathtub and his chin propped on them, they talked about their favorite movies. He'd stretched his long legs as far as possible in the cramped space.

His hair was shaggier than when she first met him, and the ends of it curled against his shoulders. Her fingers clenched around her warm mug as she resisted brushing it off his forehead. They were together every day and had sex every morning and some nights, but touching him in such a way was a different level of intimacy and familiarity.

"You're crazy," he said. "*The Godfather* is a great movie."

Caro sipped her blood. "I'm just saying I was out when the horse head showed up. No, thank you."

Smiling, he dipped his fingers to trail them through the bubbles floating on the surface. She studied his profile as she stifled a yawn and the water eased her tension.

She wanted a bed, but a question nagged at the back of her mind—the question he had always refused to answer, but they'd grown closer, he was her mate, and she believed, or at least *hoped*, he'd finally open up to her.

"Saber?"

"Yeah?"

Caro glanced at the tiled wall of her shower and gulped as the question stuck in her throat. She closed her eyes and took a deep breath before opening them and speaking.

"Why did you leave the demons and Savages? *Why* did you stop being a Savage?"

The second she finished the first question, she knew it was the wrong thing to ask as he stiffened and his fingers stopped moving. An impenetrable coldness settled over his features as he pulled his hand from the tub.

Her fingers itched to touch him, but she dug them into her palms instead. She shouldn't have asked it, but they were mated, they were getting to know each other better, and *damn it,* she *wanted* to learn more about him.

It wasn't too much to ask... but it was because whatever happened had propelled him from a life he'd enjoyed into something else. And it was something he couldn't talk about.

"Saber—"

"I need some blood." He rose abruptly. "I'll be back."

"Wait! Where are you going?"

"To hunt."

She didn't get a chance to reply before he left the room. A second later, the glass door slid open and closed.

Though the water was still warm, a chill crept through her as she remained sitting in the tub. The silence was loud in his absence.

She shouldn't have asked the question; she didn't have all the answers to everything and never would. She would have to accept that for this too.

Rising, she grabbed a towel and wrapped it around her as she stepped from the tub. She left the bathroom behind and padded over to the glass doors. Her reflection stared back at her as she searched for Saber, but he was gone.

She wouldn't be surprised if he didn't come back tonight. "You have to let this go," she told herself as she turned away from the window.

It wasn't any of her business; it was the past and obviously bothered him, but she'd prefer not to have any barriers between them. Her parents had told each other everything, and their love had filled her home.

Despite trying to keep her distance and knowing her relationship with Saber could never be like that, she still longed for it. It was still early in their relationship, and they were getting along better than when they first met; she would have to be patient and hopeful.

Patience had never been one of her virtues, but she could do it for him because whatever happened back then was bad. She also had to face the facts that he might never tell her, and this was as close as he would ever let her get.

It's not so bad, she told herself as she turned away from the window. *You're happy.*

And she *was* happy, but if he kept a barrier between them for the rest of their lives, she didn't know if it would last. It sounded incredibly lonely, especially when she was starting to care for him more than she'd ever wanted to.

With a sigh, she finished drying off, hung the towel, and crawled into bed. She was exhausted, but sleep wouldn't come easy tonight.

She was still awake when he returned, removed his clothes, and crawled into bed. They didn't speak when he drew her into his arms and kissed her shoulder. Didn't talk when she guided one of his hands between her thighs.

A barrier might always remain between them, but she could have these moments of joining and opening to one another. It might not always be enough, but for now, it was.

CHAPTER TEN

A FEW DAYS LATER, when Caro finally finished forging the third of the first four swords, she set it down on her workbench. She planted her hands on her lower back and stretched to work out the knotted muscles there.

Like always, Saber stood alone in the doorway, but Declan, Willow, and Asher had left a few minutes ago. She'd seen little of their visitors over the past two weeks, but they stopped by a few times a day to check in with Saber, say hi, and ask if she needed anything.

She didn't know them well, but they were nice. Having them here wasn't as bad as she'd originally thought it would be, yet it was still weird to have strangers in her home.

She didn't know Brie well either, as Caro spent most of her time staring into a fire and hammering swords, but she visited the most. Brie would often come by herself, and while she and Saber barely spoke to each other, she'd sometimes stay for hours.

Caro didn't have time to look at them often, but she sometimes caught the surreptitious glances Brie gave her brother. She sensed Brie's longing to connect with him, but Saber barely acknowledged her.

Caro had debated talking to him about it, but after he walked out on her the other night, she decided to let it play out between them. If she got involved, it would only be one more thing he wouldn't discuss with her.

As she hammered the blade of sword number four, Brie appeared in the doorway. The siblings muttered hi to each other before falling silent.

Caro tried not to watch them, but she kept rooting for Brie to break through the nearly impenetrable wall Saber had erected around himself. Brie clearly wanted a relationship with her older brother, but he wasn't giving her an inch. She wasn't quitting, though, and Caro inwardly smiled over Brie's persistence.

Caro suspected the main reason he remained so unbending with her was guilt, even if he wouldn't admit it to himself. He believed he'd failed his sister and hadn't been there for her when she needed him most.

He couldn't figure out how to handle that, so he remained closed off to her. It was easier to stay distant than to face his emotions and past. She should know; she'd slammed up against that same wall more than a few times.

Saber had become far more tender to her than she ever would have believed possible when they first met, but he didn't do emotions or, heaven for-fucking-bid, deal with the past. Every mule in the world, combined, was less stubborn than him.

Caro gave the sword another whack before lifting it to examine the blade. The metal shone in the fire, as did the orange stone she'd set into the hilt. *Her* orange stone.

Twisting the sword, she turned it to look deeper into the stone. She felt almost as possessive of it as she did Saber, but whereas he was *hers,* so was this stone.

When she glanced over at him, some of her irritation softened. Despite being almost impossible to deal with sometimes and incapable of expressing himself, his good heart and innate kindness sometimes shone through his rough exterior.

He'd deny there was anything good about him, but he'd be lying. A truly horrible man wouldn't be working to save the world and wouldn't take care of her as well as he did.

Caro was doing everything she could not to fall for him; she'd end up with a shattered heart if she gave him her everything. Loving someone incapable of loving her in return would be an awful way to go through life.

She started sharpening the blade while she watched the two siblings from the corner of her eye. She bit back her impulse to tell them to leave.

She was tired of being the center of attention while they held their strange, mostly silent vigil. If she kicked them out of here, they'd go their separate ways, and though this was odd and stressful, it was good for Saber... or so she hoped.

When the sun started to set, Asher came to get Brie. They said their goodbyes, which Saber returned with a small bow of his head. Caro waved and smiled as the couple went off to hunt.

She turned her attention to sharpening another blade as night descended. With fall creeping in and the air growing colder, the crickets and peepers had stopped singing. Thankfully, her fire staved off the increasing chill of the night air.

"I can help you sharpen the blades," Saber offered.

"Once they're officially out of my possession and in the hands of their rightful owners, they can take care of them. Until then, these are still mine to finish creating, and I'm the only one who will touch them."

Saber folded his arms across his chest. "Stubborn woman."

Caro gave a humorless laugh. "Hello, pot. Have you met kettle?"

"I'm not stubborn."

"Noooo, you're not stubborn at all. You're as easygoing as the Care Bears, a rainbow of delight, and so open to everyone that I worry strangers could kidnap you with only the promise of candy."

"I don't eat candy."

"No shit."

"I would accept help if it was necessary and someone offered it to me."

"No, you wouldn't. Besides, I don't need help."

"You're working yourself into a state of exhaustion every night."

"I love what I do."

"That doesn't mean you have to do it until you're too tired to stand."

She set the sword down to look at him. "I appreciate the offer, but I'm fine."

"You're my mate. I have to make sure you're okay and safe."

A twinge of distress tugged at her heart. Was it because he felt it was his duty, or was he *maybe* starting to care for her a little too?

She squelched the hope trying to rise at that possibility; too much hope would leave her a devastated mess, and she was still grieving the loss of her parents. She couldn't take another blow to her battered heart.

"I've done this work my whole life; I'm used to it, and I'm good. As for my safety, I'm here with members of the Alliance and protected by the very elaborate security system my father installed. I'm perfectly fine."

"You may be safe, but you're not fine. You're working too much."

"It has to be done, and fast, if we're going to stop this world from burning. Besides, before we discovered we're mates, you would have been up my ass asking me if I was done yet."

He scowled at her. "I'm not that much of a tyrant."

When she quirked an eyebrow at him, his scowl deepened. The stubborn, fool woman was working herself to the brink of exhaustion... and she was right; if she was anyone else, he would be demanding more from her.

But he wouldn't do that to her when shadows lined her eyes, she'd lost weight, and she barely made it up the stairs every night. Maybe he was going easier on her because she was his mate, but she wasn't going easy on *herself*.

And he didn't like it.

CHAPTER ELEVEN

"You're not a tyrant," Caro relented. "But you are stubborn. I mean...."

Her words trailed off as she inwardly kicked herself. She'd decided to stay out of his and Brie's relationship, yet she was about to say something about it.

"You mean what?" Saber asked.

He didn't like how her eyes returned to the sword or her uneasiness. She shouldn't feel that way around him. Caro lifted the sword and skimmed her finger along the edge, but she didn't fool him; she had something else to say.

"What were you going to say?" he demanded.

Caro set the sword down again. She stared at the wall while she tried to decide what to say. Should she lie and make something else up? But the idea of lying to her mate, even a small one, didn't sit well with her. Besides, she didn't think he would buy it.

"Brie wants a relationship with you," Caro stated as she returned to working on the sword. "She comes here every day in the hopes of starting one, and you know it, but you *stubbornly* resist having one with her."

"She's better off not having one with me."

Caro kept her focus on the sword, but she really wanted to set it down and go to him. He'd become a monster all those years ago and would always believe himself to be one.

He didn't kill innocents anymore but still saw himself as broken. And maybe he was and *she* was the one trying to see something that could never be, but she wasn't ready to believe that yet.

"You've spent nearly five hundred years shutting off your emotions; it's going to be difficult to open them back up again," Caro said.

She couldn't look at him while she talked. This conversation would most likely piss him off, but he'd pushed her toward it, and now, here they were.

"I don't have emotions," he stated. "When I do, things die, because *I* kill them."

"She loves you and is trying to connect with you. She's not coming here every day because she has fun staring at me. She's here for *you*. You could try talking to her. You might find you have a lot in common and like each other, or maybe you'll discover time has made it impossible for you to be friends and close family, but it's worth a try."

When Saber didn't say anything, she lowered the sword to look at him. His eyes, and the unrelenting mask of indifference he wore, were as cold as ice. She'd pushed too far; he was shutting down, but now that she'd started, she couldn't stop.

She'd vowed not to push again, not to open this doorway into rejection, but her tongue kept going. Brie wasn't the only one trying to get through to him and who craved *more* from him.

"Try talking to her. And if it doesn't work out and she doesn't back off, then tell her to fuck off if that's what it takes to get her to stop, but tell her *something*," Caro said.

Saber's fingers dug into his palms, and his teeth ground together as she stared at him. She wasn't just talking about his sister, but he was giving her everything he could, yet she *continued* to push.

She wouldn't let it go and accept him for who he was. Did she deserve better and more? Yes, but it didn't matter because *he* was who she had, the only one she would *ever* have again, and she better get used to it. This was the way things were and always would be.

Caro held her breath as she waited for him to say *something*. And then his eyes, tinged with red around the edges, met hers.

"Caro."

She gulped at the harsh tone of his word. "Yeah?"

"Fuck off."

She recoiled as if he'd slapped her. The sword would have tumbled from her hand if her fingers hadn't locked around the hilt.

Before she could reply, he vanished from the doorway. And she was left alone... *again*.

CHAPTER TWELVE

SABER WATCHED from the shadows as Caro trudged toward her apartment above the barn. Her head was bowed, and her shoulders hunched as exhaustion weighed heavily on her. And he was sure it was more than physical exhaustion but also an emotional one taking its toll on her.

Most of that was because of him. He hated the guilt and irritation tugging at him like incessant rats gnawing away at his insides. Fuck the guilt and the rats; he'd never hidden who he was, yet she wanted more than he could *ever* give.

She should be happy with what he could give her; *he* should be happy with it, but he wasn't.

Normally, he was there to carry her upstairs. It had become the favorite part of his day, and he looked forward to when she finally agreed to stop working, so they could spend time together.

Nothing was better than having her in his arms, snuggled against him, all safe, warm, and trusting. He couldn't bring himself to go to her now.

He'd told his *mate* to fuck off. It was bad enough that her bright soul was shackled to a monster, but he never should have spoken to her in such a way, even if she was pushing for something he couldn't give her.

It was weird for him to regret anything, but it weighed heavily on his conscience. He shouldn't have said that to her, but his relationship with his sister was none of her business.

The fact she couldn't understand it was better for Brie to keep her distance from him boggled his mind. Couldn't she see it was better for all involved if he stayed away?

But still, he shouldn't talk to *Caro* like that. Anyone else, fine, but she was his mate and deserved better.

As Caro reached the steps leading to her apartment, he emerged from the woods, raced across the distance separating them, and swept her into his arms. She released a small squeak as he rolled her up to embrace her against his chest.

Caught up in her exhaustion and heartache over what transpired earlier, Caro never heard him coming. That pissed her off almost as much as what happened earlier.

She planted her hands against his chest. "Put me down!"

"You're exhausted," Saber said.

"That's nothing new. *Put. Me. Down.*"

"Caro—"

"I meant it, Saber. You don't get to take off on me like that… *again* and then come back here like everything is all roses and candy. It is *not* roses and candy. It's more like a steaming pile of dog shit."

He was startled by the amount of distress her words created. "That's not how you really see what this is between us, is it?"

"I'm not sure what this is between us, Saber, other than sex. We don't talk—"

"We talk."

"Not about anything of worth. Not about anything substantial."

"I shouldn't have told you to fuck off."

"I don't care about that!"

"Then why are you so upset?"

Caro rolled her eyes as she resisted hitting his chest. She wouldn't give this exasperating, obtuse man the satisfaction of watching her lose control..

"Because you keep walking away from any conversation you don't like," she said. "I'm tired of talking to thin air."

"There are some things I don't wish to discuss."

Caro sighed as she tried to keep her patience under wraps. She knew this, and she'd known not to push him; she'd done this to herself, but, like an idiot, she kept battering herself against his wall in the hopes it would one day crack.

"I shouldn't have talked to you like that and walked away afterward," he said.

Caro crossed her arms over her chest as she glowered at him. "And?"

"And what?"

"That's not much of an apology."

"I'm not apologizing."

"Then I'll start. I shouldn't have talked to you about your sister. I knew it was a touchy subject and shouldn't have pushed it. Now you."

Saber made it to the top of the stairs and stopped walking. He was almost amused by how she stared at him with her chin raised and turquoise eyes burning with indignation, but hurt also shone in them, and he didn't find that amusing.

For the first time, some of his walls crumbled. "I don't know how to be the man you *need* me to be... the one... the one you deserve."

His voice was so low and ragged that it tore at Caro's heart and melted the last of her anger. When she rested her hand against his chest, the rapid beat of his heart pulsed against her palm.

"You're already the man I deserve," she assured him. "I just... you have to stop walking away from me. I understand you can't talk to me about some things, even if it's difficult for me not to press you about it. I want to know more about you; I'll *always* want that, but if you can't give it to me, I'll live with it."

"Why?"

"Why what?"

"Why do you want to know these things? Why do you want me to talk to Brie?"

Caro blinked away the tears burning her eyes. He really didn't understand and couldn't see how much she'd come to care for him or how much his sister loved him.

"Because I care about you, because Brie loves you, and because I'd like to know you better… to understand…."

"Understand what?"

Caro was trying to keep her patience, but if she emerged from this relationship with her sanity intact, it would be a miracle. "*You!* I want to understand *you*. It's why I ask you these things. I also want you to be happy, and I think Brie could help you heal old wounds."

"Those wounds healed years ago."

When Caro rested her hand against his cheek, he recoiled a little. "No, they didn't, but I'm not going to push you on that either. I'm not asking you to change; I don't want that. I was asking for more of you, but… but…."

Her words trailed off as she looked away, but Saber heard the words she didn't say. *You can't give it to me.*

His teeth clamped together against the fury building inside him. Why couldn't he give her what she asked for? Why couldn't he be the man she needed?

Determined to give her at least some of the answers she sought, no matter how terrible they were, and even if it meant she hated him after, he set her down. When she staggered a bit at the abruptness of it, he gently righted her. Her fingers curled around his as she gazed at him.

"Sometimes you regret the things you ask," he said.

"Sometimes you do."

"Yet you still want to know. Because once I tell you, you can't go back to not knowing."

Caro swallowed at the steely gleam in his eyes. "I'm only asking to know what you're willing to tell me."

Saber looked at the stars twinkling in the curtain of black. He didn't see a moon, but it was somewhere, hiding as things often did in the night.

Just as he once hid and continued to hide from the memory of that awful night. He was being a coward.

Tonight, he would stop hiding.

CHAPTER THIRTEEN

"They slaughtered dozens of children."

Caro's forehead furrowed at this unexpected statement. "What? Who?"

When his eyes met hers again, red filled them. "You asked why I left them and went my own way. *That's* why. They attacked an orphanage one night. They stole the innocence and life from children who had never known anything other than sadness and adversity. They killed almost every child and nun residing within."

"The demons did this?" Caro squeaked.

"One demon went with them. They rarely go above ground and prefer to have the Savages do their dirty work and bring them back victims, but Kirkau decided to join the fun that night."

"Who is Kirkau?"

"The leader, the worst of them, the thing demons fear."

Caro gulped as the hair on her nape rose. Though it couldn't be true, she felt eyes on her, watching and waiting to pounce. She restrained herself from rubbing her neck.

She didn't want to ask her next question, but she had to. "And you didn't approve?"

Saber prickled over her question, but he'd always told her what a monster he was back then. It was only right that she questioned him on it now.

"I don't kill children... *ever*," he said. "No matter how lost I was to the rage that turned me Savage, I would *never* harm a child. I like kids; they've always held a special place in my heart."

Before becoming a Savage, he'd always dreamed of children and a family. Now, he didn't dream of such things. He had a mate but would be a horrible father; he was too broken to love a child the way they should be loved.

This revelation softened Caro's heart. She *never* would have pegged him as someone who liked children.

And then, her hand went to her mouth as the full horror of his words sank in. She'd seen a demon and Savages in action, knew what they could do to their victims, and imagined they took great joy in the death of those children.

"Why would they do such a thing?" she whispered.

"Do you really have to ask?"

"No, it was a stupid question. You left after that?"

"I left the Savages after that night. I was with them when it started; I tried to stop it. I told them not to go in, that we'd find others to kill. But to evil, and I mean the *true* evil like the demons possess, the innocence and joy of children is the worst kind of offense. It's also something they love to destroy."

Saber had spent centuries burying this memory and doing everything he could to stay far from its hideous grasp. But now that he'd opened the road to it, he couldn't stop traveling its bloody, excruciating terrain.

"I couldn't stop all of them; I killed some as I made my way out with the children I could save, but I didn't kill enough to stop it, and I should have saved more of them."

"You did the best you could."

Did I? That question continued to haunt him.

"How many did you save?" she asked.

"Only five," he murmured. "And I remember every one of their terrified faces. One little girl never cried; she just held hands with her little sister as she clutched her teddy and followed me out of the building. She was the only one who didn't sob, but her eyes…."

His words trailed off as he recalled those warm brown eyes with too much knowledge of everything bad in the world. She'd maybe been seven, and even before that night, she'd seen too much of the brutality life had to offer.

"I took them to another orphanage an hour away and left them there," he said.

"Do you know what became of them?"

"Most grew up to lead normal lives and raise families."

She wasn't surprised he knew what had become of those children. He would never be the monster he believed himself to be.

"That little girl had three girls of her own before dying in childbirth. Her eyes were always well beyond her years. The screams of the rest of those children will haunt me forever, but I walked out that door and never looked back."

Caro slid her fingers into his hand. Her heart broke when anguish etched his face before he covered it up. He may be the most stubborn, closed-off, pain-in-the-ass man she'd ever encountered, but no matter how much he denied it, his heart was bigger than most.

"You saved *five* of them," she said. "If you hadn't left with them, they would have died too. You were one man against Savages and a demon; you couldn't have done anything more."

But she knew he would always question and doubt that.

"Do you hate me?" he asked.

Caro hadn't known she could hurt for him any more than she

already did until that question. This beautiful, broken man was stealing her heart, and she longed to help him heal.

"I could never hate you," she said honestly.

"I failed Brie by giving in to my bloodlust and not looking for her more that day," he said. "And because of that, I went on to slaughter hundreds. I took the lives of *so* many."

"You didn't fail her; you saw a body and didn't know she was alive. You're trying to make up for what happened afterward."

"*Nothing* could atone for that or bring those people back."

"No, but many more would be dead right now if it wasn't for you. Think of the lives you've saved too."

Saber shrugged. "Maybe, but none of it should have happened. I let my emotions rule me that day, and many people died. Maybe, if I'd paid more attention while I was in the fire, I would have seen it wasn't her body."

"You were burning too."

"Not so badly that I couldn't survive it. I should have taken more time and examined the body closer."

"You're too hard on yourself. Your mother was dead, you believed your sister was dead, and your father was on a rampage. Many would have reacted the same way as you, and some would have been worse after witnessing and losing everything you did that day. You couldn't have done anything else."

"There were plenty of things I could have done; I made the wrong choice. At the time, it was a relief. I'd been fighting my increasing urge to kill since reaching maturity, and I was glad to stop."

She didn't know what to say to this admission. "Saber—"

"I'm not going to talk about this anymore. I don't regret my choices or despise myself for them. It's a part of my past, and the humans who killed my mother deserved to die. Now, you asked what happened with the demons and have your answer. Rehashing more of the past won't do any good."

"Okay. If you ever want to talk about it more, we will, but I won't mention it again. And I don't hate you; I could *never* hate you."

Saber wasn't so sure, but she knew the worst of him and still hadn't run screaming. It was more than he deserved from this life, but he would protect her with *everything* he had.

He closed his eyes as his fingers tightened around hers. When he opened them again, the red was gone, but his sorrow remained.

Caro regretted pushing him on this. Was talking about it the way to help him care for others again?

She had no idea, but didn't the experts say talking about things was the way to heal? Then why did she feel so awful? And why did he look anything but relieved to have gotten this off his chest?

His eyes flickered to her before going over her head once more. "It's time for you to rest."

Caro turned away from him, but before she could open the door, his next words stopped her. "I am sorry, Caro. I shouldn't have told you to fuck off."

Tears burned her eyes as she turned back to him. "I shouldn't have called you an asshole."

A small smile tugged at the corners of his mouth. "I *am* an asshole, but I don't remember you saying that."

Caro chuckled. "You're not *always* an asshole, and you weren't there to hear it."

"That's only become true recently, and it's because of you."

Her heart melted, and she stepped closer to kiss his cheek. "Thank you for apologizing, but if you ever talk to me like that again, I'll kick your nuts into your throat again."

Saber winced, and his nuts ached from the reminder of her last blow to them.

"Also, please don't walk away from me again. You can't

storm away from every discussion and argument we have. We might never see each other," she said.

Saber laughed. "I can stop doing that."

Bending, he swept her into his arms and carried her into the apartment.

CHAPTER FOURTEEN

CARO SPENT the next week working on the second set of swords. Things with Brie and Saber mostly continued the way they had from the beginning, except now they occasionally exchanged small talk. They discussed the changing leaves, the weather, and how the swords were coming along.

And by occasional small talk, it was usually Brie who spoke, while Saber grunted, but sometimes he offered a few words in response. They hadn't discussed what he revealed to her about the Savages and children; she wouldn't bring it up again and doubted he would.

She still wasn't sure if she'd done the right thing by pushing him to reveal such a horrible memory. Guilt festered inside her, but Saber didn't seem to hold it against her.

Since then, Brie had been making *very* slow and steady progress with him. It was like pulling teeth to get him to interact with her, but the woman was as stubborn as her brother. And she would have to be if she was going to get anywhere with him.

Caro pretended to focus on hammering the blade as, in between each blow, she caught bits of their conversation.

"It's getting cold here fast," Brie said as she rubbed her arms.

"Hmm," Saber grunted.

Caro tried not to roll her eyes as she lost the next few words to more hammering. By the time she could hear them again, they'd stopped speaking. Saber was the most maddening man she'd ever encountered, but she'd decided to stay out of their relationship from now on.

She'd said her two cents, and he'd told her where he wanted her to stand on it, and she would honor that. Even if it killed her to watch this awkward, heartbreaking scene unfold day after day, she would keep her mouth shut.

She'd considered asking him to take this somewhere else. He may not want to talk to Brie, but she didn't have to watch this torture every day.

However, Saber wouldn't leave her, he would tell Brie to stop coming, and Caro didn't want that. It would upset Brie if he did, and no matter what he said, Caro believed he should have some relationship with his sister. They probably wouldn't ever be as close as when they were kids, but something was better than nothing.

So, she sweated over her fire and listened to the sound of metal ringing against metal while they continued their awkward dance. She imagined Asher was as frustrated by all this as she was, but he didn't try to intervene either.

At least he didn't interfere while they were *here*. He'd most likely said something to Brie about it since arriving here and was probably greeted with the same rebuttal as her. Although, Brie was probably nicer about her fuck off than Saber.

Asher stopped by every hour or so to check on Brie, but whereas she used to go with him after a little bit, she'd started sticking around more. Caro suspected Saber's grunts and his few words of response encouraged her to believe she was making progress with him.

It had encouraged Caro too, but it was an excruciatingly slow progress that made her yearn to scream at her mate to stop being so ridiculous and *talk* to his sister. She'd also considered slapping him upside the head, but violence, no matter how warranted, wasn't the answer here.

When she pulled the next blade from the fire and stuck it in a bucket of water, it sizzled as Brie discussed the birds she'd noted around here. Saber looked as enthused as a man walking to death row, but that didn't dissuade Brie as she chatted about the cardinals and blue jays.

This conversation had to be irritating Saber, but she didn't feel that through their bond. They'd both shut down their open connection; she couldn't have it and focus on work. And Saber would never allow something that intimate to remain open.

It should have hurt her, but it didn't; she needed her alone time too. Plus, it reopened every time they reestablished their bond, and even with the main connection closed, she sensed him all the time.

Caro glanced at them as the sun hanging behind them highlighted their figures. She shifted her attention away after taking in Saber's impassive face and Brie's almost hopeful expression as she discussed hawks, robins, and goldfinches.

Caro regretted shutting the connection down; she'd love to know what he was thinking about his lesson into birdlife. She hid her smile as she examined the blade before deciding it needed more time in the fire.

Saber had expected Brie to give up by now, but she'd dug in her heels about trying to create a relationship with him. He should tell her to go away but couldn't bring himself to do it.

However, he couldn't be held accountable for what came out of his mouth if she talked about one more fucking woodpecker and how to tell the difference between a downy and hairy one.

Is she trying to bore me into talking to her?

Caro lost track of their conversation as she plunged the sword back into the fire and tuned out the bird talk.

It was a while later before Saber said, "I always preferred standard."

"Oh, me too," Brie gushed. "What's the point of having a fast car if you don't have complete control? I never understood the humans who did that."

"I never understood humans."

Brie chuckled. "Me either."

Saber grunted in response, but that was the most Caro had heard him say so far. Progress, wasn't it grand?

But over the next few days, Brie made more headway. Caro eavesdropped on their conversations about whether they preferred cats or dogs, which breed of dog, if they liked horses, their favorite cars, favorite bands, singers, and on and on about small, simple things.

They should all be bored by now, but she wasn't, and they didn't appear to be either. Saber softened a little more with every passing day, and Brie became happier.

This wasn't what he wanted, or at least that's what he told her at night, but Caro suspected he was starting to enjoy it. He hadn't stopped it yet, which he could easily do. To her, that said more than his words about how he felt about this.

His answers remained mostly clipped, and sometimes all he issued was a grunt, but the siblings were learning about each other again and developing a new relationship. If something happened to Brie, it would devastate him, but Caro was sure he needed this.

When Brie yawned, Saber told her, "You should get some sleep."

"I'm okay."

Saber almost said more but decided against it. She was a grown woman, and years ago, it stopped being his place to take care of her.

Still, he couldn't help feeling protective of her; she was his sister, and....

When he realized the direction of his thoughts, he cut them off. This wasn't his business; Asher would take care of his mate.

"I think *she's* ready for bed," Brie said and nodded toward Caro.

Her shoulders hunched forward as she leaned against the wall near her forge and dipped a sword into water. He couldn't see her face, but the slump of her shoulders and more sluggish movements emphasized her exhaustion.

Sweat glistened along the lean muscles of her arms and adhered her hair to the back of her neck. The fire made it warm in the doorway; it had to be stifling where she stood.

He'd brought her some water and blood an hour ago, but she needed a bed. It was still too early to attempt to pull her away from her forge; he'd learned that lesson over the passing weeks.

"She is, but like you, she doesn't listen to reason," he said.

Brie chuckled. "You don't listen to reason either."

"I'm older and stronger than both of you."

"You have eighteen years on me, not centuries, and you're not stronger."

"I'm wiser."

"Bullshit."

Saber couldn't stop himself from laughing. As much as he didn't want to admit it, he liked his sister.

When she was a child, he loved her deeply, and she loved him. He'd never stopped loving her, even if he would have preferred it if he had. Their family had been so close, so happy, until that awful day when the humans tore it all apart.

That kind of love didn't die because the object of it did. Or, in Brie's case, didn't.

So many times, they'd sat before the fire, telling stories, playing games, and singing songs. His mother and father had incredible voices that filled their home with love and warmth.

Even after he moved out and started battling the more sinister urges that intensified when a purebred, male vampire reached maturity, he always felt comforted by home—his mother's touch, his father's laughter, and Brie's giggles as she flung herself into his arms.

"Do you blame me for their deaths?" Brie asked.

CHAPTER FIFTEEN

THE QUESTION STARTLED HIM. She couldn't read minds, he was sure of it, but her thoughts must have traveled the same path as his, and now here they were.

Until now, they'd only talked about mundane things. And they'd never mention the past. Now, with that single question, she'd turned it into a guillotine hanging over their heads.

"No," he said honestly. "Not once."

"The humans came because of *me*. They killed her because of *me* and tried to kill me because they believed I was a witch."

And she'd gone on to do something to help ensure the survival of the human race. She'd never turned on them and slaughtered them like she so easily could have, but he did. The stark differences between them widened the gulf that, despite his best intentions not to let it happen, had been closing over the past week.

"And that makes it *their* fault," he said in a tone far more clipped than he'd intended.

"They did it because of my gift... or curse... or whatever it is."

"What do you think it is?"

"Many times over the years, I've considered it a curse. Often, I was sure the weight of it would destroy me, especially when I stood by while others died and did nothing to intervene. But it also led me to the stones, my good friends Cabo and Zina, and also Asher. Now, it's also led me back to you. How could something that does such wonderful things be a curse?"

"It could be both. You must have the bad to have the good that comes with it."

"True."

"Because of your gift, you've always borne more responsibility than one should have to, especially a child so young. But you're strong enough to handle its weight. You've proven that by still being here after all these years, continuing to fight, and bringing the stones together. It *is* a curse, but it's also a blessing, and something selected you to bear it because you can."

Saber looked away when tears bloomed in his sister's eyes, and she ducked her head. He focused on Caro, who was pretending to study the blade, but her attention was on them.

"I've seen Asher's death too," Brie whispered.

The admission jerked his attention away from Caro and back to his sister. If Asher died, he would lose her all over again.

Her skin had paled to the point where he could see the faint scars marking her flesh. His jaw clenched at the sight of those marks; the humans who killed their parents did that to her.

Why are we helping them?

Right now, he didn't have an answer for that question, but they were fighting for more than the humans; they were also fighting for *their* lives. And Brie would lose hers if Asher died.

"I won't let that happen," he vowed.

He'd just gotten her back and wouldn't let their relationship develop into something more, but he'd believed her dead once; he wouldn't let there be a next time. And he certainly wouldn't lose her in the same way they lost their father.

"I won't let that happen," he vowed again.

"I don't know where it happens, but it's coming soon. I suspect it will happen when we go up against the demons, as there's darkness around us in my vision, but he says he won't stay out of the fight."

"Of course he won't. There's no way he'll let his mate go in there alone."

"And that's foolish, because if he dies, then he's condemning us both to death."

Saber would prefer to stay out of it too. It was a simple, easy solution to the problem, but it wasn't a solution. The hunter-turned-vamp would never agree to it, and Saber didn't blame him. He *never* would have agreed to let Caro go in without him.

"You won't stay out of it either," he said to her.

"I don't have a choice. The stone found me."

"Is that how you see what happens with the stones? They find us?"

"Isn't that how *you* see it?"

"I don't know. I never really thought about it until now."

"The Alliance and stones have brought us all together. There's a reason why the stones belong to so many in the Alliance."

"And that reason is…?"

Brie hesitated before replying. "Fate. All of us finding each other, my visions, and the stones all boil down to fate. Whether that means we'll be successful against the demons or not, I don't know, but fate brought us together to fight them. I firmly believe that."

"And what about the final stone? We've found someone for nine of them, but where's the vampire or hunter who will claim the final one?"

CHAPTER SIXTEEN

"I've been thinking about that," Brie said. "Elena never touched any of the stones. She never went near any of them. Everyone was too busy celebrating her miraculous return, and then she and Logan locked themselves away. We didn't see them again before we packed up and came here. The final stone could be hers."

"What do you think the chances of that are?"

"Pretty good. I never expected almost *all* the stones to get claimed once we went to the Alliance with them. I wasn't granted a vision of that happening, but it makes sense. My collection of stones was always leading to something, and now, I know what it was. And then, we came here; I wasn't expecting Caro to claim another stone *or* to discover you with a mate."

"I didn't expect that either," he muttered.

And he wouldn't change a thing. Well, he would have preferred it if she wasn't working herself into a state of exhaustion every day, but he was glad she was his, and he wasn't going to let her go.

He still wasn't sure how she felt over what he told her about the demons and the orphanage. It had upset her, that much was clear, but she didn't hate him for it or hold him responsible for what happened.

He would always hold himself responsible. They would have killed him if he'd gone after more children, but the what-ifs were reawakened with the memory. He was glad he'd told her; while it hadn't lifted the weight of that night from him, at least he wasn't still upsetting her by keeping it from her.

Before her, his incessant need for death was the only thing driving him. With her, the thrum of that compulsion was much quieter and far more controllable. Now, he had to ensure she survived the coming battle, and his sister and her mate did too.

Caro lowered the sword and used the back of her arm to wipe sweat from her brow. She planted her hands on her lower back as she stretched.

She went to pick up the sword again, but Saber's strong hand encased her wrist, stopping her. Scowling, she shifted her attention to him as he stepped closer.

"Enough," he said. "That's enough for today. It's time for you to rest."

"I normally work for at least another hour," she said.

"Not today; we're calling it an early night. You're exhausted, and the swords will still be here tomorrow."

She glanced over his shoulder to the doorway, but Brie was gone. She'd left them to their moment like Caro had left them alone for weeks.

She wanted to argue with him, but the feel of his hand around her wrist sent a shiver of anticipation down her spine. Instead of fighting with him, she stepped into his arms, wrapped hers around his waist, and clung to him.

Saber stood uncertainly for a minute. They continued to have sex, and they'd grown closer, but she'd never sought comfort from him like this before.

At first, he didn't know how to react. Then his arms slid around her waist, and he drew her closer. She fit perfectly against his chest as he buried his nose in her hair and inhaled her ocean scent.

She was as full of life as the sea aroma she emitted and as beautiful as the sun glinting off the waves. She was wild, tumultuous, and a force to be reckoned with, but best of all, she was *his* force, *his* mate, and the woman who completed him.

He wouldn't change a thing.

Caro stifled a yawn as Saber lifted her into his arms and carried her from the workshop. "I can walk," she murmured.

"You can, but do you want to?"

Caro smiled as she snuggled closer; he had her there. "No."

CHAPTER SEVENTEEN

As Caro rose from the tub, water ran off her in rivulets that emphasized her lean muscles and soft curves. Saber's eyes followed as they ran down her flat belly and between her legs.

His mouth watered, but he tamped down his desire. She required rest more than sex right now.

Still, being this close to his mate and seeing her like this had kicked his hunger for her into hyperdrive. Fighting against his growing erection, he draped a thick towel around her as she stepped from the tub.

"Feel better?" he asked.

"Yes."

The warm bath had relaxed her stiff muscles and revitalized her a little. The scent of blood lured her from the room as she toweled herself off.

When she finished, she dried her wet hair while hungrily eyeing the steam rising from the mug of blood Saber had set on the table. She was ravenous, but that wasn't the blood she craved. Scenting his arousal, she tossed the towel onto her green armchair before turning to face him.

Saber tried to tear his attention away from where she stood in the center of the room, bathed in moonlight, her hip stuck slightly out. Lifting her finger, she smiled as she crooked it and beckoned him forth.

Saber wanted to resist, she should sleep, but she had a better idea of what she needed than he did. Instead of telling her to rest, he strode toward her as she backed away with a mischievous twinkle in her eyes.

Her smile never vanished as she sat on the bed and pushed herself back to perch near the headboard. Saber nearly tripped over his feet when her legs parted a little. He tugged off his sweatpants, kicked them aside, and climbed onto the bed to crawl toward her. Caro leaned against the headboard and lifted her arms over her head to proudly display every curve and hollow of her splendid body.

"You're magnificent," he murmured as he stopped in front of her.

"I know. You're not so bad yourself."

Saber chuckled as he rested his hands on the insides of her knees and pushed her legs a little wider. He met her eyes again as his finger rubbed her clit. They darkened as her mouth parted and her head tipped further back.

When he removed his hand from between her legs, irritation flashed over her features. Her hands rested against his chest as he leaned over to open her nightstand drawer.

"What are you doing?" she inquired.

Saber sorted through some of her things before locating what he sought. When he pulled the vibrator free, he held it up, and she lifted an eyebrow.

"Going through my things?" she inquired.

"I was looking for a pen and ended up checking out the competition."

Her laughter was music to his ears. Had there ever been a more lovely sound? He didn't think so.

"A girl's gotta stay happy," she said.

"You'll get no arguments from me."

With that, he switched it on. Caro's mouth parted as he brought the head to her clit and caressed her. She gasped as he teased and played while leaning closer to kiss her.

And what a kiss it was. Saber kissed her like he would never get the opportunity again, kissed her as if she were the only thing in this world and he'd lost himself to her. And she most certainly lost herself to him.

He grasped her hair and pulled her head back as he slid the vibrator into her. She arched toward him as their tongues entwined. The sensation between her legs and the intensity of his kiss caused her body to spiral toward ecstasy.

She'd never done anything like this with someone before, and she wanted more as she came so hard white spots burst behind her closed eyes. She cried out against his mouth as her toes curled and her fingers dug into his hair.

She was trembling and trying to catch her breath when he tossed the vibrator aside. She had no idea where it landed and didn't care as he grasped her legs, pulled her down the bed, and settled between her thighs.

Before she could fully come down from her orgasm, he thrust into her, and she cried out from the breathtaking sensation of their bodies joining. As the world faded away, there were no demons, swords, and death lurking around the corner. It was just them and the pleasure they gave each other.

It was everything she'd ever wanted and more as her fangs pierced his neck and his blood filled her. Passion and emotion clamored through her, and when he renewed his bite on her, love rushed forth.

It was so sudden and unexpected that she hadn't known it was coming. But while trying to protect her heart, she'd also been falling for this powerful, broken, stubborn, and often obtuse man.

His tender care for her, inability to see how much his sister loved him and how good of a man he actually was, and his wounded spirit had entangled themselves around her heart. Until, gradually and unbeknownst to her, she'd fallen for the man.

There was a good chance he'd break her heart, but there was no changing this. She loved him.

And she couldn't let him know. She kept her emotions locked away, contained by a wall, and the mental bond between them closed. If he sensed her feelings, he would pull away from her.

Maybe one day he could know, but he wasn't ready for that, and she refused to reveal how in love she was with him when he didn't love her back. He may not love her, but he wouldn't want to hurt her by not returning her feelings.

Becoming more distant would be his way to solve the problem, and she wouldn't let that happen. At one time, she'd regretted that fate had chosen him for her; now, she was glad it did. She never would have chosen anyone else.

Grasping her hips, he rolled so she was on top while they continued to feed on each other. Releasing her bite on his neck, she rose over him, and her head fell back as she planted her hands on his chest and came again with a loud cry.

Saber drove into her, and as her sheath clenched around his cock, he pulled out. When he came, his back arched off the bed, a tingle raced down his spine, and he shouted as she collapsed onto his chest.

CHAPTER EIGHTEEN

Caro set the last sword on the workbench inside her forge and stepped back to examine them. Their stones glimmered in the sun streaming down on them.

It was a little cramped around the bench as the core members of the Alliance had gathered around to examine the final products. Some lower-level members hovered outside the doorway of the forge, curious to see what was happening. Brie's friends, Cabo and Zina, were in front of them and a little inside the forge.

The king had arrived with a lot of their fighters last week. They'd reassembled all those who had scattered after the attack on the compound. Twenty of their soldiers remained behind to guard the injected who were still imprisoned in their cages.

Nathan had also contacted Juan in Arizona. The leader of the hunters there was sending fighters to join them. He'd spoken with some of the other hunter compounds who had agreed to help the Alliance, but they were also experiencing a surge in Savage activity and were unwilling to send fighters.

War loomed on the horizon, and they needed all the help they could get to wage it. Juan's hunters would arrive in a couple of days, and some of Willow's family would join them in this battle.

They had a lot of fighters, but would they be enough? And would they be able to find whoever the remaining stone belonged to?

She had a feeling that, without them, their battle wasn't worth waging. These stones, and the fighters they chose to wield them, should be together.

Caro eyed the swords as she recalled Brie's words about Elena. Had the woman touched the sword containing the light pink stone yet? She hadn't seen it if she had.

But if it wasn't Elena, then who else could it be? Maybe they'd get lucky and it would be someone else in the Alliance or one of Juan's hunters, but they had to find them before going after the demons.

"Impressive," Ronan murmured as he examined the weapons.

"They are," Saber agreed.

He looked at Caro as her attention shifted to Elena. Saber couldn't believe the difference in Logan's mate. The last time he saw her, Elena's eyes were completely black and a black liquid filled her veins.

She'd been crazed, pale, and completely different from the serene, healthy-looking woman with glowing, golden skin and normal, black eyes. Logan stood protectively against her side, his hand on her waist as they surveyed the weapons.

The difference in her was amazing, but it had been almost two months since he last saw her and a month since she awakened from her demon-imposed prison. Seeing her like this gave him hope they could destroy these things.

"We have to find the owner of the pink stone," Brie said.

"Have you had a vision?" Killean asked.

"No, but I *feel* that if they all find their rightful owners, they'll be much stronger, and so will we."

"How do we find who that stone belongs to?" Kadence asked.

Brie pinned Elena with her stare. "You're the only one here who hasn't touched it. If it's not you, then we'll have to find its owner, but you have to try."

"It can't be," Elena murmured in her accented voice as she shifted her attention to the swords.

Stepping closer to the table, she stretched her fingers toward the unclaimed one. Her hand hovered over the blade before she lowered it and clasped the hilt.

When a spark of light flashed through the stone, she let out a little gasp. Brie smiled as Elena lifted the sword and twisted it before her.

"There's a reason we were all brought together," Brie whispered.

Saber stared at where his sword lay on the table before shifting his attention to Brie. She knew far too much of this world, yet not enough.

It would be much easier if her gift could reveal all they needed to know to stop the demons, but things were never that easy. They were lucky her gift had brought these stones into their lives; it was selfish to ask for more, but that's what he'd always been.

There were still so many unanswered questions, and death loomed on the horizon... for the whole world if they didn't succeed.

He glanced toward the serene woods, but in his memory, he saw the fires devouring them. The screams would never go away.

There was a reason he'd shared a vision with his sister. He didn't know what it was. He was pretty sure he'd never get a true answer, but he suspected it had something to do with his relationship with Brie.

He didn't know why fate would care if they talked, but

maybe he was meant to save Asher or *her*. She was important to this; even though she'd gathered the stones already, fate might still have plans for her.

And then he looked to Caro, who stared at the blades. Sorrow radiated from her, and though their ability to communicate and experience each other's feelings remained locked down, he knew it was because she wished her father could see this.

He settled his hand on the small of her back and stroked it with his thumb. His chest constricted when she lifted her head and smiled at him. A little tug pulled at his heart, but he buried it.

Now was not the time for emotion of any kind. They would soon be going to war, and he would remain focused on winning and keeping her safe.

"Okay, so we have the rightful owner of each stone," Simone said. "Now what?"

"We wait for the others to arrive and bring the war to the demons. We've spent too much time on the defensive; it's time to go on the offensive," Ronan said.

CHAPTER NINETEEN

"How do we take the battle to them when we don't know where they are?" Lucien inquired.

"I've been thinking about that," Saber said. "We killed a demon in the storm drain, we found Willow's sword in Maine, and there has been a lot of activity in the Northeast."

"I saw a demon in Vermont; his name was Kirkau," Killean said.

"He's their leader, and they'll congregate where he is."

"I encountered him years ago."

"But they're after the sword," Saber said. "And as far as they know, only *one* of those stones has been found, and Willow has it. They know she's in the Northeast and won't go far from it."

"So wouldn't they be in Boston or the surrounding area?" Willow asked. "That's where they found us last time."

"They could be," Saber said, "but I have a feeling they somehow knew the sword was in Maine and decided to establish their central location around here while they looked for it. They wouldn't pick it up and move it, even after they lost the sword.

"They're not so far from where the compound was, or where they think we could be, that it's difficult for them to travel there.

Besides, I killed that demon in the storm drain; they'll expect it to be the work of an Alliance member, as almost no other vampire, without the training, could have pulled it off.

"They'll start grouping together around here in the hopes that maybe we've moved, and they can find us again. They'll also do it to protect themselves. But I suspect they're centered here and have tunneled out to other locations from those drains."

"But hunters in Arizona were also injected with their blood," Saxon said.

"It's easier to transport their blood than them," Saber said. "They could have also traveled there at night or in some container that kept them out of the sun's rays. It's not difficult for them to do, but I'm not sure they'd venture that far from their main base."

"Did they when you were a Savage?" Ronan asked.

"I don't know. That's not something they would let me in on. Plus, there were fewer of them when I was a Savage."

"Or so you think," Caro said. "They might not have let you know how many of them there were."

"Or they could have been spread out to all different locations," Elyse said.

"They could have," Saber agreed, "and it is possible we'll have to track them worldwide, but I believe their main focus is in this area. There's too much activity here; if there wasn't a reason for them to stay here, they would have left after Willow claimed the sword."

Willow's hand rested on the hilt of her sword as it lay before her on the table. A small spark ran through the red-orange stone.

"Going into those tunnels after them could prove to be a death sentence," Nathan said. "Who knows how many tunnels they have down there."

"That's *if* they're camped out down there," Killean said. "We can't go down there for nothing."

"We'll have to draw them out," Saber said.

"How do we do that?" Vicky asked.

"By using me," Saber said.

Caro stiffened beside him, and her head turned his way. He could feel her staring daggers into him but didn't look at her.

"They want me," he continued. "As far as I know, I'm the only one who got away from them and forsook their ways. They don't like that. If they know where I am, they'll send Savages for me, but they'll come too. They won't be able to resist."

"No," Caro said.

"And how would you lure them out?" Logan inquired.

No," Caro said again, and Brie was shaking her head.

Saber moved his hand from the small of Caro's back to her hip as he pulled her closer. It didn't matter what she or Brie thought about this; *he* was the best way to draw the demons and Savages out, and they had to use him.

"I believe they're in those drainage tunnels. I'll go in there alone, take some explosives with me, and use them to piss them off and draw them out. Once they realize *I* did it, they'll turn the Savages loose on me, but they'll also come for me. I know they will."

"And how will they know it was you?" Killean asked.

"I'll make sure someone sees me and lives to track me."

"You can't do that alone," Caro said.

"I agree," Brie said.

"I'll go with him," Saxon offered.

"So will I," Lucien said.

Ronan held up a hand when Elyse and Callie started protesting. "Let's discuss this without arguing over it."

"If he sets off a bomb below the city, people will die," Kadence said.

"No one is going to set off a bomb beneath the city," Ronan assured her.

"I can make it so it's not big enough to go beyond the tunnels," Saber said. "I'm good with bombs."

"He is," Declan agreed.

"If there's some way to lure them out of those tunnels instead of going down there, it would be better for us," Ronan said.

"Even if we did that," Asher said, "we'll never know if they all came out after him. We have no idea how many of them are down there."

They all pondered his words as Declan removed a lollipop from his pocket. He twisted the stick between his fingers while eyeing the swords.

"I don't think we have to do any of those things," Declan said. "We'll use the swords to draw them out."

"And how do we do that?" Willow inquired.

Declan shifted his attention to Caro. "How fond are you of this place?"

CHAPTER TWENTY

CARO RECOILED a little at the question. It was all she had left of her parents and the life she'd treasured. They'd been so happy here; memories lurked around every corner, and she could still hear the laughter rebounding off the walls.

But she couldn't stay here forever. Before she met Saber, she'd known her time here was ending. Locking herself away here would be a slow form of death. Her parents wouldn't appreciate it if she followed them into the grave, even if she still lived.

However, to see this place destroyed wasn't something she wanted either. She rubbed her chest over her heart as she thought about it.

"Why are you asking?" she whispered.

"I've checked this place out since arriving here," Declan said. "Your father did an amazing job with the security. The woods would be a great place to set traps and ambush anyone who comes over the wall.

"The electricity running through those metal spikes will keep some from getting over, but, as we learned with the compound, if there's enough of them, they will get over. And there will be enough of them; they'll come with everything they have, especially if they know we have all the stones."

Around the table, the Alliance scowled, and some of them shifted at the reminder of their lost home. Caro sensed their bitterness in the air and their desire for revenge. The ones in the doorway muttered something, and a ripple went through the crowd behind them.

"The rest will come through, and over, the gates. Which, despite their thickness, are the weakest entry points because there's no electricity running through them," Declan continued. "But we'll have more traps ready for them there. By the time they get to the house, and they will get to the house, there's enough cleared land here for us to make a solid stand against them. If we kill enough of them before drawing them here, we have a good chance of winning."

"He's right," Saber said. He didn't like saying it as he sensed Caro's distress, but they had to explore all options. "Charles did a great job with the security, and there are enough cameras that we'll see them coming and know where they are throughout the invasion."

"If all goes well, we could kill hundreds of them without ever having to engage them," Nathan said. "And once we kill the ones here, the tunnels will be safer to enter, and the demons will be weaker with fewer fighters. We can go in and clear out anyone left behind afterward."

Caro bit her bottom lip while pondering this. She'd already lost her parents, the store, her van, and the statues and weapons she melted to create the swords. Before this, she would have been certain she couldn't take any more loss, but she had to.

Drawing them here to make a stand against them was a far better option than having Saber go into those tunnels to lure them out on his own. She'd already lost so much; she couldn't lose him too.

If she could stop that from happening, then she would. And

this plan was better than having *all* of them file into the drainage tunnels that went who knew where and could have any number of side tunnels branching out from them.

That would be like shooting fish in a barrel and a good way to get them all killed. Watching the demons and Savages destroy her home would be horrible, but watching the world burn would be far worse.

"How do we lure them here?" she asked.

Some of the tension eased from the group when they realized she was agreeing to this plan. Declan unwrapped his lollipop and stuck it in his mouth.

"We can't make it look obvious," Callie said. "They'll suspect a trap if we're not careful."

Ronan rested his hands on the workbench as he studied the weapons. "Once they see a couple of these stones set into the swords, they'll be determined to take them from us. We only have to tease them with a couple of swords that aren't Willow's."

"Even if they don't assume we have all of them, they'll come for these," Killean said. "They want them… *badly*."

"And they won't get them," Willow said. "Since each of these weapons has been claimed by one of us, they can't take any away unless we're dead."

Caro gulped. "That means the demons will come after us the hardest."

Simone rested her hand on Killean's arm. "Yes, it does."

No one spoke until Caro broke the silence. "There's a bunker on the property too. I'm not sure if it will do us any good, but it's there."

"We could turn it into another trap," Saber said. "I could put some explosives down there and blow it up when the demons and Savages approached. They'd never see it coming."

Caro winced at the prospect but bit her tongue. She'd resigned herself to this destruction and wouldn't change it, no matter how much it hurt.

"So," Ronan said, "we'll spend the next few days setting traps and waiting for the rest of our fighters to arrive. And then, a few of us will go into the city of White Bridge, let the Savages see what we have, and lure them back here without making it look obvious. After that, we'll go to war."

CHAPTER TWENTY-ONE

THEY SPENT the next week digging holes, making traps, and setting up wires. Saber was also preparing explosives for when they drew the demons here.

While they worked, more hunters arrived from Arizona, along with some of Willow and Vicky's family. Their parents, Sera and Liam, and brothers, Ethan, Ian, and Aiden, arrived with their mates Emma, Paige, and Maggie.

Their sister, Abby, who was Vicky's twin, also arrived with her mate, Brian, who Saber said possessed a unique ability to track others. Their adopted uncles, Jack and Mike, came with their mates, Charlie and Mollie.

They also said their brother Julian and his mate, Aida, Mollie's younger sister, would be coming soon, as would their sister Isabelle and her mate, Stefan. They'd stayed behind to ensure all the children were settled before leaving.

The family had decided against splitting up the mated pairs, and though they all wanted to come, they left the other mated adults home to care for the children. They also stayed behind to help protect the female hunters and all the hunter children who traveled there after the compound fell. Some of those female hunters had also come to join the fight.

Every day, their numbers swelled until they had a small army stationed within the walls of her family property. Tents and sleeping bags were scattered through the yard and hidden amongst the trees beneath the thick canopy of pines.

Some newly arrived fighters slept in the barn, vehicles, and the bunker, but most were in the woods. They had to make sure that, when the Savages or demons trailed them here, they couldn't see how big their army was.

They needed the demons to bring enough fighters that they could decimate their numbers, but not so many they were overrun. The demons and Savages could never see beyond the gates and walls, but if they had drones or some other aerial surveillance, many of their fighters would be hidden. Lucien and Saxon confirmed this after flying drones over the property.

Once they went to White Bridge, everyone here would go to their designated places until the demons and Savages breached the walls. And then, the blood would flow.

It was so strange for Caro to see her home, one that, before Saber, had only ever known her and her parents, overrun with so many vampires and hunters. It was also empowering.

At first, she wasn't sure this would work, but she was beginning to think they could pull it off. The demons would never expect the sheer number of traps and fighters they had.

If, for some reason, they did suspect a trap, Saber had told her the demons would underestimate them. They were too arrogant not to.

Toward the end of the week, their numbers had swelled to well over two hundred. There were a lot more Savages in the world, but they wouldn't all come here with the demons as they were spread out across the country.

"What about the demons in the other countries?" she asked

Saber as they dug a hole in the woods on their final day of preparations.

"*If* there are any demons in other countries, and I'm not sure there are, I believe they would stick closer together, a strength-in-numbers thing. But they will come too, once they receive word of the swords. It will take them time; they'll have to travel at night and probably enclosed in something—"

"Like a coffin?"

"Yeah, pretty much."

Caro couldn't help but chuckle as she threw a shovel full of dirt and tree roots out of the hole. "Maybe we should try throwing garlic, holy water, and crosses at them too."

"I doubt those would work, but sunlight will."

They exchanged a look as they smiled at each other in amusement before returning to digging.

"What if the ones traveling here don't get here in time?" Caro asked.

"I really don't think that's something we have to worry about. They may not all live in the same place, but I think they'll all be in the same area. They're stronger together. If for some reason I'm wrong, then I think they'll wait to attack.

"Once they know where we are, if they expect more demons to arrive, they won't come for us immediately. They'll monitor us to make sure we don't leave while they grow their army before trying to enter. When they *do* come for us, they'll accept nothing less than death, and there will be no mercy."

Caro already knew all this, but hearing him say it in that flat, assured tone made her gulp. "No mercy."

"And we won't show them any either."

She had no intention of doing that, but she was unsure how she would handle killing something. Though she'd stabbed some of them before, none had died at her hand. It wouldn't be easy, but she'd do whatever it took to stay alive and protect Saber.

"We're going to have to be careful not to become injected, too," Saber continued. "We know how to cure those who are now, or at least we're pretty sure we do, but it will slow us down."

"And be just awful," Caro said with a shudder.

"That too."

When the hole was deep enough, Caro set her shovel aside and scrambled out to retrieve the wooden stakes they'd sharpened into lethal points. She returned to the trap with them.

She handed some to Saber, and together they hammered them into the ground. Careful not to accidentally fall onto one of the stakes, Caro tiptoed around the wood as it filled more and more of the hole.

When they finished, they tossed their tools out and pulled themselves out of the hole. Caro's heart hammered as she tried not to picture losing her grip and tumbling back onto the stakes, but she managed to escape the death trap without any holes in her body.

Once outside the pit, they carefully placed the sticks, leaves, dirt, and branches they'd gathered over top of it. When they finished, Caro stepped back to admire their handiwork. If someone wasn't aware of the trap, they'd never know it was there.

Caro wiped her hands on her jeans as Saber lifted the map Declan, Julian, and Roland had printed out from the numerous computers they brought in. It laid out, in intricate detail, every inch of her property.

Xs marked the places to set traps. The numbers next to each trap indicated which team was supposed to create them. They were DT3, also known as the Death Trap Three team.

Any X with a circle around it meant the job was complete. The Xs didn't start until a few hundred feet from the wall. They would lure the demons and Savages into a false sense of security before unleashing a ton of death in the form of clustered Xs that would be impossible for all of them to evade.

Saber circled the X they were working on now and pulled out his handheld radio from where it hung in a holster at his hip. He hit the button to inform the other twenty groups in the woods that they'd set trap number two hundred.

Those twenty groups would circle it off on their maps, and back at the main base of operations, her parents' dining room, Roland would mark the large map hanging on the wall. They had to make sure no one else accidentally wandered into one of them.

Not all the traps were full of stakes. Saber had also established land mines throughout the woods. It was now more dangerous to stroll through her woods than to steal a bear cub from its mama while running through a nest of vipers.

Caro leaned on her shovel's handle while she surveyed the trees that once offered solace and limitless places to hide as a child. She'd daydreamed about ghosts, trolls, ogres, and all sorts of fantastical creatures beneath these boughs. Some were her friends, some were not, but all of them made each day more fun.

"Ready?" Saber asked.

His question tore Caro from her reverie. To hide her sadness, she smiled at him as she pulled her shovel from the earth. "On to the next death trap."

CHAPTER TWENTY-TWO

THEY WALKED to the next X designated for them on the map. It was the last one they had to set today, which meant the other teams would finish soon too.

And once they finished with this, they'd shower and eat before heading to White Bridge with Declan and Willow. She hoped they'd have some time to sit and relax first, but she wasn't going to rush Saber through setting the land mine.

Not having much experience with the damn things, she hovered twenty feet away as he worked with the ease of someone with a lot of experience. That didn't ease her anxiety as she chewed on her bottom lip and gripped her shovel so tightly her hands ached.

One wrong move... Stop it! she scolded herself. *He knows what he's doing.*

Still, it killed her to watch her mate working with something that could tear away pieces of him. Instead, she focused on their plan for tonight in the hopes of calming the wild flutter of her heart.

They'd decided against bringing any more than the four of

them tonight. It would be too obvious to the demons if a bunch of Alliance members suddenly showed up with swords.

However, they already knew she and Saber were in Maine. The Savages, who arrived at her parents' store to try taking her, would have gotten word back to the demons about who they were hunting and what they looked like. The demons would recognize Saber.

Plus, the dead demon and Savages in the storm drain were a good indicator someone powerful was nearby.

The demons and Savages expected them to be around, and they already knew Willow had a sword, so they wouldn't be surprised to see hers. Plus, she was someone they *really* wanted too. She'd kept that sword from them, and they were eager to get it back.

The four of them would go to the city tonight but wouldn't do much while there. They needed the Savages to see them with the swords and report to their masters.

Seeing so many swords with stones would lure the demons into following them… or, at least, that's what they hoped. If not, they were doing a whole lot of work for nothing.

It was a terrifying prospect.

After tonight, half of their numbers would go into hiding around the property, in the woods, and the bunker with enough blood for two weeks. If it took the demons that long to attack, it would be miserable for them, but they'd get through it.

When Saber finished with the mine, he marked it on the map before radioing it in. They returned to her apartment, cleaned themselves, and had sex like it was the last time, which it might be.

They didn't expect anything to go wrong tonight; they weren't going there to fight. They'd have to kill some Savages if they encountered them, but they expected it to be a simple mission.

She and Saber barely spoke as he drove her car toward White

Bridge. Declan and Willow were also on their way but had taken a different vehicle.

Declan and Willow would be the ones to "accidentally" lead them back to her house. Saber didn't think the demons would buy it if he was the one to do it.

The demons knew Declan and Willow a little, but not as well as they knew him and his reputation. He wouldn't fuck up like that, few members of the Alliance would, but it was bound to happen on occasion. They'd found the compound somehow.

To the Savages and demons, it should look like nothing more than a divide-and-conquer mission. The demons would believe it if Declan and Willow didn't make it obvious. And two cars would make sense as they'd park in different areas and enter the city from those locations… or so they all hoped.

CHAPTER TWENTY-THREE

ONCE THEY MADE it to White Bridge and exited the car, she and Saber stayed mostly in the shadows and were careful not to draw too much attention to themselves. They could have pulled off wearing the swords if there was some cosplay thing going on, or if it was Halloween, but neither of those were true.

Neither she nor Saber wanted to deal with the police, even if they could send them on their merry way with relative ease. It was a hassle they'd prefer to avoid.

While staying mostly out of the public eye, they strolled through the waterfront section of the city. They used the buildings and shadows to help keep them hidden but drew the attention of some people.

Those people mostly gave them strange looks, openly admired Saber, or leered at her, but none ran away, and she didn't see anyone pull out their phones to call the police. So far, they were attracting enough attention but not so much to cause a scene.

They didn't see Willow and Declan, but that was part of the plan. They were on their mission to attract the right amount of attention while also seeking out Savages to follow them from there.

After a couple of hours and many winding trips down side streets and alleys, Saber *finally* scented rot on the air. When his steps slowed, so did Caro's.

They'd left the busier waterfront area behind and were on a quiet side street with a single bar toward the end and a restaurant in the middle. Light poured from the only two open establishments. It spilled across the sidewalk and street, with a few cars parked along the curbs.

The scents of cooking meat and humans mingled in the air, but neither were strong enough to drown out the fetid, garbage aroma of a nearby Savage. Saber listened for the sound of approaching footsteps, but the laughter of a group of friends and the hum of an approaching vehicle were the only noises.

The friends turned to the bar doorway. A second later, when the door opened, the beat of music increased, as did the din of conversation, until the door closed again.

They continued walking as Saber glanced around but didn't see anyone on the street. Then, recalling what happened to Caro, his gaze fell.

He gripped her arm, pulling her to a stop a few feet away from the roadside storm drain. With no cars parked over them, the drain grates were clearly visible.

Holding up a hand, he tried to reestablish a connection to Caro through their bond. Instead, he came up against a wall as she shut him out.

Gritting his teeth, Saber buried his irritation over this discovery. He'd been keeping her shut out but hadn't realized she was doing the same. It shouldn't annoy him that she was doing the same thing as him; it did.

He was the one who was supposed to be closed off, not her. He shouldn't expect her to be open to him when he wasn't to her, but he did. Yep, he was an asshole who couldn't communicate with his mate when necessary.

He refused to admit finding her shut off hurt, but a pang tugged at his heart. Saber resisted his urge to rub his chest right over the beating organ.

Taking a deep breath, he held up his hand to indicate for her to stay here. She opened her mouth to say something but closed it again. She glared at him before nodding.

He crept closer to the drain and was only a few feet away when a face emerged from the shadows below. Red eyes blinked at him, and a snarl curved the Savage's mouth as it bared its fangs and smiled.

When the creature's fingers gripped the grate as if it were going to lift it away, Saber smiled as he pulled his sword free. The black stone glistened in the glow from the restaurant.

Despite its obvious bloodlust, the Savage stopped moving as its eyes fastened on the stone. Then its gaze flicked to Saber, and instead of emerging from the storm drain, it ducked down and vanished into the shadows.

Saber closed the distance between him and the drain. The slap of feet pounding against concrete retreated as the Savage disappeared into the maze of tunnels that he was sure the demons had built below.

This whole city probably sat over the top of a pit leading straight into Hell, and they had *no* idea. When he was with them, the demons moved around a lot, but he was beginning to think things had changed.

Saber wasn't surprised when Caro came to stand beside him. He'd known she wouldn't stay away for long, not his mate.

"There's something down there," he said.

"We already knew that."

"No. It's more than anything I ever experienced with them before. I have no idea how I know it, but I do. There's something down there, and it's bad."

Caro gazed into the grate as she processed this information. "Do you think you're somehow sharing Brie's gift or tapping into it? I know she receives visions, and I assume they make her more intuitive."

He would have vehemently denied it at any other time, but he'd never get the image of those burning woods from his mind. It remained so vivid he could smell the fire and hear the crack of the falling trees.

"I don't know," he muttered. "But I haven't survived five hundred years because I can't spot danger, and it's down there… building."

"To what?"

"To the end."

CHAPTER TWENTY-FOUR

CARO GULPED AS SHE SHIVERED. She could picture a sea of lava and death building beneath them as Hell threatened to take over.

"We should have brought Brie here," she said. "Maybe she could have seen something to help us."

"I don't want her here."

"She's going to have to fight, Saber. She has no choice, and neither do I."

He scowled as he pulled her away from the grate. "I know that."

"There's a difference between knowing and accepting. It's time to start accepting it. Maybe we should call and have her and Asher join us."

"No, it's too late to deviate from the plan. If no Savages follow us back tonight, then we'll bring her with us tomorrow."

The Savage had run, but it would spread the word of what it saw. The demons would soon know he was here and possessed something they craved.

"Let's head back toward the waterfront," he told Caro.

She released the breath she hadn't realized she was holding.

Together, they walked back to the waterfront, where the streetlights and glow from the open businesses sparkled off the water.

The boats docked in the marina bobbed on the gentle rhythm of a waveless sea. Now that summer was over, there weren't as many boats, but they still decorated the water.

The cobblestone streets were filled with cars and people as they strolled from one place to another, laughed, and danced in the night. It was all so beautiful and peaceful despite the noise and music.

It was almost impossible for Caro to believe monsters lurked beneath them, but she'd been down there. This beauty was hiding an insidious evil just waiting to spring.

She recalled Saber telling her the demons and Savages had taken over some towns. Had they moved in and taken many of the residents here too?

It wasn't a large city, but it was still a lot bigger than some small town in the boondocks, but had they gotten their tentacles into the people here? She gulped as she realized it was a good possibility.

"Some of these people might be working for them too and reporting about us," she whispered.

"I know."

"I hate this shit."

"So do I."

As they made their way through the crowd, Caro became more determined than ever to ensure a future for this world. If the demons had some of these people, they needed to be set free, and the rest of this beautiful, crazy, magnificent world had to be saved.

The demons had planned a fate worse than death for these people, and she wouldn't allow it to befall them. She also wasn't about to let penguins be wiped off the Earth. Those cute, waddling little animals deserved better, as did *every* other animal on this planet.

"Hey, you've got a sword!" a young, drunken man declared while he staggered toward her. "Are you like Wonder Woman or something?"

When Saber clasped her wrist and pulled her away from the kid's drunken lurch, Caro rolled her eyes; she was out here hunting demons, and he was trying to protect her from a twenty-something kid.

"Oh cool, you have a sword too," the kid slurred as he eyed Saber's sword.

Saber stared unrelentingly at him, but the kid was too drunk to notice as he stretched a hand toward the sword on Saber's back. When Saber snarled at him, the kid's precarious position finally registered.

"Back off," Saber warned.

The kid's hand dropped, and he stumbled back. "Sorry, man."

A young woman rushed over and seized his wrist. She eyed him and Caro as she tugged the young man away. "Come on, Duane. Let's get you some water."

"They have swords. They're like superheroes or something," Duane said.

Fear flashed over the woman's face when she glanced back at them, and she hurried her friend a little faster. "They could be killers, you idiot."

"Oh shit," Duane slurred. "They could be. That's pretty cool!"

"I think Duane needs more than water," Caro muttered.

"I agree, but killing him on the street would be frowned upon, and, unfortunately, I've vowed not to kill any more humans."

Saber sounded entirely too disappointed about this. Caro poked him in the ribs. "That's a good thing."

He grunted in response.

"Also," Caro stepped out from behind him, "you don't have to protect me from humans."

Saber rested a hand possessively on her hip. "I don't care if they're humans, Savages, or vampires; no man will get too close to you."

"Okay, Captain Neanderthal, but I can take care of myself, especially from a human. So don't do that again."

When he growled, she rolled her eyes but decided against pushing the issue further. She was very aware of how possessive mated males were, and if she was honest with herself, if some drunken female approached him, she'd be tempted to kick that woman's ass, even if she wasn't hitting on him.

"Come on," she said. "We should keep moving."

CHAPTER TWENTY-FIVE

THEY DIDN'T TRY to enter any of the establishments; there was no way they were getting their swords inside. They could change the minds of the bouncers or hostesses they encountered, but there were too many other patrons for them to do anything about.

So instead, they moved through the shadows on the main thoroughfare. After a while, they headed for the side roads and alleys again. They walked along them before returning to the busier area once more.

When they got there, she spotted Willow and Declan ahead of them. They were stopped outside a darkened store, leaning against the wall while Willow examined her phone.

"Let's go this way," Saber said.

Clasping her elbow, he turned and led her in a different direction. They only strolled a few feet before the stench of rot filled her nostrils.

When she glanced down, she saw the storm drain in the sidewalk. Unlike the one along the streets, this one was a cover and not grates, but that cover could easily come off. The Savages had already dragged her into one; she wouldn't go into another.

"They're following us from underneath," Saber said. "We're catching their scent when they move closer to the surface."

"They're like rats," she muttered.

"Stay away from the drains."

"Believe me, I know that better than anyone."

His thumb caressed her arm as he steered her into another alley. They spent another hour walking through side streets and alleys before returning to the main road.

As they moved, the stench of rot followed them with more frequency. And after a while, it stopped coming from beneath them.

They'd picked up a Savage who weaved in and out of the people as it trailed them through the crowd. Saber wasn't sure if Caro had detected it yet, but without looking at it, he knew where it was.

The night was growing late, and businesses were starting to close. The main street was much more subdued, though some die-hard humans continued to party as they traversed the roads and lingered in the few remaining bars still open.

"It's time to go," Saber said.

Keeping her close by his side, he remained acutely aware of the Savage while leading her back to the car. When they crossed the road, the Savage hid in the shadows while it remained on the opposite side, but he spotted another as it ducked behind a car in the parking lot.

They wouldn't make a move against the Savages, but soon, these bastards would follow them to their deaths. Saber hid a smile over the fate awaiting these murderous fuckers.

Once settled in the car, Caro put on her seat belt and pulled out her phone to text Willow. "What should I tell her?"

"We have two of them following us," Saber said.

Caro hid her shock about this revelation. She knew about the one still loitering on the other side of the street, but where was the other one?

Just when she thought she was getting the hang of all this covert shit, the reminder she still sucked slapped her in the head.

With a sigh, she turned her attention to her phone and typed. *Leaving now. There's 2 following us.*

She hit send. Almost immediately, three dots materialized at the bottom of the screen while Willow typed her reply.

Heading for the car now. We have 3.

So far, the plan was going well, but that made her more nervous. Had it gone too well?

She tried to bury her unease as Saber pulled out of the parking lot, but it refused to die as another vehicle fell in a hundred feet behind them.

CHAPTER TWENTY-SIX

Caro never saw it coming. One minute, they were in the fast lane on the highway, and the next, a set of headlights was coming straight at them.

She had only a second to gasp and brace herself as Saber's arm shot across her chest, pinning her against the seat. He jerked the wheel, and the tires squealed as the car turned sideways so his side would take most of the impact.

And then the other vehicle slammed into the backend of the car. Her head bounced like a ping-pong ball between opponents as tortured metal screeched, bent, and folded like some sick, twisted accordion. White dust exploded around her and filled the air when the airbags released.

A scream caught in her throat. Saber's arm pressed into her chest when it became pinned between her and the airbag. It kept her pinned to the seat as the car spun in faster and faster circles.

Glass flew through the air. It rattled as it bounced off the inside of the car, her face, arms, and fell down her shirt.

She tried to reach out to him, but the spinning kept her arms pinned as the ass end of the car found a hill and it lurched down the side of it. Caro's heart leapt as the car teetered, and in a split second of certainty, she knew it would flip before it did.

A startled squeak escaped her as the car flipped once. The metal screeched as the ceiling caved in and the car slid down the hill, teetering toward another flip, but the tree they crashed into stopped it.

Her head pounded, her stomach lurched, and instincts screamed at her to jump up and run, but as the notion spun through her mind, she lost it. It felt like someone was hammering away at her skull; she felt chunks of it splintering away.

She couldn't think coherently, she smelled blood, and something tasted awful on her lips. The warmth against her chest slid away.

"Caro?" Saber demanded. "Caro, are you okay?"

She couldn't find words to answer him. They were there, on the tip of her tongue, but her tongue was too heavy to move.

Saber tore at the airbags, ripping them away from his face and side as he sought to break free. When he finally pulled them out, he turned to Caro but could barely see her through the white surrounding her.

Grasping the airbag in front of her, he wrenched it free, along with part of the dashboard. Her head fell forward and lolled for a second before rising. She blinked at him, but her eyes remained unfocused.

"We have to go," he said.

He fumbled for her seat belt and unclicked it before removing his. She leaned back against the seat and closed her eyes. He wanted to check on her again, to assure her it would all be okay, but there wasn't time.

That had *not* been an accident.

Putting his shoulder into the door, he shoved against it. Metal screeched, but his side of the car was so indented that it wouldn't budge much.

Turning sideways, he planted his feet against the door and his back against the console as he shoved with his legs. The door twisted, with a sound like that of nails on a chalkboard, as it bent outward.

Sweat beaded his brow, and his muscles strained as he pushed. The door gave way so suddenly that it flew away from the car and crashed into a tree. His feet hit the ground with a thump.

Saber lifted his sword from where it landed in the back seat and shrugged it on. Caro's was on the other side, lying half in and half out of the back window.

Saber scrambled out of the car and reclaimed Caro's sword while he ran to her side and slid it onto his back. When he got to her door, he paused to search the woods for Savages.

There was no sign of them yet, but they were coming. That wasn't a random accident; some human didn't cross the centerline and plow into them.

He hadn't seen it coming, but the demons weren't taking any chances he might get away again. Their antipathy for him outweighed their desire to locate more of the Alliance.

And they had to know there were other members of the Alliance with them in the city tonight; Willow and Declan had shadows too. It wouldn't be a big jump to assume that others were nearby too.

They could have attacked Willow and Declan too; they could be on the run or in the hands of the demons right now. But he suspected they'd decided to attack him and trail them. If the Savages lost Willow and Declan, it would piss off the demons, but having him and Caro and their swords in their possession would ease their wrath.

The demons had ordered this hit and would unleash hell on them when they arrived.

Kicking himself for not seeing this, for being so sure they would follow them to see what they were doing and how many more they could kill, he pulled Caro's door open. Without meaning to, he ripped it off the hinges. Tossing it aside, he bent and slid his arm under her to lift her from the car.

As he did so, headlights flashed across the highway, and vehicles screeched to a stop on the roadside a hundred feet above them. Doors opened and closed; words and the scent of rot drifted down to greet him.

Caro's phone lay in a puddle of glass beneath where her feet were. He wasn't sure, but he didn't feel the weight of his phone in his pocket anymore; it must have fallen out somewhere.

He snatched up Caro's phone and shoved it in his pocket as he cradled her against his chest and fled into the trees. Behind him, shouts filled the air before it went deathly quiet.

Darting in and out of trees, his fear for his mate and determination to keep her safe propelled him to faster and faster speeds. He instinctively dodged the trees rushing toward him as he leapt over fallen logs and rocks. The hunt was on, and they were the hunted.

Caro leaned her head against Saber's shoulder as she tried to understand what was happening. Her brain felt rattled, and her body was out of control as her fingers twitched uselessly but didn't rise to touch him as she commanded.

Were they in a car accident? Was that why she kept hearing a god-awful screeching sound in her head?

"Are you okay?" Saber demanded.

The urgency in his voice pierced through some of the fog and confusion encompassing her. Something was wrong, but of course, something was wrong, she couldn't think straight, and he was running.

Is he running?

Caro narrowed her eyes as she tried to make out the blurs rushing past them and why they were blurs. His long strides ate up the ground as his powerful body flexed around hers.

Yes, he's running.

She felt better and more coherent when she confirmed this for herself. And they were running because....

Small parts of the picture started fitting together. Red eyes glowed from beneath the storm drain, a city full of laughter and good cheer, a loud bang and then spinning, so much spinning.

Her fingers finally worked enough to touch her forehead as the pounding there became a cacophony that drowned out the memories. She squeezed her eyes shut as she tried to ease the pain.

Sensing her distress, Saber lifted her until her mouth rested against his throat. "Feed," he commanded.

CHAPTER TWENTY-SEVEN

Despite the agony of her battered brain, Caro couldn't refuse the overwhelming temptation of his blood. It pulsed against her lips with every rapid beat of his heart; its scent teased her fangs into elongating.

Running on instinct, she sank them into his throat and groaned when his blood filled her mouth. She drew him closer as his power swelled in her veins and flowed through her body.

While it filled her, her thoughts became less scattered and chaotic. Her memories returned, and the knowledge of what happened hit her like a hammer to the chest.

They'd been attacked, someone was hunting them, and they would die if she didn't get down and run. Feeling a lot stronger and afraid of weakening him, she released her bite on his neck.

Leaning back, she studied his handsome face as terror curdled in her belly. Anger simmered in his red eyes, and determination etched his features as he sprinted through the woods.

"I'm okay; you can put me down," she told him.

He glanced at her but couldn't look away from the forest too long, or he'd plow into a tree. If he did that, he'd cause a *lot* of damage to them, and they'd never get away. "Are you sure?"

"Yes."

Dirt and leaves kicked up from beneath his feet when he skidded to a stop. He shrugged off her sword and handed it to her before pulling out her phone.

They didn't have time to waste, but he had to get a message out in case they didn't escape this. He went straight to her texts; the one she'd exchanged with Willow was still on the screen.

Car down. After us.

It wasn't much, but they'd get the gist of it. He hit send, clasped Caro's elbow, and turned her to face the woods. No matter how badly he wanted to, he couldn't keep holding her while they were running, so he released her as they raced through the trees.

Caro's heart hammered as she dodged trees, leapt over fallen logs, scaled massive rocks, and clambered up a hill. Debris slid out from beneath her feet as they climbed the steep hill together.

It was so steep, she had to bend forward and use her hands to grasp the sticks and rocks jutting from the earth. She slipped a few times and almost face-planted but managed to catch herself in time.

When they finally reached the top, sweat cleaved her clothes to her body, and her legs ached from exertion, but she didn't dare rest. During their climb, the woods had gone completely silent.

Not even the rustle of a field mouse could be heard as none of the animals stirred. There were bigger and worse predators than foxes and coyotes out there tonight, and they all knew it.

And that predator was closing in on *them*.

Leaving the hill behind, she ran past the blurred trees with Saber a few feet away but parallel to her though he could move faster. She ducked branches that tore at her hair and clothes and avoided boulders that would have shattered her bones.

The branches she didn't completely miss welted her arms as they slapped against her skin. Some of them broke open her skin, and blood seeped from the welts inflicted on her, but they didn't slow her.

The sound of running water reached her seconds before they plunged into a small stream winding its way through the hilly and rocky countryside. Their feet kicking and splashing through the water caused her to wince, but they couldn't do anything about it as they trudged to the other side of the bank and ran onward.

Saber glanced behind him as they skated down another hill; he didn't see anyone, but their scent gave them away. The Savages were still coming.

They were halfway down the hill when lights shone in the distance and the hum of tires against asphalt drifted in the air. Another road lay ahead; if they could get to it, they might find a ride away.

He reclaimed Caro's hand, and his body immediately reacted to the warmth of her touch. The blood on his skin from her injuries caused a haze of red to blur his vision. He knew she was hurt; he'd scented it on the air, but feeling it made it worse.

They'd pay for doing this to her, and he would get her out of this. If it was the last thing he did, he would make sure they didn't get their hands on her.

The idea of those filthy creatures laying one finger on her spurred him faster. She couldn't survive without him, but he'd sacrifice himself to get her out of here.

It would be much easier if she got to choose her death; the demons would torture her until nothing remained but a groveling, incoherent mess. It would take a lot to break Caro's spirit, but he'd seen them in action, and they would do it, he had no doubt.

They were almost to the roadside when gravel crunched beneath tires and a car screeched to a halt. For a second, hope leapt in Saber's chest.

Is it Willow and Declan? Did they somehow track Caro's phone to our location?

Then, three more cars stopped behind it, and his hope deflated. The Savages were communicating with each other, sending backup, and trying to trap them between one group and another.

Instead of continuing down the hill, Saber switched direction and went sideways across it as he sought to outrun the Savages unloading from the vehicles below. When he glanced back, the doors of a van opened, and a demon glided out. From behind it came another.

The demons' stench of rot and fire and brimstone permeated the air. Not much unnerved him, but the hair on his nape rose when he spotted those cloaked figures. It was extremely rare when the demons joined in on the chase, but they sought his blood, and if he didn't come up with a plan, they would have it.

Now that their creators had joined the chase, getting away would be tougher.

CHAPTER TWENTY-EIGHT

THEY STAYED parallel to the road as the Savages separated into groups, and more cars screeched to a stop below them. They were trying to cut off their exit at every opportunity.

Saber knew they didn't have much time or many options, but the best one was to get to the road before the Savages squeezed them in. They could flag down a passing motorist or cross the highway to hopefully more woods where they could keep running. At least then, they wouldn't have Savages in front and behind them like they did now.

They could stay in the woods and try to outrun them, but they were becoming increasingly outnumbered. It was only a matter of time before their enemies found them.

The woods seemed endless, but he suspected they weren't as vast as he would have liked, and with both of them bleeding, they'd never cover their scents enough to hide. And with demons tracking them, the hiding option was far from good. Those monsters would find them.

When they were far enough away from the demons' vehicles, Saber started down the hill with Caro again. They would have to get a car as fast as possible or get across the road in a hurry, but he'd worry about that after they broke through the line of monsters running parallel to them below.

But as he pondered it, he knew it wouldn't work. There were too many of them; they were too bloodthirsty, and he and Caro didn't have enough options for escape. There was only one way Caro was getting out of this.

"You have to keep running straight this way," he said to Caro. "Go parallel to the road. I'm going down the hill."

Everything inside Caro rebelled against this ludicrous statement. "Absolutely not. We're *not* splitting up. We're in this together, and it will stay that way."

"Some of them will still come for you, but most will come for *me*. You have a chance to get away."

"And do what? You're going to sacrifice yourself? You do remember that if you die, I die, right?"

"Of course I do!" Despite these past weeks being some of the best of his life, he regretted what they'd done. She could survive if she wasn't bound to him, but he couldn't change that now. "But I'd rather have you die a painless death than have them torture you."

"A stake to the heart isn't exactly painless."

"It's much better than being cut to tiny pieces while they rape and brutalize you. I won't have it."

Caro's breath caught at his words. Yes, she'd prefer a stake through the heart than that, but she couldn't let him go alone. With the two of them fighting, they had a better chance of getting away. With only one, even with his sword, they'd eventually overpower him.

"Listen to me." He seized her wrist, but neither of them stopped running. "If they catch you, they'll torture you until they break you."

"And what are they going to do to you?"

"The same, but if they catch you, they'll realize you're my

mate and know the real way to make *me* suffer is through *you*. They'll make it worse for *both* of us. Do you understand?"

He was right, but she couldn't let him face these monsters alone. "You wouldn't leave me."

"I plan on leaving you. Once I do, they'll focus on me. *I'm* the one they're really after; you'll be nothing more than a missed opportunity if you keep running. And you can make it if you do. I'll keep them distracted and buy you time to get away."

Caro's heart was already pounding from exertion and terror, but the idea of leaving him caused it to pick up even as it started to shatter. "I can't lose you."

Those four words crushed him in a way he hadn't experienced since he lost his mother and thought he discovered Brie's body in the fire.

There was nothing left of it to ever break again... or so he thought, until now.

"I know, but they can't get their hands on you. It will be far worse," he said. "You have to go. Besides, you'll be the one who can find me when they take me. Our bond will lead you to me; you just have to open up to me."

"You have to do the same."

"I will."

He wouldn't let her in completely because he expected a lot of suffering in his future, but he'd let her in enough to find him.

"Brian can find you too," she reminded him.

"Not as fast as a mate could, and you know it."

She did; she felt it deep in her bones. She'd find him faster than Brian, but leaving him here would be the toughest thing she'd ever done.

"I can't watch them take you; it would be like carving out my heart," she said.

He shouldn't do it, but they had a little time, and he needed to *really* touch her one last time. Clasping her cheeks in his palms, he gazed into her beautiful, turquoise eyes. She'd tied her hair back into a ponytail, but strands had fallen free to cling to her face.

"Don't watch; keep running," he whispered against her lips as he kissed her.

A small sob worked through Caro and burst free before she could stop it. "Saber—"

"Run, Caro. Run faster than you've ever run before. As long as you remain free, I'll have a chance." He thrust his sword out to her. "And take this with you."

"No! I'm not taking your best weapon and defense against them."

"They can't get their hands on it. Now go."

He gave her a little shove that staggered her back a step. Righting herself, she lifted her head to meet his cobalt eyes that were turning red. He was so handsome and fierce in the little radiance the moon shone down on them.

"Saber—"

"You have to take it, Caro. They can't have those swords."

Her heart broke as a sob lodged in her throat, and she whispered, "I love you."

He flinched at her words, but she hadn't expected anything else. Did she wish he returned the feeling?

Absolutely. But she'd known what she was facing when it came to those words. She'd held them back and kept him shut out for a reason, but her pride and possible heartbreak didn't matter in this situation.

He'd told her he was incapable of love, and while she hoped one day it wouldn't be true, he still wasn't ready for it. But he *had* to know how she felt before she lost him... possibly forever.

Saber opened his mouth to reply but had no idea what to say. He cared for her deeply, but he wasn't capable of love. And he couldn't speak the words just to make her happy.

He really was a monster. He should at least say them to her; he *should* give her this, but he couldn't get them out.

And he didn't understand how it was possible that she loved *him*. How had such a thing come to be when he'd done everything to keep her at a distance? He'd held her back to protect her from this.

Yet, it had still happened, and he was upsetting her more with his complete inability to utter the words. He seethed against his failure to open himself to another as grief clawed its way into his chest.

He'd never felt for anyone the way he felt for Caro, but it wasn't love, was it? It didn't matter; they didn't have time for him to sort his shit out.

Cupping her cheek, he kissed her nose before turning away. "Run!"

He didn't look back as he sprinted down the hill and toward certain death.

CHAPTER TWENTY-NINE

The swords banged accusingly against Caro's back with every step she took. Every clicking bounce of them as they clanked together was a reminder she'd left her mate to face a fate worse than death, but if she didn't keep going, they would both end up dead.

At least, if she remained free, she *would* find him again and bring an army to him. Leading that army, she'd carve her way through all those demons and Savages if that was what it took to get him back.

That was the only thing propelling her onward. She could leave him now because she'd find him again later and make all those who harmed him pay for it.

If she was going to do that, she couldn't keep running with the swords like this. They were noisy, homing beacons for the monsters pursuing her.

Most of the Savages had gone for Saber, but enough still followed her to be a threat. If she didn't do something soon to stop the swords from bouncing against each other, those bastards would be on her in a matter of minutes.

As she ran, she tugged her sword free of its sheath. She

didn't like running with the blade in her hand, there were far too many obstacles coming at her too fast for it to be safe, but she had no other choice.

She had to rely on her amazing vision and instincts to keep her from plunging the blade into a tree and getting stuck there. But at least the swords stopped banging against each other, and she'd stopped leaving a clattering trail to follow.

She loathed that he'd given her his sword, it was his best weapon against the demons, but she understood his reasoning. She would have sacrificed her sword, too, before letting them get their hands on it.

Caro sprinted around fallen debris and more trees. The branches snagged in her hair and clothes. They slapped at her as she plunged onward at a speed she hadn't believed possible, but her mate being in jeopardy had awakened something primal and powerful inside her.

I will save him!

She was sure she'd almost lost them when headlights bounced across the road on her left again and three more cars screeched to a halt. She didn't have to look at those who exited the vehicles to know they were the enemy; their *stench* carried in the air to her.

Her heart sank, and everything inside her screamed against the unfairness of it all, but she refused to give in. She could still get away, get help, and bring back an army for Saber.

She glanced at the trees, but there wasn't enough time to scale one of them. And they would all know what general area she'd vanished in and be on her in minutes. Her only option was to keep running.

And then, like the animals they were, the newly arrived Savages released a series of yelps, squeals, and shouts of joy before plunging into the woods after her. They'd been so quiet until now as their bloodlust emanated through each of their screams.

Their noise was more unnerving than the hush, and she wished they'd shut up, but they were doing this to rattle her, and she wouldn't let them succeed. Knowing she had to get away from the road, Caro veered to the right and started back up the hill.

The climb hindered her progress, but it would slow them too, and the demons couldn't continue unleashing Savages on her if she was away from the road. The only problem was she could be heading straight back toward the highway they'd left behind and *more* of the monsters.

Those *things* were extremely brazen to go after her and Saber like this. Countless humans traversed the highway; someone might call the police when they saw the number of vehicles parked on the roadside.

Or worse, someone could stop to offer assistance; she doubted they'd survive it, and neither would any police who might arrive. These things didn't care who they killed, and that was nearly as unnerving as the creatures screeching like hyenas behind her.

She'd seen so many horror movies over the years, and now all she could think about were the ones with the inbred creatures who lived in the mountains and ate any unsuspecting people who accidentally stumbled across them. These things sounded exactly like those deformed cannibals.

However, she couldn't focus on the problem of police and bystanders getting killed. She didn't want any innocents to die, but she'd prefer not to die too.

Sprinting up the steep incline the best she could, she went as far as she could before requiring her hands to help her. Propping her blade under her armpit, she used her fingers to help propel her faster as she dug them into the earth and grasped rocks.

She was near the top when the smell of those things overwhelmed her. Her breath caught as her nose refused to inhale any more of that awful *reek*, but it didn't matter, the taste of their rot lingered on her tongue.

The Savages were closing in on her, and her precarious position on the hill was *not* a good place to fight them. She also couldn't keep going up; she couldn't see them, but they were already there.

Changing course, she ran parallel to the road and the top of the hill. She went another hundred feet before stones started rattling down from above.

She didn't have to look up to know they were coming for her.

CHAPTER THIRTY

SABER PUNCHED one Savage in the face before using his haladie knife to slice the throat of another. He ducked and spun as he kicked out the feet of a Savage running toward him. They'd swarmed like locusts to surround him, but, for now, he was keeping them at bay.

He would have preferred to have his sword, but there was no turning back, and he'd done the right thing by giving it to Caro. The demons couldn't get their hands on it.

He wasn't sure how it worked, but he suspected his death would release the stone to be claimed by another. If they had been used to defeat the demons before, they must have belonged to others who could draw on the full power of the stones.

And those others were all dead, leaving the stones to be claimed by them. If they killed him and had possession of the sword, then the Alliance and the world would fall.

They'd have to find someone else to wield his sword, but they still had a chance while they possessed *all* the weapons. They might have to find someone for Caro's sword too, but she was strong, and revenge against the demons would give her a good reason to keep living.

It might not be a good life without her mate, and it would still be short, but at least she would get to *live*. He wished he could give her everything she deserved, but he'd learned years ago that wanting something didn't always make it happen.

Hands tore at his back, shredded his shirt, and sliced open his skin. The sounds the Savages emitted mimicked ravenous animals fighting over their prey.

He'd once been one of these things, obsessed with the kill and endlessly excited by blood. He'd thrived on the hunt and distress of his victims. It was his sole reason for living, but these things disgusted him now.

No matter what they did to him, he would *never* be one of them again. They could inject him with their blood, it could rot his mind and steal his body, but he would find some way to stop that madness from ruling him again.

Despite not having his sword, he still had his knife and stakes. He wielded his blade with the most effect as he ducked a Savage charging at him and swung out to eviscerate the idiot.

When another emerged from the crowd, he spun his knife and plunged it into the creature's thigh. The Savage howled as he twisted the blade before ripping it free.

Blood sprayed into his face from the severed artery, but he barely noticed its sticky warmth as he cut the Achilles tendon of another. It went down like a tree felled by a saw.

He ducked the next one, but the following Savage hit him with a punch that knocked his head to the side, rattled his teeth, and cracked his cheekbone. Knocked backward, he was still trying to clear his blurred vision when the Savage leapt at him.

He regained enough of his senses to plunge his knife into its belly as the creature's fingers clamped around his throat. When Saber thrust upward, intestines spilled over his hand.

The Savage howled and leaned back. Jerking his knife from the creature's belly, he plunged it up and into the Savage's chin.

Prying the beast off him, he yanked the blade free and watched it fall like a sack of potatoes.

Before he could completely recover, another one gripped his throat from behind. A second one wrapped its arms around his waist and shoved him to the side.

Saber plunged his blade into the back of the one trying to tackle him while the one behind him cut off his air supply. He tried to wheeze in a breath but barely got enough air as its skeletal fingers bit into his windpipe and white stars erupted before his eyes.

Swinging his arm up behind him, he plunged the blade into the Savage. He wasn't sure where he got the thing, but it screeched as its fingers eased enough for him to gasp in oxygen.

His vision cleared enough for him to see a cloaked figure emerging from the trees and gliding toward him. From behind it, more cloaked figures spread out through the woods.

They kept their hands clasped within the bell sleeves of their robes. Their hoods hid their faces, but their brilliant, white-blue eyes shone out from the shadows.

Saber didn't have to see its face to know the one in the lead was Kirkau. That beast had led the demons and Savages when he was one of them, he wouldn't have given up his position, and his vast height gave him away; the beast was over seven feet tall.

It was only a matter of time before the sheer number of all these Savages overwhelmed and took him down, but the arrival of the demons intensified their fight. It also intensified *his*.

Saber smiled at Kirkau and waved before shifting his attention back to the fight. If Kirkau was here, then he'd been right about the demons centering themselves in this area. At least the Alliance might still have a chance of defeating them, especially if the monsters killed him and they found someone else to claim his sword.

It probably wasn't the best idea to antagonize Kirkau, but he didn't give a shit. He was going to die.

It would be a *horrible* death, but these fuckers wouldn't have the satisfaction of thinking he was afraid of them. As long as Caro was free, he didn't care what they did to him.

He spun and plunged his knife into the eye of another attacker while two others tore at his hair and shredded what remained of his shirt. A burst of fire drew his attention to the woods. His heart sank as he realized Caro hadn't gotten away.

The agony that clenched his heart and stole his breath made the pain of the injuries the Savages inflicted on him vanish. *No.*

The word was a broken whisper in his mind. She hadn't gotten away, and these things were hunting her through the trees, pushing her back toward him. He'd hoped to become their main focus and to buy her time to get her free, but he'd failed.

With renewed vigor, Saber ignored his growing number of wounds, and as the Savages beat, kicked, and stabbed him, he unleashed more brutality upon them. They weren't trying to kill him; the demons wanted him alive, but they had no problems weakening and incapacitating him.

Grabbing two Savages, he smashed their heads together. The impact shattered their skulls and rendered them useless as he dropped them to the ground.

He tore free of the other hands clawing at his back before backhanding the one chewing on his leg. He knocked the thing aside as Caro sprinted toward him with a horde of Savages on her heels.

Managing to tear himself free, he raced for Caro. Her hair had come mostly free of its ponytail, blood and dirt streaked her face, and her eyes were a virulent shade of red.

When she was close enough, she threw his sword at him. "They cut me off," she panted. "More of them pulled up in cars. There's so many and no escape."

"I know," he said.

Instead of crushing her against him and kissing her as he

longed to do, he turned and put his back to her as a wave of Savages bounded toward him.

CHAPTER THIRTY-ONE

Saber wouldn't allow them to take her; he'd fight to the absolute death before that happened. He swung his sword as he kept his back to Caro and his senses attuned to how she was faring.

As he worked, he carved through Savages and joyfully watched as they burst into flames and ash. He'd happily destroy every last one of them.

Unlike before, when they had less to fear, the swords kept them at bay, but the Savages circled as they tried to find a weakness in their defense. Behind them, the demons watched and waited for the inevitable fall.

But as they circled, more descended from the hillside that Caro had gone down. The demons weren't taking any chances on losing them; they'd unleashed an army.

Caro's father had trained her how to fight with swords, as well as countless other weapons. She should be tired from this night's emotional and physical drain, but the adrenaline pulsing through her made sure she was wide awake and ready to kill any who dared to threaten her or Saber.

Her fear for him also had her moving with a speed and

strength she'd never experienced before becoming mated to him. Their chances of making it out of this were smaller than a snowball's chance of surviving Hell, but she'd fight to the last second.

She swung, lunged, and hacked at the monsters closing in on her. The sword made them a little less brave, but their rapidly increasing numbers helped build their confidence. Of course, none wanted to die, but they'd sacrifice some of the weaker ones to take them down.

She wondered if those soon-to-be sacrificial lambs had any idea it would be them. She suspected the Savages who were already plotting this course knew who.

Sweat beaded her forehead, crept down her spine, and stuck her pants to the back of her knees. The clang of metal hitting bone filled the air, as did the hisses and screeches of the Savages.

At least the freaks had stopped shrieking like they did when they first emerged from their cars and pursued her into the woods. The near silence of so much death and brutality was strange, but she'd hated those sounds.

For every Savage she cut down, more emerged. It was as if they were pouring out of the earth, like the dead rising from their graves.

Where do they all keep coming from?

Occasionally, she glimpsed the freaks on the sidelines, standing with their arms clasped and their eyes burning out of the darkness. It was unnerving to have those demons standing there, watching them, but she tried to ignore them as spiders of unease ran down her spine.

She swung to push an overeager attacker back. As she did so, one broke through her defenses on the right and charged her. Its arms encircled her waist as it propelled her through the crowd, to the ground, and into a rock.

Pain exploded through her shoulder, but she suppressed a grunt as she commanded herself to keep moving. The rotten stench of the thing engulfed her, and she restrained a gag as she slammed an elbow into its face.

Blood gushed from its broken nose; it yelped as its hands flew to its face. With her sword in hand, she scrambled to get away from its weight, but the others descended like vultures on carrion before she could rise.

Fingers entangled in her hair and wrenched her head back as their hands pulled at her face. They shredded her shirt as they yanked her arms behind her back, tore her sword away, and lifted her from the ground.

The loss of her sword was more painful than the fingers they broke as they pulled it away. They'd taken a piece of her, and she wanted it back!

Lunging against them, she tried to break free, but there were too many, and it was impossible to break their iron hold on her.

Saber roared when they ripped Caro to her feet and surrounded her. They shouldn't be *touching* her or be anywhere near her, yet they were all over her.

With his knife in one hand and his sword in another, he hacked his way through the Savages surrounding him. Ashes filled the air, blurring his view, but he didn't care as wrath fueled him.

He was spiraling out of control as Caro's red eyes met his. He wouldn't ever be a Savage again, but he could tap into that worst part of himself and unleash it on those who deserved it most.

Power thrummed through him, his muscles swelled, and his veins hummed. When he swung his blade again, he saw the red and black color seeping through his skin. The demon part of his purebred DNA was taking control as it surged forth.

They had his mate, and he wouldn't allow that to stand.

He was about to carve into one of the Savages holding her when four shots rang out. Almost as soon as he heard the sound of them, the bullets peppered his back, tore into his spine, and his legs went numb.

Saber almost went down but somehow managed to stay up, though he couldn't feel his legs anymore. The Savages weren't trying to kill him; they would have put a bullet through his heart if they were, but they were determined to bring him down.

It was difficult, but he somehow willed one foot in front of the other as he hacked his way through the Savages surrounding her. He lost sight of her in the ash filling the air, but she was there, and he would get to her.

Then the wind shifted, and he spotted her as she lunged to break free of her captors. She bared her fangs and, like him, red and black color seeped across her face.

He wasn't the only one losing control, and he wasn't the only purebred whose mate was threatened. These demons and Savages had pushed the two of them into a whole new realm of pissed off.

If they could stay on their feet and fighting, they might have a chance of evading this. He didn't hold out much hope for that, but their unwillingness to kill them was helpful, even if it wouldn't last.

From the corner of his eye, he spotted Kirkau drifting closer. Evil radiated from the creature as he glided through the trees, past the Savages, and toward them.

Twisting, Saber battered at the Savage tearing into his arms. The creature lurched back to avoid Saber's blows before jumping forward and sinking his fangs into Saber's bicep.

His entire body reacted as if someone had shoved him into a fire, but he clamped his teeth against the agony and jerked his arm forward. He swung his free hand over and plunged his knife through the creature's back and into his chest.

Before he could jerk the knife free, more of them pounced on his back. Caro's cry of rage rebounded through the trees before abruptly cutting off.

She crumpled to the ground with blood spilling from her temple. She was alive, but the sight of her down, unmoving, and bleeding caused red to shadow the edges of Saber's vision as he roared.

Still unable to feel his legs, he lurched forward on legs as stiff as a board. His gait was awkward as he bounced off a Savage and nearly went down.

More of their enemy pounced on his back. They encircled their arms around his throat and dug their fingers into the bullet holes in his spine.

Fire lanced through his nerve endings, torching his skin and sending flames throughout his cells. He was about to tear into them when something crashed into the back of his skull.

Bone gave way with an audible crack as his head shot forward. He had no idea what they hit him with, but something caved in before the world went black.

CHAPTER THIRTY-TWO

SABER WOKE to severe pain shooting through his head. His body and brain were working to repair themselves; he could feel synapses healing and flesh knitting back together, but it was a slow process.

He remembered enough to know it wasn't happening fast enough. He had to be fully coherent and at top strength for what was about to come.

Lifting his head, he tried to take in his surroundings, but his vision blurred, and a cloudy haze surrounded everything. He could see little more than a pinpoint of only a few feet before him.

No matter how much he blinked, he couldn't get anything more to come into focus. His ears rang; occasionally, the ringing would stop, and he'd catch the drip of something in the distance, but then the ringing returned, and it became all he heard.

The stenches of rot, brimstone, and sulfur permeated the air. Beneath it all, he detected the ocean's faint aroma on Caro.

His teeth grated together as his heart contracted in his chest. She shouldn't be here. She deserved far better than this, but he'd failed to help her get away, and now, here they were, and the demons were going to make him wish he'd died centuries ago.

His chest ached with the knowledge of what they would do to her. Everything in him screamed against it; he cared too much for her to see her hurt.

The realization of how much he cared hit him as hard as whatever they used to bash his skull. Part of him recoiled from it and tried to deny it was true, but it was.

He cared for her; he didn't know if it was love, he still didn't believe himself capable of it, but she'd somehow dug her way into his heart… and they were going to make her pay for it.

Saber blinked again as he tried to focus, but it did him little good. He had to see her, assure himself she was okay, and somehow get her out of this.

She was still alive; even if they remained closed off from each other, he felt her life pulsating across their bond. If she was already dead, he would have felt the severing and not cared about what was to come.

He jerked at the wrists the demons had bound behind his back. Thick chains rattled when he moved. His legs remained numb, but the bullets were making their way out of his spine, which meant he would soon walk normally again… if they didn't break all the bones in his body first.

"He's awake," a voice hissed.

When he recognized Kirkau's voice, the hair on his nape rose. Kirkau was pure evil and would take great pleasure in making Saber suffer. The best way for him to ensure that was to go after Caro; they all knew it.

They would have seen the marks on both their necks now, would have recognized them as a mated pair, and would take great joy in exploiting it.

Blinking again, he started bringing the room into focus, but it still wasn't enough for him to see where he was or what was happening. He sensed something only a few feet away from him.

"I'm awake." Saber's words came out slurred as his tongue didn't work properly.

But as he spoke, his mind started processing how bad this was for them. He had no idea how long they'd been in the hands of the demons and Savages or where they were.

Even if the Alliance could find them, and they could with Brian's ability to track others, they might not come. Brian could lead them right here, it might take some time, but it could happen… if the Alliance allowed it.

He was one of them, but he was still an outsider. They needed the swords to have a chance of defeating the demons, but was that enough for them to risk their lives, and the lives of their mates, to save them?

Before Caro, he would have gone after one of them. What did he have to lose? His life was no great thing, so it didn't make any difference.

After Caro, he didn't know if he would risk it because doing so would also jeopardize her life if something happened to him. They would all feel the same way, and he didn't blame them.

He also had no idea where they were. It might be too risky to come after them if they were beneath the ground. And they had to be below ground as, through the stench of decay, he detected the mineral aroma of earth and limestone. Cool, damp air adhered to his skin and created a small sheen across his flesh.

Coming here could be a death sentence for every member of the Alliance, even if it meant sacrificing him, Caro, and their swords. That might be their only option.

Saber wouldn't blame them for it either. They had to remain alive to continue a fight whose outcome would be much bleaker without the swords to help, but hope remained while they lived.

However, there wasn't any for him and Caro. He didn't see how they would make it out of this alive.

The demons wouldn't try to change him back into a Savage.

He'd broken free once; they wouldn't take the chance of him doing so again.

Maybe they'd turn him into one of the injected, but he doubted it. They wanted the swords, and he suspected he and Caro would have to die for the weapons to work for the demons.

They could turn *her* into one of them. They wouldn't want to wait the month or so it would take to turn her into a Savage, but they could inject her with their blood and turn her loose on him. Or they could do the same to him.

He'd fight it with everything he was, but he didn't think that would be enough for the demons. It would be over too quickly, and they wouldn't get a chance to unleash the full amount of suffering they intended for him.

It had taken centuries, but they would finally get the chance to make him pay for leaving them. And they would do it by starting with *her*.

CHAPTER THIRTY-THREE

Ronan walked beside Brian as he led them through the city. Thankfully, it was early in the morning and the sun was just starting to rise, or their large group would have drawn a lot more attention as they strolled past businesses and people gathered on the streets.

As it was, they'd already had to send two police officers away when they questioned their presence here. A bunch of men and women with weapons didn't go unnoticed, but with fewer people around, there would be less calls and a smaller chance the police would return.

Saber had told them he'd encountered a demon in the storm drains beneath White Bridge, but Ronan hadn't expected the monsters to bring them back to the city. He'd been certain they would have gone to a less populated area, beneath some woods or in a cave.

He supposed they could still be in one of those offshoots, but Brian led them straight through the city to get there. And they had no choice but to follow as the demons would have taken Saber and Caro back to their main base of operations.

In many ways, it made sense that they'd started to branch out from beneath this city. It was a smaller city, but there was a ready blood supply here to keep the Savages happy and fed.

It would be more difficult to cover their tracks and hide the missing people disappearing from here, but they were doing a good job. A large increase in missing people hadn't attracted the attention of the Alliance to this place. Whatever they were doing here, it was working.

But, if this went well, it wouldn't work much longer. He just wasn't sure how well this could go if they all had to funnel beneath the earth and into the storm drains to go after them.

They'd purposely tried to lure the demons away from here to avoid such a thing happening. Now, they had no choice but to meet them on their ground.

At least the demons didn't know of Brian's existence or talent and wouldn't expect the Alliance to locate them. If they had known about Brian, they would have gone after him years ago. An ability like his was rare and coveted.

They *did* know about Elyse, but she'd never encountered Saber or Caro's blood. The demons couldn't know that and might suspect they were on their way. However, he'd bet they didn't think Saber would allow another to have the ability to track him in such a way.

Brian didn't need blood; he sensed a soul and homed in on it. It had taken him a while to get them this far, and they'd taken a few winding trails through the city, sometimes doubling back over ways they'd already come.

But if the demons were underground and moving Saber and Caro around, the backtracking made sense.

Brian's forehead furrowed as he pushed his platinum hair out of his ice-blue eyes. "It's difficult to get a read on them."

"Is that because they're underground?" Lucien asked.

"No, it's because there are a lot of other souls around them."

Ronan resisted the impulse to grasp Kadence's shoulders, turn her around, and tell her to go back. She wouldn't leave, and she had a sword, which meant she was supposed to be in this fight. Fate, or something else, had chosen her; he hated them for it.

"Are they still alive?" Ronan asked.

"I think so," Brian replied. "I'm getting something from Saber, but not Caro."

"I hope she's not dead," Brie whispered.

"Like I said, there's a lot of souls around them. They could be throwing me off."

Ronan glanced back at the army following them. Once beneath the earth, they would be funneled like rats toward the death and destruction waiting for them.

If there were enough Savages and demons around Saber and Caro to throw off Brian's ability, they were most likely in a large, open area. They'd be able to stand and fight there if that was the case.

Getting there alive would be the problem.

From the second Declan called to report Saber and Caro were taken almost two hours ago, he'd known they would have to go after them. They couldn't leave a member of the Alliance, and someone who helped them, behind.

This wasn't his first choice for facing the demons, but this day had been coming for centuries. And now it was time to put an end to all of this.

~

EVERYTHING IN CARO HURT. Her toenails and hair throbbed as she kept her head bowed and listened to the conversation swirling around her.

She kept her breathing steady as she commanded herself to remain still and not react to anything. She'd give anything to shift to alleviate her discomfort, but they would know she was awake if she moved.

And the torture would soon follow. She could remain still for however long it took to avoid that.

They might start attacking her before she indicated she was awake, but for now, they were leaving her and Saber alone. She didn't know how much time they had before that changed.

"You're such a disappointment," Kirkau said.

Saber shrugged the best he could with his arms chained behind him. He stretched his legs casually before him, but the chains pulled taut before he could fully extend them.

Leaning back in the chair, he smiled at Kirkau as his vision finally returned. Instigating the demon wasn't the best way to handle this, but he would *not* cower before this monster.

It was easy not to when he was the only one dealing with the fucker, but once they realized Caro was awake, it would be an entirely different ball game. For now, he could give the metaphorical finger since he couldn't see the one behind Saber's back.

In all honesty, if it was just him, he wouldn't care about what was to come. Yes, they were going to carve him into small pieces before killing him, but death wasn't the worst thing in this world.

There were far more horrible things one could endure, like the loss of all those he loved and *himself.* His soul shattered the day they murdered his mother and he lost his father. After years of being a soulless monstrosity, he'd finally pieced what remained of it together, but he'd never be the same man.

That man was good, kind, and caring. The one he built himself into was cold, relentless, and indifferent to the world. He wasn't indifferent to Caro though.

Unwilling to give anything away, he kept his gaze focused on Kirkau. Caro was doing a good job of pretending to still be knocked out, but it was only a matter of time before Kirkau's attention shifted to her. And once it did, things would get ugly.

CHAPTER THIRTY-FOUR

"I suppose I can thank you for bringing the stones back to me, especially *my* stone," Kirkau said.

His insidious voice crept into the soul and awoke a fear that existed when predators hunted humans and people lived in caves and hunted for food; it was the voice of evil. It was the serpent offering Eve the apple, the boogeyman, and the predators that drove humans to their knees while they begged for mercy.

It would not make him plead. Saber kept his face impassive as the demon lifted *his* sword from where someone had leaned it against the wall.

"How do you know it's yours?" Saber inquired.

Kirkau caressed the sword as he studied it. "I just know."

He wasn't surprised *his* stone belonged to the most powerful demon he'd ever encountered. It made sense to him; he wasn't the most powerful vampire, that title went to Ronan, but his soul was more malevolent than the other Alliance members. Of course, he and Kirkau would share this connection.

There was a time when he would have considered this monstrosity almost a friend. Except, he'd never kid himself into believing the demons considered anyone a friend, not even each other.

But they had plotted to murder others together, which was the closest thing he had to friends back in the day.

Now that he could finally see better, he took in more of his surroundings. They were in a large, cavernous space. Assorted debris, such as concrete blocks, pallets, and anything else the Savages could find, propped up the dirt walls surrounding them.

Tree roots dangled from the ceiling twenty feet over his head. Lanterns cast shadows around the space as their flames danced from where they hung near the walls.

Those tiny flames did little to penetrate all the shadows, and he sensed countless others hiding in the shadows, waiting. Kirkau was the only one he could see, something the demon had intended to try to unnerve him. It wouldn't have worked if Caro wasn't here, but he couldn't deny that it did.

He purposely kept his gaze away from her as he smiled at Kirkau.

"You're pathetic," Kirkau hissed.

"What can I say? I aim to please," Saber retorted.

From beneath Kirkau's hood, Saber couldn't see much of his hideous face, but the demon's white-blue eyes gazed out at him as it issued a throaty chortle. "And you always did, until you turned against us."

"I don't kill children."

"You should try it one day; they're quite a delicacy, so tender, especially when they're terrified. But you won't live long enough to get that chance. I can't thank you enough, as not only did you bring me my sword and *you*, but you brought your mate to me too. How kind of you."

"Like I said, I aim to please, Kirkau."

He tried to remain casual but couldn't stop himself from tensing when Kirkau turned his attention to Caro. Shifting on his chair, he tried to judge how solid it was. The thing was made of metal as thick as his thigh; he couldn't break it.

Caro kept her breathing steady as dirt crunched beneath the weight of the footsteps coming toward her. The pounding that rattled her head when she first woke had dulled to a throb, but her senses still weren't running at full capacity.

She could hear and smell enough to know one of those things approached. She suspected it was the demon talking to Saber... Kirkau.

Though she didn't move and showed no outward reaction, her heartbeat doubled when a massive hand rested on top of her head. It was so large it encompassed her entire skull as its claws slid through her hair before biting into the base of her neck.

It took everything she had not to flinch when they pierced her flesh. This new discomfort was nothing compared to her numerous others, but as blood trickled down her nape, the bitter taste of fear filled her mouth.

A warm, fetid breath tickled her ear a second before that awful voice whispered, "I know you're awake."

Caro didn't know how to respond. If she shot up now and recoiled as she yearned to do, he would think she was scared of him, but if she remained meek and immobile, he would believe the same.

In the end, she decided playing possum wasn't for her. Lifting her head, she glared at the hooded figure beside her as every part of her shrieked to RUN!

Adrenaline flooded her until it pounded in her temples. She forgot all her injuries in the face of her desperation to evade this thing. Its white-blue eyes made her bladder clench, and for the first time, she glimpsed the revolting face hidden beneath the hood.

Its face was so pale it was nearly translucent, and its human-like features were distorted. It was like someone had taken silly putty and spread it across its face to make its features less discernible but still recognizable.

Two hooked fangs jetted out from its nearly lipless mouth when it smiled at her. This thing would have no problem devouring her, bones and all, and would probably use some smaller bones as a toothpick afterward.

And then, before she could say anything more, it struck. Those abnormally long fangs pierced her neck so deeply she swore they hit bone.

She'd been adamant she wouldn't show any weakness or fear to this thing or the others she sensed watching from the shadows. No matter what they did, she'd remain strong. She would not cry, scream, or beg.

And while she didn't humiliate herself by releasing the scream lodged in her throat or pissing her pants, it was only because the demon's strike and the intense pain accompanying it was so unexpected. She couldn't react as all her muscles and bones went ramrod straight, and her throat closed.

A little piece of her withered and died as fire scorched her veins and torched her bones as he drained her blood against her will. This monster could destroy her by just doing *this*.

Her mind recoiled into the darkness, where it attempted to hide, but the demon wouldn't let her go. She could never escape this.

The chair thumped against the rocky, dirt floor as Saber yanked against his chains, but he couldn't break free. "Get off of her!"

He jerked at his restraints as he threw all his weight into trying to break free. He'd forgotten all about trying to remain nonplussed when this beast attacked his mate. Kirkau was feeding on *his* mate.

It was something he wouldn't let stand under any circumstance, but her anguish radiating across their bond made it worse.

They still weren't completely open to each other, but her pain was so severe that it battered him.

When he leaned forward and strained against the chains behind his back, something in his shoulder cracked as it dislocated. The relentless battering of her pain buried his as he twisted to the side while trying to use a different angle to break free.

He'd tear his arm off if it meant getting to her and killing this monster.

Kirkau lifted his head from Caro's throat; his pointed tongue flicked out to lick away the blood staining his lips. If rage could rip out of a chest, it would have torn him in two as Caro's head fell and her shoulders hunched up. He felt the inward sobs shaking her, but she didn't make a sound.

When Kirkau laid his hand over the top of hers, she recoiled from his cool, clammy flesh. It was like touching a worm crawling from beneath the earth—if that worm was also like touching death.

Her skin crawled as Kirkau rubbed the back of her hand. When he grasped a finger, she was still so caught up in the memory of his bite, she didn't react when he yanked it backward.

Oddly, the sound of her bones breaking bothered her the most. A broken bone was nothing compared to this monster's bite, and she almost laughed but found no humor in this.

She was still completely numb after his bite, but that wouldn't last, and this was only the beginning.

"I'm going to kill you!" Saber bellowed.

CHAPTER THIRTY-FIVE

SABER'S WORDS rebounded throughout the storm drain as they bounced off the concrete around them. Declan froze when Ronan held up a hand to stop him and the rest of the Alliance, including the hunters from Arizona, Willow's family, and Brie's friends.

Beside Ronan, Brian cocked his head as he turned to where his mate, Abby, stood with Vicky and Nathan. Willow was a few feet in front of her sisters while the rest of their family remained a little further back in the tunnels.

Declan met Ronan's eyes. Ronan didn't have to say anything; Declan could tell his friend was thinking the same thing as him —a vampire only sounded that anguished when their mate was suffering.

So far, they'd gotten lucky and hadn't encountered anyone in the tunnels. He suspected that was because those monsters had all gathered to watch the "torture Saber" show, but their luck might not last.

The Alliance couldn't rush in there to stop them; they could get killed if they did, but they had to hurry. There was a chance they were already too late to save Saber and Caro.

Not only would that mean they'd lost a member of the

Alliance, a brother-in-arms, and one of their best fighters, but they would also lose the vampire who helped create the weapons that could destroy these beasts. For now, they knew Saber lived, but Caro could already be dead.

He didn't like thinking about it; he couldn't imagine losing Willow. It was too difficult to fathom, and he certainly didn't want anyone else to suffer such a horrendous loss.

Declan kept his empath ability shut down. If he allowed it to open in here, it would overwhelm him. That would only jeopardize Willow and his friends, and he couldn't risk it.

But even with it shut down, he sensed the distress and fury vibrating the tunnels. And not all of it was from Saber. The beasts who lived down here were so fueled by it that it had permeated this place.

When Ronan jerked his head to the right, they started down the tunnel once more. They rounded a corner, and the storm drain diverged.

One pathway still consisted of concrete walls as it faded into the shadows of this abysmal place. The other way was made of dirt and boards that helped shore up the tunnel.

It would *never* pass any inspection, and he was sure more than a few collapses had occurred, but the ground had been beaten down beneath the weight of numerous footprints. Before Brian pointed to the dirt corridor, Declan knew it was the one they would take.

Ronan kept his flashlight pointed at the ground as he led the way, with Kadence behind him and Declan at his side. They'd be better off if they didn't have any light, but they required at least a little to navigate this strange world.

They probably shouldn't have come here. For the safety of everyone, it would have been better to write Saber and Caro off, but they couldn't throw them, and their swords to the wolves, while they scurried away to wait for the demons to attack.

It might never happen.

They had left some Alliance members behind with the injected and left more above to kill anything that emerged. He'd commanded them to retreat if they didn't survive this. And none of them could live with themselves if they left behind some of their own because they didn't want to go beneath the earth.

The Alliance would certainly fall without its core members leading it, but at least fighters would remain to carry on. He didn't know how much longer that fight would last without an army to back them.

One way or another, it was all coming to a head. And instead of it being in a wide open, booby trapped, and protected area like they planned at Caro's property, it was beneath the earth in this cramped, damp space.

The scent of dirt and rocks grew stronger as they shuffled cautiously forward. They couldn't go too fast. The demons and Savages would see their light coming, but they couldn't see much beyond the rays of the beam.

The reek of the Savages and demons increased as they moved. He briefly contemplated pinching his nose closed to block it out.

He was used to the stench of these things, but he'd never been bombarded with it before. The brimstone, sulfur, and decay scent seared into his nostrils until he tasted it on his lips and tongue.

When this was done, he would brush his teeth for hours, gurgle a bottle of mouthwash, and scrub himself until his skin was raw. He had to survive for that to happen, and he planned to walk out of here with Willow and as many Alliance members as possible.

As they went deeper beneath the ground, the chill in the air increased. The weight of the earth pressed further down on them as they had to duck to avoid the beams running across the ceiling.

Bugs and worms crept through the earth and scampered into

the shadows until they ceased to exist down here. They were too low now for those creatures to thrive, and he was beginning to suspect they were descending into Hell itself.

He glanced back at Willow and reached for her hand; his fingers enclosed on hers when she took it. Declan squeezed it as he tried to convey all his love for her into this gesture.

She was the one who had healed his soul, the one he should be protecting, not leading into a possible death trap. But they'd always known this is where their journey would take them.

He hoped it wasn't the end of their journey.

CHAPTER THIRTY-SIX

KIRKAU BENT so close to Caro that his mouth and breath warmed her ear. His breath smelled like someone had left fish out in the August sun for three days as it tickled her cheek. "Did that hurt?"

At first, Caro couldn't respond. She was terrified, in the worst pain she'd ever experienced, and not in the mood to talk to this prick.

But from somewhere deep inside, she dug up a strength she hadn't known she possessed. Lifting her head, she smiled at him. "You bite like a bitch."

Kirkau's twisted smile made those monstrous fangs look bigger. She'd found the strength to respond to him, but she involuntarily flinched away from those torturous things.

Her reaction elicited a chuckle from him. He moved so fast she never saw it coming before the back of his hand smashed into her face with its lethal claws.

The blow caused blood to erupt from her nose and sent her chair skittering backward. It probably would have kept going, but the chains, bolted into some nearby rocks, stretched taut and jerked her to a stop.

The sounds coming from Saber were nearly as animalistic as the excited cries of the Savages and demons surrounding them. They were all enjoying this, and she could barely keep her eyes open as her face swelled.

Using her tongue, she felt over her teeth. The blow had knocked a couple loose, but they'd be fine if he stopped pummeling her face. She didn't know how likely it would be for that to happen.

She was pretty sure he'd broken one of her cheekbones too, but that was the least of her worries. Cracking her eyes open, she tried not to wince as the pounding in her head returned. It felt like a hundred tap dancers had taken up residence in her skull, and every one of them was trying to outdo the others with the ferocity of their kicks.

When she was sure she wouldn't vomit, she lifted her head and looked at the beast again. She glowered at him before shifting her attention to Saber.

Black and red coloring had flooded his body and turned him into something she almost didn't recognize. The veins in his arms, throat, and face bulged as he yanked against his chains, and despite the cool air, sweat coated his body and cleaved his bloody shirt to him.

She'd never seen him this wild before, but when those red eyes met hers, the soul of the man she loved so deeply shone back at her. She yearned for him, and her fingers itched to touch him, but that was impossible with her hands chained behind her back.

She held his gaze as Kirkau glided toward her. If she kept her attention on Saber, it wouldn't matter what this demon did to her; she could find the strength to withstand it.

And she knew, without a doubt, that Kirkau's cruelty would remain focused on her. She was the best way for him to punish Saber.

Her torture would be horrible, but it was far worse for a mate to sit by and watch it unfold. She would hate this more if she had to sit and watch Kirkau do it to Saber instead.

Though her lips were swollen and blood streaked her teeth when she pulled them back, Caro smiled at Saber. "It's okay."

The fuck it is! Saber jerked against his restraints until they tore away the flesh on his wrist, and blood spilled to coat his hands before dripping onto the floor.

None of this was okay. He twisted as the bones in his wrists cracked. Fire surged through his hands and up his arms, but he didn't stop trying to break free as Kirkau approached Caro.

He should be the one suffering Kirkau's cruelty, not Caro. She was practically an innocent and far too kind to endure this. She'd already lost and suffered so much; she didn't deserve this.

The increasingly excited noises and shouts of the Savages and demons helped stifle the noise he created as he struggled to break free. Kirkau wouldn't get away with this. He would get Caro free if he had to tear off his own hands to do it. She would die if he died, but it wouldn't be at the hands of that thing.

I love her too much for that to happen.

The realization was almost as jaw-dropping as when she told him she loved him in the woods. After his parents' deaths, he hadn't believed he could love anyone again.

He was too broken, vicious, and too much of a monster to experience love. He'd also believed no one could ever love him again; why would someone love a man who thrived on killing and once relished the deaths of innocents?

But somehow, Caro, the strongest, most enduring, and most wonderful soul he'd ever encountered, knew all that he had been and still *was* and loved him anyway. She'd told him so, and he hadn't said a word.

Now, she would die without ever knowing he loved her. He always would and was sure he had since she kicked his nuts into his chest.

It was a weird time to fall in love with someone, but he'd

never been normal, and despite his suffering, he was amused and impressed by her. She'd done more than bash his nuts; she'd also battered his walls and somehow slipped inside without him realizing it.

He tried to whisper the words into her mind, but she remained blocked though he'd finally opened himself to her. He could sense her suffering through their bond but couldn't talk to her.

Saber opened his mouth to tell her how he felt and bit back the words. They would give Kirkau more incentive to torture her if he said them.

He couldn't let his selfishness be the cause of that. After all these years, he finally regretted his actions and cursed himself for his stupidity. He should have told her, but if they got out of this, he might have the chance to do so.

Jerking against his chains again, something else gave way in one of his arms, and his legs finally regained their full feeling. The color seeping through his skin and taking him over made him stronger as the skin on his hands peeled away beneath the manacles.

When Kirkau snapped another one of her fingers, Caro didn't make a sound, but she flinched. Saber threw himself forward, and the manacle around his right wrist tore away more of his flesh to expose his muscle as he twisted his hand to rip it free.

Kirkau chortled as he gave Saber a disdainful look. "Seize him."

CHAPTER THIRTY-SEVEN

When Savages rushed toward him, Saber grasped the cuff he'd shed and jerked it forward. He tore the bolt free of the ground and swung the thick metal cuff at the Savages.

The cuff bashed three in the face; it sliced open their skin, and their blood spilled free. That didn't deter the others, and as they came at him in a rush, he released the cuff and turned his attention to his other wrist.

Gritting his teeth, he twisted his wrist until it snapped, and his skin peeled away as he wrenched his other hand free. His feet remained shackled, but when he lunged toward Kirkau and Caro, the heavy metal chair scraped across the ground behind him.

He made it three feet before the horde of Savages pounced on him. Five landed on his back, clawed at his face, and shredded his flesh. He didn't try to stop them as he struggled to remain standing beneath their weight and trudged toward his mate.

Kirkau laughed as he clasped Caro's throat and lifted her until she hung in the air. Her toes dangled above the ground, and the chains around her ankles rattled beneath her. His fingers constricted on her windpipe as her face turned red and her hands grasped Kirkau's.

Caro labored to breathe as the demon's hold cut off her air supply. Her lungs burned, and she couldn't stop the awful wheezing sounds she emitted every time her lungs sought oxygen.

Spinning, she kicked at the monster, but he laughed as he caught her leg and sank his claws into her thigh. She choked back a cry as he tore into flesh and muscle while dragging his fingers across her leg and toward each other.

This was far from the position she wanted to be in, but relief filled her when she saw her sword on the ground behind the chair. She had no idea why the demons had left the weapon so close, probably to torture her with it, but maybe she could get to it.

That didn't seem likely as all around them more Savages and demons emerged from the shadows. The scent of blood, the excitement of the fight, and the possibility of impending death were like the Pied Piper luring them forth.

Nausea twisted in her belly as their thirst for death and destruction pulsated in the air until it vibrated the cavern and pulsed through her body. These repulsive *things* were the worst form of life on this planet.

Using his claws in her legs, Kirkau spun her back toward where Saber was laboring to escape the Savages trying to bring him down. The scent of his blood on the air and the suffering he endured as they punched, kicked, and bit into him brought tears to her eyes.

She blinked those tears away; the bastard holding her couldn't think they were because of the torment he was inflicting on her. Her physical agony was still intense, but it was nothing compared to the melancholy pummeling her.

And she wouldn't give in to the hopelessness trying to engulf her. Yes, they were vastly outnumbered and at the mercy of these things, but they weren't dead yet. And Saber had proven there was a way to break free.

With renewed vigor, she kicked at Kirkau. She ignored the sensation of his claws tearing through her flesh as she sought to kick this motherfucker anywhere she could.

Around them, the chatter of hundreds of Savages and demons filled the air as they emerged from the shadows like bats from a cave. The dim light flickered over hundreds of them as they laughed, screamed, and hunted.

Why are there so many of these monsters?

But the demons had been working to recruit, forcing others to join them, and for some vampires, it was easier to give in to their bloodlust than to fight it.

When the Savages succeeded in bringing Saber to his knees, rage flooded Caro's veins. Grasping Kirkau's wrist, she squeezed as she dug her short nails into his moist flesh.

The monster laughed as the same black and red color covering Saber seeped across her hand, up her arms, and through her. She couldn't see where it moved through the rest of her body, but it flooded her with strength as it spread further.

Saber rolled beneath the pile, taking some of the Savages with him and flinging others aside. Her heart jumped when she lost him beneath the mass of monsters crawling over him.

The Savages were having a blast, but the demons hung back, watching the show. It was as if they believed all of this was beneath them; as far as Caro was concerned, there was slimy, filthy bacteria climbing through pond scum right now who were on a higher level than those things.

Twisting to face Kirkau again, she pulled back her fist and slammed it into his revolting face. She'd always been fast and strong, but the threat to her mate and the color flooding her had doubled her strength as she hit him repeatedly.

Something crunched as Kirkau staggered back but didn't

release her. His hooked fangs sliced her skin and spilled more blood as she fought him.

The chains around Saber's ankles jerked to a halt. He tossed aside another Savage as he sat up. His broken fingers and wrists made movement difficult, but he managed to grasp the manacles locked around his ankles.

Metal twisted, and pieces broke off as more Savages piled onto him. Yanking the chains toward him, he didn't get a chance to use the newly removed shackles as a weapon before the Savages pinned his arms to the floor.

But he did get his feet braced underneath him, and shoving up with his hips, he threw some of them off enough to free a hand. With quick movements, he encircled the chain around one of their necks and pulled the Savage over the top of him.

The Savage's legs kicked a few of his brethren in the head and knocked some of the others back as Saber used its body to batter some of the other Savages off him. He needed to clear enough of a path to get to his sword and Caro.

If he could get to his sword, they could get away. Spinning toward his mate, he launched to his feet as a new sound emerged.

It took him a few seconds to realize the walls were pulsing with the beat of approaching footsteps. At first, he thought more Savages were descending on them, but then fire erupted from the crowd, and ashes flew into the air.

The Alliance! Saber was too stunned to move. He'd hoped they would come if only to save Caro, but he hadn't expected them to do so.

If he'd been Declan, Killean, or any other Alliance member with a mate, he wouldn't have doubted the Alliance would do everything they could to save them. But he'd been one of them for years and never truly considered himself one of them.

He'd never allowed them to become his friends or allowed himself to experience the bond they all shared. But they'd still come for him and Caro.

He'd never felt more humbled in his life. He wanted to sink to his knees and thank whatever brought them here, but the fight was only beginning.

They were vastly outnumbered, but the presence of the Alliance buoyed his strength and determination. Wrapping the chains around his hands, he fisted them as he punched the two Savages who were closest to him.

CHAPTER THIRTY-EIGHT

Willow hacked her way through the Savages closest to her, but the overwhelming stench of them told her there were plenty more of them ahead. The muted lighting didn't reveal much, but what it did expose was an army coming at them.

The Savages outnumbered them at least two to one, and if she factored in the demons....

She decided not to do the math as she focused on fighting instead. She'd trained for years for this; this sword had claimed her because it believed she was strong enough to harvest its power.

It's what she'd been born to do, and she would do it. She couldn't think about her family, somewhere in the middle of this fray, or the possibility of losing one of them. Her parents were here, as were her siblings and adopted uncles. She'd lost sight of them as the Savages poured forth, but they were here.

She shut off her connection to Declan; if her family couldn't distract her right now, neither could he. If he was there and they were too entangled, she'd never keep her concentration, but she missed him.

At least they stayed close enough she could see him as the

monsters continued to pour over the cavern and toward them. The sea of their faces blended into a blur until she couldn't separate one from the other, but she didn't want to separate them; she just wanted to kill them.

Battle cries filled the cavern. They mingled with the screams of the injured and dying as steel clashed against steel and the twang of arrows releasing filled the air. The coppery tang of blood had started to mingle with the rot of the Savages.

A hideous face emerged from the crowd. It was so disfigured it stood out from the others, and she couldn't help noticing it as there was something oddly familiar about it.

She swung her sword repeatedly as she worked her way through the Savages. Fire and ash surrounded her. Pieces of those she killed stuck to her lashes and coated her face, but she didn't try to wipe them away.

Most of her remained focused on killing, but though the sea of Savages had swallowed that face, a part of her brain concentrated on it. *Where do I know it from?*

Then it hit her. *Derrick!*

He was the Savage who relentlessly hunted her and Declan through that town. The one who tried to take *her* sword from her and failed.

Half of his face was the one she remembered. The one who made their lives a living hell and had done everything he could to destroy them.

The other half.... She inwardly shuddered as she recalled the other half she'd seen in the crowd before it vanished.

That half of his face was like something out of a horror movie or Batman. *Yes! That's exactly what it was like!* she realized as she cut down two more Savages.

He was like Two-Face from Batman.

On one side of his face, the flesh had been peeled away to reveal the bone beneath. His remaining eye bulged grotesquely from its socket, though it was probably the same size. The lack of flesh and eyelids surrounding it made it so awful.

The other half of Derrick's face remained untouched. It was a horrible disfigurement and would eventually heal. Still, the fact it hadn't meant it was new or the demons inflicted this atrocity on him regularly.

Eventually, it would cease trying to heal and might have already stopped doing so. It was how a vampire got a tattoo, after all. They did them repeatedly until their bodies stopped rejecting the ink and accepted the new intrusion into their system.

No one had to tell her; she *knew* Derrick had this punishment repeatedly inflicted on him for a massive wrongdoing. She suspected that wrongdoing was failing to bring her sword to the demons.

It must have been an awful torture to endure, but she didn't feel pity for him. He chose to align himself with these fuckers, but it was still the most atrocious thing she'd ever seen, and she'd seen *many* horrible things, including this place.

The cruelty and evil that had driven such an act as this was something she couldn't imagine.

But she would be the one to end it as the crowd parted and she came face-to-face with the shithead who once tried to kill her and Declan. When he spotted her, Derrick's mouth pulled into a grotesque smile.

The open view of his teeth on one side of his mouth was unnerving, but it wouldn't distract her. That grotesque, bulging eye was the white-blue color the hunters' eyes became after turning and when they were enraged. The other eye was the same color but far less noticeable.

When Derrick lifted a crossbow and fired an arrow at her, Willow stepped to the side and swung up her sword to knock the projectile away. From the corner of her eye, she saw Declan spin toward them.

Shock registered on his face when he spotted Derrick, but he still charged forward. Willow tried to control the uptick of her heartbeat as her mate went after the Savage, but it was impossible to remain calm and focused while watching her mate attack their enemy.

The disfigured Savage fired another bolt at Declan before tossing aside his crossbow. Knowing he could never defeat Declan, Derrick tried to blend in with the fighters around him, but the crush of bodies knocked him back toward Declan.

The ex-hunter suppressed his irritation over this development, but he couldn't hide his apprehension. He'd intended to turn and run like the coward he was, and now he'd have to stay and play.

Derrick pulled his sword from where it hung on his back and swung it at Declan, who dodged the blade with lethal speed and expertise. When his sword clashed against Derrick's, sparks flew.

They became locked in a deadly battle as their swords pressed against each other and Declan pushed the Savage toward the ground. Unable to withstand Declan's superior strength, Derrick's knees started to bow as his back bent before he hit the ground.

Willow went in low after Derrick, but she wasn't so focused on him that she missed the deadly threats surrounding her. Twisting, she managed to mostly avoid a knife that shot out of the mob.

Its tip sliced across her shirt and belly, severed her clothing, and spilled her blood, but she didn't feel the sting of the gash across her stomach. She was too focused on killing the man who had nearly destroyed them.

Smashing her hand down on the arm holding the knife, she knocked the blade free as the arm snapped beneath her blow. The Savage tried to recoil, but it didn't get far enough to avoid her sword as she plunged it into the creature's leg.

Ashes and fire erupted as Derrick hit the ground. Spinning

toward him, she saw the flicker of alarm in his eyes as they briefly met hers.

She grinned as she plunged her sword into Derrick's stomach and out his other side. He screamed as the stone's power burned through his insides and erupted out of him.

Willow didn't have time to feel any satisfaction over watching that bastard burn; there were too many other Savages closing in on them. They'd destroyed Derrick, but that didn't mean they would make it out of here alive.

CHAPTER THIRTY-NINE

Over Kirkau's shoulder, Caro spotted Brie and Asher carving their way through the Savages and toward them. All around her, the Alliance and Savages fell as death rained down on those inside the cavernous space.

She'd been too focused on Kirkau and his torment to notice the table behind him before, but as Brie leapt onto it, she realized there were dozens of chairs surrounding the long table. Some skittered backward beneath the weight of the bodies hitting them, and others became weapons.

Caro was about to hit Kirkau again when something crashed into her back. Thrust forward by the weight, she slammed into the demon whose fingers dug into her throat as hands enclosed around her ankle and yanked.

"Brie, watch out!" Asher yelled.

Caro couldn't see what was happening with Brie anymore as another weight shoved into her back and kept pushing. Unable to stay upright beneath the force of the blow and the crowd pressing against them, Kirkau toppled to the ground.

The inhuman sound the demon released sent a chill up her spine as she fell on top of him. This was a horrible position to be in, even if it seemed like she had the advantage, because she didn't.

This was an embarrassment, and he would destroy all those who caused him to hit the ground... including *her*. Planting her palms on the hollow cavity of his chest, Caro ignored the discomfort in her broken fingers as she pushed herself up to tear free of the hand on her neck.

She tore his grip on her free, but not without skin and blood loss. She didn't think he'd torn open her artery. Blood spilled down on top of them, but it wasn't the torrential, pulsing wave it would have been if he'd sliced her artery.

But it would weaken her soon, if she didn't get away. Just when she believed she might succeed in breaking free, Kirkau ensnared her wrist.

She nearly screamed *no*, but yelling at him wouldn't help. She didn't have time to look for her sword; it was beneath the feet of those surging around them.

Her fingers itched to reclaim her weapon, but first, she had to escape this *thing*. Kirkau started pulling her closer, and she saw in those awful, sunken eyes that this would be the end for her.

It wasn't the way he intended to kill her, as he'd planned to drag it out for *much* longer, but he would make sure she died, and now might be the only chance he got. With her heart pumping adrenaline through her system at an alarming rate, Caro unleashed everything she had on the beast.

She kicked at the demon and drove her knee into his belly. He grunted when she hit the area of his groin.

They must have some reproductive organs if they once bred with humans to create the vampire line, but she wasn't sure if she hit them or if they were even outside the demon's body. His dick could be retractable, which somehow made this monster worse.

She jerked against his hold until something broke in her wrist, and she bit her lip to keep from crying. Determined to break free, she kicked out again but didn't make contact.

She was about to plunge her fingers into his eyes when a Savage grabbed her hair, yanked her head back, and seized her wrist. The foul-smelling thing leaned over her as it pulled her hand back, and its mouth rested against her throat.

"No!" Kirkau barked. "I'll be the one to kill her."

The Savage hesitated before reluctantly pulling away. Caro writhed against the hands lifting her from Kirkau and winced as they tore out her hair.

Like a puppet on a string, Kirkau rose in one fluid motion to stand before her. More Savages grasped her arms and pulled them out at her sides as they shoved her to her knees.

Her struggles increased as he approached, but the Savages wouldn't release her. Caro gathered spit in her mouth; if it was the last thing she did, she would show this thing how little she cared about whatever it did to her.

When Kirkau stopped before her, she spit on him and tipped her head back to smile. He stared at the blood and saliva running down his cloak before lifting his eyes to hers again.

From beneath his hood, his fangs glinted as the monster smiled while raising his hand. His arm started to descend in a deadly arc that would knock her head off her shoulders.

Caro refused to flinch away as she tilted her chin up to meet the blow. But a second before Kirkau hit her, a sword pierced through his back and out his stomach. It sliced upward as whoever held the sword jerked Kirkau back a step.

The demon's arm fell uselessly to his side, but the wind of it caressed her face. As the blade cleaved the demon in two, Kirkau released a sound she'd equate with an animal being skinned alive.

The ear-piercing sound rebounded off the walls and rose in pitch until it nearly deafened her. It also drew the attention of almost everyone in the cavern as Kirkau's screech drowned out all other sounds.

Fights waged around her, but some stopped to watch, and

everyone was aware of what was happening. A demon was dying. And not just any demon but the one Saber considered their leader.

Kirkau didn't go quietly or alone, as the other demons took up his call until the horrible sound vibrated her bones and rattled her soul. It was the most awful thing she'd ever heard, and they seemed to have no intention of stopping.

Kirkau's screech finally died off as flames burst from his mouth, erupted out of his eyeballs, and broke free of his skull. They consumed him until he was nothing more than a pile of ash falling before her and sticking to her face.

She blinked away the ash to discover Saber standing on the other side of where Kirkau once did. He held his sword in hand and had hers draped over his back.

As the screaming continued around them, he swung his sword across the Savages holding her. More ash rained down as her captors became nothing more than dust in the wind.

Free of those things, Caro pushed herself unsteadily to her feet and would have thrown herself into his arms, but more of their enemies were already coming at them.

Shrugging off her sword, Saber tossed it to her. "Are you okay to fight?"

Caro took stock of her broken fingers and wrist as she swung the sheath onto her back and pulled her sword free. Blood continued to drip from the holes in her neck, but they were healing. She could use some blood, but it would have to wait.

"I'm fine!" she called over the cacophony filling the cavern.

She longed to reach out to Saber and assure herself he was okay. Instead, they turned their backs to each other as the Savages approached.

CHAPTER FORTY

FIGHTING BESIDE SAXON, Elyse fired the remaining rounds in her gun at the Savages crawling over the dead to get to them. As the screams of the demons continued to reverberate around her, she worked to shut them out while remaining focused on killing all those bent on destroying them.

Dead bodies littered the ground around them, yet more continued to come. She didn't see any break in the wave and had lost sight of many of the Alliance members, but they had to run out of Savages eventually... didn't they?

She wasn't sure she'd like the answer to that question, so Elyse didn't ponder it as, out of ammo, she released the gun. From the holster strapped around her waist, she pulled out a stake and dagger.

She kept close to Saxon as she prepared for hand-to-hand combat. Her mind brushed against his as they worked to destroy the Savages.

It would probably be better if she shut him out. It would be a huge distraction if he went down, but she couldn't close the bond. She had to know he was okay.

And he must have felt the same way as he kept the thread

between them open. What she couldn't think about was their daughter.

No thoughts of Madison could enter her mind, or she might run screaming from this place. The idea of her child growing up without them was crippling, but if they didn't fight this war, she would grow up in a world far worse than the one they lived in now.

Madison was safe with her dad and Willow's family. If she and Saxon didn't survive this fight, then Kadence, Simone, or some other member of the Alliance would take Maddie in and love her as their own.

Elyse did not doubt that, even if the idea of it destroyed her. No one could ever love her daughter as much as she and Saxon did.

When she realized her mind was wandering a treacherous pathway, she shut it down. She focused on fighting her way back to her daughter and for a life, while not filled with peace, that would offer more security and fewer monsters.

Just when her ears finally started to adjust to the deafening screeches of the demons, their cries abruptly cut off. For a few seconds, they rebounded around the cavern so much it was almost as if the monsters were still yelling, but then their echoes died away.

Though guns continued to fire, the wounded and dying still screamed, and steel clanged off steel, the absence of the demons' twisted voices made it oddly hushed in the enormous cavern.

Fighters went down all around them, yet no matter how many fell, they continued to come. And the Savages and demons weren't the only ones dying.

She recognized plenty of Alliance members and hunters from Arizona succumbing to the crush of Savages and demons. Willow's brother, Ethan, went down beneath a horde of Savages, but his mate, Emma, stabbed the creature through the back and pulled him out from under its body.

Then, a familiar face swam into view through the endless sea of monsters. Elyse's heart hit her ribs, and the world collapsed around her as that face threw her back into the horrible uncertainty of her teen years.

Misery filled those years. Her mother had treated her like nothing more than a sideshow as they traveled from one place to another. The woman was so bent on showing off her daughter's unique gift, she hadn't bothered to think about how it would affect Elyse or the consequences of her actions....

Such as Savages and demons who would do anything to get their hands on her. They'd twisted her strange gift of being able to track others through their blood into a monstrous thing.

They imprisoned and tortured her by sending her *pieces* of her father to make her do their bidding. And they would have killed her when they were finished with her if Saxon hadn't found her first.

Her mother, already one of them, had stood by and watched it happen. She hadn't understood it then, but as a mother now, she *really* didn't get it.

There wasn't anything she wouldn't do for Maddie, including die to keep her safe from these monsters. And she would gladly destroy anyone who dared to touch a hair on her daughter's head.

But her mother used Elyse and rarely considered her feelings in anything, even before she became a Savage. She made her life a living hell years before the Savages captured her.

Elyse hadn't realized how much she'd grown to hate her mother until she saw her face again. And when her mother's red eyes met hers, a cruel smile curved the woman's mouth.

But though she hated her mother, she didn't want to see the woman die, and she certainly didn't want to be in the same place as her.

So stunned by the sudden presence of her mother, Elyse didn't realize she'd stopped moving until Saxon bellowed. "*Elyse*! Look out!"

She tried to turn to face what was coming at her, but it was already too late. She couldn't move out of the way in time to avoid the Savage behind her.

The one who plunged a stake through her back and into her chest.

CHAPTER FORTY-ONE

"They're leaving!" Ronan shouted as the demons, in their hooded cloaks, started funneling toward a side tunnel.

It was another pathway they'd carved out for themselves and one he hadn't seen until the creatures disappeared into the shadows. They couldn't let those fuckers get away, but the Savages were doing everything they could to keep them from pursuing their masters.

He glanced over at Kadence; blood and ash covered her as Savages hovered beyond the reach of her powerful blade. Her silvery blonde hair hung in a matted braid over her shoulder, and her white-blue eyes shone with determination.

She was his warrior queen, and though he hated having her in danger, they would have to follow the demons toward whatever hell they were escaping to. And they might have to do it alone as he'd lost sight of the other members of the Alliance.

Then, Killean, Simone, Asher, Brie, Nathan, Vicky, Brian, Abby, Saber, and Caro broke free of the crowd and rushed into the tunnel after the demons. They must have seen the monsters trying to flee too, but they were few against powerful beings who outnumbered them at least three to one.

"We have to help them!" he shouted to Kadence.

She didn't look up from the Savage whose head she'd chopped off as more rose to replace it. He didn't know how they would get free of this mess, but they would.

He wouldn't let his fighters go on without him.

From the back of the pack of Savages surrounding them, heads started to fall and Savages crumpled to the ground. He couldn't see who through the massive throng, but someone was hacking their way through them from behind.

The demons had probably commanded the Savages to focus on him and Kadence. The monsters had spread out to kill all of them and had a higher number.

The demons probably believed that the others would fall or run if they killed the king. He'd trained his men too well for that.

One of them would rise to take his place, most likely Declan, even if leading the Alliance was never something he wanted. The others all saw Declan as his second-in-command, and Declan would take the position if it meant keeping the Alliance going.

As he and Kadence used their swords to fend off the rest of the Savages and slaughter all those who got too close, he spotted Logan and Elena, with a large group of hunters from the Arizona compound and Willow's family, working to take out the Savages surrounding them. He searched for Saxon and Elyse but didn't see them anywhere.

He fought a sinking feeling in his gut as a Savage leapt from the shoulders of one of its cohorts and flew toward him. Ronan ducked its grasping hands and plunged his sword straight into the Savage's heart.

As it burst into flames, another Savage lunged forward and buried its blade in his stomach. Ronan grunted as the blade tore through his flesh.

Kadence cried out and jumped toward him; her fingers reached for him but never connected as hands grasped her shoulders and tore her away. Ronan yanked the blade from his stomach and plunged into the chaos after her.

He lost her when she became swallowed by a sea of Savages.

CHAPTER FORTY-TWO

Brie rushed down the hallway after the retreating demons. It was so dark she couldn't see her hand in front of her face as the mineral scent of the dirt surrounding them engulfed her.

As she ran, she couldn't help recalling a dream she had. In the dream, demon hands broke through the earth as they tried to grasp her.

Now, in this place, surrounded by the dirt aroma that had followed her from the dream, she realized it might not have been a dream but a *warning*.

Her heart hammered, and her instincts screamed at her to go back. Because of her ability, she'd always tried to listen to her instincts the best she could. She was more intuitive and saw more than most; it would only make sense her instincts were stronger.

But they couldn't turn back. They'd come this far, lost so many, and were so close to ending those dipshits.

Her body screamed at her to turn around, but she pushed it faster as the tunnel plunged deeper into the earth, and the path took a sharp, downward dive. Her heart thudded with every step, and sweat coated her body as she became more certain they were running straight toward Hell with every step.

But though she sensed the unease of the others, none of them stopped. They continued onward, unrelenting in their pursuit, and from behind, she heard the steps of others who had followed.

Amongst them were Cabo and Zina; she'd recognize their smell anywhere. She wanted to stop and let them catch up so she could tell her friends to go back, but they wouldn't listen, and she'd only waste time.

Besides, she would have followed them into Hell too.

The scenery around them started changing as they ran deeper into the earth. Colored stones began to fill the spaces between the dirt, and the air went from being cooler to increasingly warmer.

The flashlights some of them held reflected off the translucent stones to cast an array of colors across the ground. At first, she thought the floor was hardpacked dirt, but the distinct slap of their footsteps landing against something rock made her realize it was black stone.

When they rounded a corner and the rocks became a deeper black, something inside her broke as she glanced at Asher. The determination etched onto his handsome face told her that he would see this through to the end… no matter what she said.

But he had to know *this* was *it*. In this shithole beneath the earth was where he would die.

"Asher, I saw this in my vision. This is where you die."

Her voice came out far steadier than she'd expected, considering they were running, and she felt like screaming as she dragged him away from this place.

Asher barely glanced at her before replying. "No, it's not."

"He's right," Saber said.

Oh, how she wished her mate and brother were right, but she couldn't shake the impending doom enveloping her in a blanket of uncertainty and heartbreak. He wasn't right, and if they didn't do something, Asher would die.

CHAPTER FORTY-THREE

SAXON CAUGHT Elyse before she hit the ground. Terror pulsed through every part of him; his heart shattered as blood spilled from her mouth, and she coughed out a clump.

Her beautiful, arctic blue eyes met his as her chocolate brown braid spilled over his hands. He couldn't tell if it was a death blow, but it was close, she was suffering, and if he didn't get her away from these things, she would die.

"No," he said. "I'm not going to let this happen."

He didn't know how he could stop it as Savages surrounded them. As he tried to remove the stake from her back, they clawed at his arms and yanked at her, trying to rip them apart.

Saxon snapped and snarled while swinging his fists to hold them back. The color flooding his skin and the rush of power accompanying it coursed through his system, but there were far too many of them.

He wouldn't let them take his mate from him. If they were going to die, then they would do so together.

Reaching into his jacket, he pulled out the remaining gun from his shoulder holster and fired at those closest to him. It drove some of them back as they sought to evade the wooden bullets, but the gun emptied too soon, and the Savages lunged back at them.

When one of them tried to pull her away, his muscles swelled with power as he carefully set Elyse on the ground. He leapt to his feet and planted himself over her as he took on anyone who would dare harm her.

He plunged his fist through the chest of one and tore out its heart as he grabbed the throat of another. He smashed the second Savage's head into the one whose heart he'd crushed, shattering his skull.

More Savages pounced on him, and though the full extent of his demon ancestry flowed through him, there were too many for him to hold back. He felt like more monster than man as he somehow managed to hold his ground against them with nothing more than his bare hands.

He couldn't see beyond the Savages tearing and beating at him. They were all he knew as they battered and stabbed him with blades and stakes until he had more holes than a net.

They hadn't gotten his heart yet, and he didn't feel any weakness from blood loss as his need to save Elyse propelled him onward. He couldn't feel anything other than his increasing impulse to murder.

But the more they piled on him, the harder it became to fight as their weight dragged him downward. One of them managed to grab Elyse and pull her from between his feet.

Saxon lunged toward the Savage. He was slower with the ones clinging to his neck and stabbing him in the back, but he managed to pull her back.

A stake broke through his ribs and nicked the corner of his heart. With every beat, warm blood pooled in his chest cavity and squeezed his lungs until it became difficult to breathe.

Blood filled his mouth and spilled over his lips; weakness finally started seeping through him as his legs wobbled, but he retained enough strength to stay upright. He wouldn't for much longer.

When another Savage jumped on his back, he almost went down as one of them burst into ash in his face. The debris momentarily blinded him, but when he blinked it free, he discovered Kadence using her weapon to slice and dice the Savages hanging from him.

When the main crush was either dead or retreating, she wiped away the blood and ash coating her face. "Are you okay?" Kadence's white-blue eyes fell on Elyse's blood-soaked body between his legs. "No!"

When she dropped to the ground beside Elyse, Saxon finally had the chance to notice the fight was waning. The bodies of dead Savages and Alliance members littered the ground, but Logan, Elena, Ronan, and other members of the Alliance worked to take out the few who remained.

Most of the Savages were either dead or had fled after the demons or away from them. But from what he could see, much of the Alliance had fallen too.

Is that Roland?

It was. The head of security, an older hunter who had survived longer than most hunter men and who mainly monitored their security systems, had insisted on being in on what he called the final battle.

And for him, it was.

Saxon had liked the gruff, no-nonsense man with a heart of gold. He shouldn't have been here, but Saxon had no doubt the mostly retired hunter had taken more than his share of Savages with him before he died.

His gaze fell to Elyse, and with a sinking feeling in his blood-filled chest, he knelt at her side and rested his hand against the beautiful face of the only woman he'd ever loved.

CHAPTER FORTY-FOUR

"A lot of the others went into the tunnel after the demons," Kadence said as she tore open Elyse's shirt. "We have to help them."

Kadence ripped Elyse's shirt into pieces before wrapping one around her friend. She cinched the shirt and looked at Saxon as he knelt at Elyse's side.

Pale and bleeding profusely, he looked about to fall apart as he cradled Elyse's cheek. Kadence fought back a wave of anguish as she tore her attention away from them.

Elyse was still alive, which meant there was hope even as blood stained the shirt and continued to pool around them. She wouldn't let Elyse or Saxon die, just as she'd refused to die when the Savages pulled her away from Ronan.

At first, when they finally succeeded in separating them, she was convinced her end had come. But the idea of losing her mate had sent her into a fury that would make a berserker cower. She would *not* die in this place, and neither would Ronan.

As the Savages tried to tear her sword away, she struck out with fists and fangs. As she bit into them and gleefully inflicted pain, their putrid essence hit her tongue.

That taste lingered, and she was certain she'd always recall it. But that bite had set her free as it immobilized the Savage trying to take her sword.

Once he released her arm, she went after the others carrying her. She hacked and carved at them with the ferocity of a cornered tiger until nothing but ash remained of them.

When the last one holding her dissipated into ash, she hit the ground with a thud that knocked the air from her. But knowing those things would come back at her propelled her to her feet.

She stabbed the next Savage who lunged at her as Ronan broke free of the mass surrounding him. His chest heaved, and blood coated him, but when their eyes locked, she felt his relief.

All she wanted was to reconnect with her mate, but as the Savages started to fall in between them again, she spotted the monsters overtaking Saxon and Elyse. She looked back to Ronan, but the Savages had thinned out enough that he easily slaughtered them.

Feeling like she was leaving a piece of her soul, Kadence turned away from Ronan to help save the friends who had become family.

Now, she leaned protectively over Elyse as Ronan, Logan, Elena, other members of the Alliance, and Vicky and Willow's family worked to destroy the remaining Savages. She turned away from Roland's body as tears stung her eyes.

She'd spent so much time with the man over the years, he'd become like an uncle to her, and she loved him. She'd told him not to come here, they needed him to help lead if they didn't return, but he'd strapped on his best prosthetic leg and told her there were plenty of other hunter elders and Alliance members to lead if he died.

He'd always been so stubborn. And he'd died exactly how he wanted to, in the field and fighting against their enemies.

She'd miss him so much, but he'd gone out on his terms. It

was what he deserved, even if she wished it hadn't been at the hands of these bastards.

But there was nothing they could do for Roland anymore. They could still save Elyse and Saxon if they got them out of here and they received some blood.

"We have to move," she told Saxon though she wasn't sure how capable he was as he swayed a little.

"She's... she's—"

"She's going to live," Kadence assured him when his words slurred. "She's losing a lot of blood and needs more. The stake nicked her heart, but it wasn't a direct hit; she'd be dead if it was. So would you."

Straightening his shoulders, Saxon slid his arms under his mate to lift her. Kadence rested her hand on his shoulder to stop him.

"Let someone else carry her."

"No," Saxon hissed from between his teeth.

It was pointless to argue with him; besides, she would have insisted on carrying Ronan out of here too. Bringing his wrist to his mouth, he bit down and drew blood before placing it over Elyse's mouth.

"You need blood too." It was pointless to tell him this, he'd drain himself dry to save Elyse, but it wouldn't do either of them any good if he dropped before getting her to safety. "Take her above. Take as many injured with you as possible, and don't forget there's blood in the vehicles."

She had no idea how they'd get out of here without drawing the attention of the humans. They were all a bloody, filthy mess, but Saxon and whoever went with him would have to handle that.

"I can't leave this fight," Saxon said.

"Yes, you can," Ronan said as he stalked toward them.

He had a strip of cloth tied around him to staunch some of his bleeding. Red stained the fabric, but it wasn't a big stain. He limped a little as he walked, but fire burned in his eyes, and he was far from out of this battle.

"Take her somewhere she can heal and get some of the other wounded out of here. You also have to do it before you're too weak to change the humans' memories." Ronan clasped Saxon on the shoulder and squeezed it. "You've done all you can to help here. Now it's time for you to help in another way."

Saxon looked about to protest, but he closed his eyes before giving a brisk nod. "I'll return as soon as I can."

"Do what's best for you, your mate, and the Alliance," Ronan said. "A couple of leaders have to escape this and continue the fight if we lose. You are a leader, Saxon."

The look in Saxon's eyes said he didn't agree, but he didn't argue. Kadence didn't doubt that once he got Elyse and any other injured he could get out of here, he would be back as soon as he was sure his mate was okay.

"We have to go," Ronan said.

Kadence thrust out her arm and turned her wrist toward him. "You should drink some of my blood first."

"There's no time for that."

"There is, and we need you at full strength."

"You're hurt too."

"Nowhere near as bad as you; now stop being stubborn."

She assumed he would continue arguing, but he took her wrist and brought it to his mouth. He didn't drink as much as he should have.

Trying to get him to take more was a battle she'd never win, so she grabbed his hand and followed him into the tunnel.

CHAPTER FORTY-FIVE

As the tunnel continued to plunge downward, heat enveloped Saber. Sweat cleaved what remained of his clothes to his body.

In all his time with the demons, he'd never been anywhere like this. He'd never known such a place could exist, but as the rocks around them became a deeper red in hue, he had no doubt what they were rushing toward…

The entrance of Hell.

When he glanced at Caro, their eyes locked, and he saw the same realization within them. If they kept going, they could plunge into an ambush of demons, but if they stopped now, everyone they'd lost would have died in vain.

And they would lose this war. They couldn't come back after the demons again; they didn't have the numbers.

They'd decimated some of the demons' army today too, but it was a lot easier to recruit and make Savages than it was members of the Alliance. There was no turning back, even if certain death lay ahead.

His injuries had mostly healed, something that wouldn't continue to happen if he received many more. For now, he could take these things on again, as could Caro; he still scented her blood on the air, but it wasn't as strong as before.

When they turned another corner, the demons came into view. They didn't rush; they were fleeing the battle but had little fear of those pursuing them. They simply glided along as they descended further into the earth.

He didn't like it. Yes, they were all weaker than the demons, but with the swords, they were stronger and more capable of taking these demons down.

They're leading us into a trap.

He was certain of it, but the demons would also be trapped. They could wait for the others with the swords to catch up, but there was no guarantee they were coming. For all he knew, they were dead.

He glanced over at Brie and Asher as they ran beside him. The hunter couldn't die here; he wouldn't allow it, but if they kept going, it could mean his death.

Saber's mind spun as he tried to figure out a plan. Going back wasn't an option, but was going forward?

When the demons vanished around a corner, they gave chase, but as they rounded the bend, it was to discover the demons had turned to face them. They'd entered a larger area, one more suited for battle, and that was where the demons waited before what could only be a gate to Hell.

A fiery opening, no bigger than a doorway, stood behind them. Waves of fire rolled behind it, illuminating the jagged edges of the rocks sticking out from the edges of the opening.

From within the fire came screams of torment. They weren't loud and didn't reverberate around the black stone walls surrounding them, but those cries cut into Saber in a way no sword or blade ever could.

They were the cries of the lost and eternally bound to Hell, of those who did so wrong in life, their souls were forever tortured. They were the cries of the damned.

And they flitted across the fire like spirits floating through the air. They couldn't escape as they burned in the fires that would consume them for eternity… or however many years they were bound to Hell.

And facing them were even more demons than the ones they pursued here.

Saber skidded to a halt as he jerked Caro to a stop. Beside him, Brie released a cry of such despair that Saber knew she was coming face-to-face with her worst nightmare.

She pulled Asher back as she jumped protectively in front of him. When she moved, so did the demons.

At least fifty of them struck at once.

Caro barely got her sword up to fend off the monsters, who released a murderous hiss. They were the most awful things she'd ever seen, and they descended like a pack of wild wolves seeking to destroy.

Saber pulled her closer as some demons scampered across the ceiling like crazed spiders. Others ran up the walls until the monstrosities surrounded them while continuing to make that awful noise.

Their claws clicked against the rocks, and the strangest, guttural noises issued from them. She'd never heard them make those noises before, but then, like they were a unit operating with one brain, they fell from the walls and ceiling while the ones still running toward them pounced.

CHAPTER FORTY-SIX

Brie bit back a scream when one of the demons landed on Asher. She couldn't lose him, not here, not like this. She lashed out with her sword, but the demon was already leaping off Asher and coming at her. It was so fast, so inhuman, and something that shouldn't be a part of this world.

She had no idea how they'd opened this doorway onto their world, but she'd see it closed before this was over. The demon knocked her blade aside as it seized her throat and pounced, shoving her back.

Beneath her hands, its bones protruded from its slender body. Despite its lean build, it hit her with the force of a wrecking ball. Her fingers tangled in its cloak; she tried to pull it free, but the creature caught her wrist, slammed it into the ground, and sank its fangs into her throat.

A scream reverberated in her head but didn't break free. It couldn't, as her throat closed up the second the demon's fangs pierced her neck.

She struggled to lift her hand, but it had gone numb from his bite. When Asher leapt onto the creature's back, his face emerged over the demon's shoulder as he enclosed his arm around the monster's neck and yanked it back.

Its fangs tore across her throat, but blessed relief followed the release of its bite. Gasping in air, Brie labored to get her wits as her body relaxed, and she took in the fullness of what Asher was doing.

NO! Asher couldn't put himself in further danger by trying to protect anyone from this thing. Unless she did something to stop it, he would die in this place, and jumping onto the back of a demon was *not* doing something to stop it.

When Asher jerked the demon's head back, he exposed its throat. Brie used her free hand to punch the creature in its windpipe. The awful sound it emitted choked off as it swung a clawed hand at her face.

Its claws sliced through her skin and cleaved through half her face. Cool air flowed across her tongue and teeth from a direction it never should, but she refused to let the pain slow her down as the demon reached over its head and seized Asher's skull.

She inwardly screamed as the monster ripped Asher over its shoulder.

∼

THE SCENT of Brie's blood filled the air as Asher hit the ground with a thud. Saber's heart lurched, and a fresh wave of adrenaline flooded his system. By now, he would have understood if his body had stopped producing the stuff, but it hadn't.

He'd failed his sister once before; he wouldn't do it again. But three demons had descended on him and Caro, cutting him off from his sibling.

Caro held off one of the demons with her sword while the other two dodged his blade and came in low. Saber couldn't get his sword into either of them, but he spun his knife around and plunged the blade into the creature's stomach.

The pitch of the demon's cry increased until the others matched it. As their screams grew louder, Saber was certain his eardrums would explode.

Caro started to cover her ears against the awful noise before catching herself. She steadied her nerves and used her sword to deflect the demon's grasping hand.

When the blade sliced across its pale skin, three of its fingers fell to the ground before turning to ash. The creature squealed as it yanked its hand back and, clasping its wrist, held its mutilated hand up before her as its flesh and bones became ash.

Caro tried not to scream as their squeals grew louder. The sound was so awful, but she couldn't do anything to block it out.

The demon she'd cut staggered backward as fire erupted from its eyes. She had no idea what these stones were or how exactly they worked, but she *loved* them.

With a burst of flame, the demon evaporated into nothing more than ash. All around them, the others worked to slaughter those who'd sprung this trap, but though they had the stones, the demons outnumbered them.

"Asher," Saber growled as he cut another demon with his knife.

Caro turned at Saber's voice and nearly screamed when she saw the demon feasting on Asher as another tore Brie's sword from her hand. The demon spun the sword around and plunged the blade *she'd* crafted into Asher's chest.

Brie's scream nearly drowned out the cries of the feasting demons. Caro leapt toward them and, swinging out her sword, slashed it across the demon's back.

Asher clawed at the sword still in his chest while Brie wiggled to get free. Caro kept waiting for Asher to erupt into flames, but he wasn't burning up like the others.

That stone and sword don't belong to the demon. Brie would have to die for that to happen.

The demon must have come to the same conclusion as her;

he ripped the blade free and turned his attention to Brie. When the demon swung down with Brie's sword blade, Caro lifted hers to deflect the blow.

They crashed against each other with a shower of sparks, and the demon's blade shot up as Brie threw herself on top of Asher.

As the demon recovered his hold and stance, another blade arced out and sliced across the creature's throat. Blood sprayed from the creature's neck as its head was effectively severed.

Its head landed on the rocks with a plop before rolling a few feet and erupting into flames. The demon's still-standing body caught fire before turning to ash.

Brie's sword clattered when it hit the ground, and another demon pounced on Caro's back.

CHAPTER FORTY-SEVEN

Saber threw himself forward and away from the demons closing in on him as the one on Caro's back drove her into the ground and bashed her forehead into the earth. Blood broke free, she tried to roll, but it seized her hair and lifted her head to smash it again.

"Caro!" Saber shouted.

A demon lunged out of the masses at him, but he dodged its claws as he raced toward Caro. Lifting his sword, he went to plunge it into the creature's back, but it shoved off her and launched itself onto the ceiling.

Saber took Caro's hand and pulled her to her feet. Blood smeared her forehead from where the skin had broken open, and a bruise was already forming, but her eyes remained clear and her feet steady.

"Asher!" Brie cried.

Brie grasped her mate's shoulder and turned him over. Asher's hands covered his chest as he sought to staunch the blood flowing from him, but it wasn't helping.

"Get your sword!" Saber commanded.

He understood her need to help her mate, but the best way to protect him was to reclaim her weapon. Brie didn't seem to hear him at first, and then her eyes darted frantically around as she searched for her blade.

"It's okay. It's okay," Brie repeated as she secured her sword at her side and rested her hands over Asher's.

The increased shrieks of the demons coming toward them drowned out most of her words. They had to get Asher up and out of here, or he *would* die if they didn't.

Keeping his sword in hand, Saber bent and gripped Asher under the arm. Brie grabbed her sword and jumped up as Saber hauled his brother-in-law to his feet.

As Brie rose, their swords clashed together. When they did, a spark of power raced from their blades and into his arm. The power arc was so strong it quivered the muscles in his arm as his hand clamped around the hilt.

When his sister's awe-filled eyes met his, he knew she'd felt it too. They stared at each other before Saber shifted his attention to the stone. A dim glow emanated from its center.

"Shit," he breathed. "Caro put your sword against ours."

Saber doubted demons wanted anything to do with the blades and would avoid them if possible. Caro frowned at him as she edged away from the demons prowling toward them. One scampered over their heads and went for Cabo and Zina.

Caro lifted her sword and brought it closer to theirs. The second their three blades touched, power coursed between them, the demons' screaming increased, and the stones glowed brighter.

"Zina!" Cabo shouted.

Saber and Brie turned as the large, black man pulled Zina from beneath a demon. It was too late, they could all see the gaping hole where her heart once beat, but he flung Zina's body over his shoulder as he punched another demon in the chest.

"Run, Cabo!" Brie shouted. "Get her out of here, and you go too!"

When Cabo's red eyes met Brie's, Saber saw the man's unwillingness to leave his sister behind. He admired it, but if Cabo didn't go, he would die.

"Don't let this be her final burial place!" Brie yelled.

Cabo stood there before nodding. Though two demons surrounded him, he lowered his shoulder and charged through them. He didn't escape unscathed as the demons tore at his sides and shredded his flesh, but he returned to the tunnel with Zina.

A few seconds later, Ronan and some of the others arrived. Saber hadn't believed it possible, but the demons' screams grew louder.

Everyone who controlled a stone was here, and those stones needed to be together. They were *far* more powerful that way; the demons didn't like it, but they didn't retreat.

Those monsters still outnumbered them two to one; the demons still believed they could win this, and maybe they could, but a sliver of hope grew in Saber that they could stop this. They just had to keep the demons from escaping through the doorway to Hell and had to get everyone who didn't have a stone away.

"Get him out of here," he said to Brie. "We'll cover you."

Brie looked to Asher, and though sadness filled her eyes, she smiled. His sister understood what Saber did; Asher would walk out of here, but probably not her or anyone else the stones had chosen.

~

BRIE DRAPED Asher's arm around her shoulders and hugged his waist as she hurried him toward the entrance. Her heart hadn't hurt this much since she lost the life she'd cherished as a child.

Zina, one of her best friends and loyal companions, was dead. Zina had kept her going forward, become her family, and been the source of a lot of smiles and laughter; now, she was gone.

Tears choked her eyes and throat, but she couldn't shed them here. She'd die too if she stopped to scream out her grief as she longed to do.

And she had to get Asher out of here. He was injured but *alive*. That might not last, as this was most likely the last time she'd see him.

She didn't expect to walk out of this cavern or away from these demons. She'd prefer if this wasn't her grave but didn't see how she could break free.

The power that thrummed through her when those swords connected still hummed across her veins. It was right and what they required to defeat these monsters, but a power that strong couldn't be easily controlled.

Of course, that meant Asher would die, but it wouldn't be here. It wouldn't be in this awful place she'd seen in her vision.

The appalling noise of the screeching demons increased as they approached the exit. They swarmed over the ceiling and up the walls.

Some of them tried to drop down, but when Saber lashed out with his sword, they retreated. Brie swore they laughed when they did. It was the worst maniacal laugh she'd ever heard, and it caused goose bumps to pepper her flesh.

These things were toying with them; she was certain of it.

"Fall back!" Saber shouted to everyone else.

He waved his arm in the air, gesturing for the others to follow him. Most of them were already retreating, but Declan and Willow continued to fight as they tried to clear a path for Jack, Mike, Charlie, and Mollie.

The demons didn't chase anyone into the tunnel. They wanted the stones and would destroy anyone who possessed them, but they also wanted the vampires who controlled them to be alone. It was much easier that way.

"We have to get everyone, except for those of us with

swords, out of here," Saber told Ronan when they arrived at his side.

Brie kissed Asher's cheek. "I love you."

Before he could do anything, she handed him over to Logan.

"No," Asher said as he stretched a hand out for her, but he was too weak to put up much of a fight.

"Get him *out* of here," Brie said to Logan. "I've had numerous visions of him dying down here."

"I'll get him out," Logan said.

"I'm staying," Asher protested.

"You have to go," Brie insisted. "The stones—"

Before she could finish, the demons charged.

"Everyone without a sword, get OUT!" Ronan bellowed.

CHAPTER FORTY-EIGHT

Nathan kissed Vicky and nudged her toward the exit as, behind them, the sounds of clashing steel, the demons' shrieks, and cries of suffering erupted again.

"No, wait!" she protested as she grabbed his hand.

"You have to go."

"I'm dead without you."

"You'll die if you stay." He had no idea how he knew it; he just did. "We have a chance to survive if you leave."

She clung to him as he pushed her toward the door, but instead of fighting him again, she rose onto her toes and kissed him. "If you die, I'll kick your ass."

He chuckled as he clasped her chin and kissed her. "I have no doubt. Now, go."

"I love you."

"I love you too."

She turned and ran toward Asher and Logan. She grasped Asher's other arm and helped lead him toward the exit.

Nathan's heart broke as he watched his mate go, and though he would give anything to follow her, he turned to face the demons.

KILLEAN KISSED Simone goodbye as he adjusted his grip on his sword. She clung to his hand, reluctant to let go, but grasping her shoulders, Lucien pulled her away, and Callie took her hand.

Lucien met Killean's eyes before guiding Simone away. No matter what, Lucien would protect her, and if Killean perished down here, they would see that Simone didn't suffer before dying.

Feeling as if a blade had pierced his heart, Killean tore his attention away from Simone's tears. She was so beautiful and much more than he'd ever deserved in this life. And for her, he would survive this… somehow.

The demons hissed in unison, and someone cried out as he gripped his sword, braced his feet apart, and prepared to fight to the death. When he briefly spotted Elena, she was staring after Logan with the same yearning in her eyes that filled his heart.

They'd just found each other again and were being torn apart once more. When she finally looked away from Logan, their gazes briefly met. Resolve filled her eyes as she stepped closer to him.

"Let's kill these fuckers," he said.

"Gladly."

LOGAN GLANCED BACK at Elena as she stepped closer to Killean. More demons were pouring out of the entrance to Hell. They'd been waiting for them to leave so they could unleash Hell on those with the stones.

He looked around for someone to take Asher so he could go back. He'd told Brie he would get Asher out of here, but Elena had *just* returned to him, and he couldn't walk away from her.

Before he could hand Asher off to Jack, Lucien grasped his shoulder. "We can't go back."

"The demons—"

Lucien's fingers dug into his skin a little. "I know, but we can't go back. There's a reason they were chosen and not us. They have a chance of surviving it; we don't."

"You can't know that."

"Don't you know it?"

Logan started to protest his words, but Asher leaned more heavily against his side as he spoke. "He's right. I hate it as much as you do, but he's right. We have to leave."

Before he could protest further, some of the hunters from the Arizona compound fell in behind him, blocking his way.

"If you start a fight here, it will only distract her," Lucien said. "Keep walking, Logan."

"That's easy for you to say; you have your mate with you."

"But my family remains in that cavern. *Keep walking.*"

Knowing it was useless to protest and unwilling to distract Elena from the horde racing toward her, Logan reluctantly turned away. He carried his friend toward freedom while the biggest part of him remained behind.

CHAPTER FORTY-NINE

THE DEMONS CONTINUED to screech in that awful way as they advanced. Saber suspected it was to distract them, drown out their thoughts, and stop them from communicating with each other.

It was too late for that; he already knew what they had to do, even as the demons poured toward them.

"The blades!" he shouted. "We have to touch them all together!"

It was easier said than done as the demons poured over them and they had to defend themselves to stay alive. They couldn't lose anyone now; they were close to uncovering more secrets of the stones.

Though the demons sought to separate them, they remained relatively close together as claws slashed at them, the screams echoed, and hooked fangs found Kadence's flesh. Ronan caught the sword she dropped at the same time he plunged his blade into the demon.

Elena nearly fell when a demon dropped from the ceiling to her shoulders. The only thing that kept her up was Killean lunging out with his sword and driving it through the demon's ribs.

The creatures all emitted an awful, eerie howl again as Killean seized Elena's wrist and pulled her out from under the dying demon.

"We're not losing you again," Killean said.

Elena smiled at him as Nathan and Kadence clustered closer to them. The twins looked at each other before touching the tips of their blades together.

A spark raced through their stones, and their eyes widened. But though amazement registered on their faces, Saber also saw their uneasiness.

Kadence and Nathan understood it now too. Once unleashed, this kind of power wasn't easily survived.

But their shoulders went back, and their hands briefly touched before the twins turned to face the demons. Ronan, Declan, Killean, Brie, Elena, and Willow worked to hold off the approaching demons as Saber pulled Caro against his side.

He kissed her hard and fast before releasing her. There was so much he wanted to share with her, but there was no time for it as he lifted his sword, and she followed suit.

He wrapped his arm around her waist, pulled her against his side, and pressed his blade to hers. Their stones sparked as power raced up his arms, but instead of feeling invigorated by it, he felt deflated.

He'd waited too long to realize what was truly in his heart for Caro and never gotten the chance to tell her. He could shout it now, over the scream of the demons and the clash of swords, but this wasn't how he wanted to say it to her.

It's better than her possibly dying without knowing.

That was true, but a sudden, unified shriek of the demons drowned out all other sounds. He tried to whisper the truth of how he felt into her mind, but she still had him shut out. He didn't blame her; he'd done the same... until now.

And now he would give anything to get into her head and tell her how much he cared.

Instead, he was left with the truth of having failed her and Brie. He was supposed to protect them, but he couldn't save anyone from fate, which brought them all to this place.

Kadence set these events in motion when she fell in love was Ronan. Brie solidified it when she brought the stones to the Alliance, and Caro unleashed it when she forged the blades that brought them here.

Somewhere, a wheel was spinning. In the beginning, it turned slowly and maybe could have been stopped, but now it spun wildly out of control as it propelled them toward the destiny no one had seen coming… not even Kadence and Brie.

Now, they had no choice but to stand and face it. If there was an afterlife, Saber would spend it burning in Hell, like those spirits he'd seen flitting through the fire, but he would take these demons back there with him.

The others remained focused on fighting off the demons while he and Caro lifted their blades to Kadence's and Nathan's. A bigger spark flashed through the air, and the wave of power it created quaked his bones and muscles until he shuddered.

Caro's fingers itched to reach for Saber; even though she stood against his side, she wanted more of a connection. She contemplated lowering the barrier she'd erected against his mind but couldn't bear to come up against his wall, so she left it intact.

Her body shook from the power coursing through it, but the tears in her eyes were for all she would lose and all they'd never have. In the end, being denied her future was worth it if the world went on.

She wished she could have had more time with Saber and could have loved him a little longer. He was a difficult man to love and wasn't one to share the emotion, but they'd found happiness together, and she knew there could have been a lot more.

But thinking about things that could never be wasn't helpful now. Besides, there was a chance they could still survive. She refused to quit clinging to that hope as rocks started falling from the ceiling and crashed around them from the demons above.

CHAPTER FIFTY

"Brie!" Saber had to scream his sister's name to be heard over the demons. "You're next."

He wasn't sure she heard him until she turned away from the demons still racing toward them and threw her sword up to join theirs.

The impact of Brie's sword joining theirs rattled Caro's teeth, and she briefly feared they might fall out of her head. It was so potent that it knocked the thoughts from her head; she didn't have time to recover before Elena's sword joined theirs.

Having the five swords together was like a punch to the gut, but she somehow managed to maintain her ground as it rocked her on her heels. Saber's arm constricted around her when Killean's blade joined the max.

An unexpected sob broke free. She hadn't known she was on the verge of releasing one until it was out. Thankfully, the increasing screams of the demons drowned it out, but when she looked at the faces surrounding her, she saw the same alarm and disbelief inside her reflected in them.

Kadence was blinking away tears, and Nathan's eyes were closed. Elena's head bowed, and Brie and Saber both had their shoulders hunched forward, and while Killean remained focused on Declan, Willow, and Ronan, he was far paler than normal.

The glow the stones emitted no longer flashed when they touched. Instead, it had become a burning thing that pulsated in the air. Demons scrambled across the ceiling, but none dropped onto them. The points of their swords, raised over their head, discouraged it.

They were still coming from all sides. And once Willow, Declan, and Ronan stopped fending them off, the demons would be on them like rats on cheese.

"We need you guys!" Killean shouted.

Ronan glanced over his shoulder at them before turning his attention to Willow and Declan. He jerked his head at them, indicating they should fall back as the demons slashed, clawed, and tried to leap over them.

Declan said something to Willow; she hesitated before turning and sprinting toward them. Saber couldn't hear what Ronan told him, but Declan fought for a few more seconds before running toward them.

When Willow made it to them, she didn't hesitate before thrusting her sword up to join theirs. They all turned their heads away when the light intensified.

The power vibrating through Saber's body quaked his core. Declan arrived and, grasping his mate's hand, lifted his sword into the air.

That wheel was spinning completely out of control and about to splinter apart. They were racing toward the end, and Saber suddenly found himself longing for more time when he'd already had so much.

He'd done nothing but push her away, but he wanted more time to get to know his sister better. And he would give anything for mornings spent in bed with his mate as their love and relationship progressed.

Watching their children play in fields of grass or run through meadows was a dream he'd never contemplated until now. He wanted to be an uncle and father, but as the power grew and the shrieks increased, he became increasingly convinced none of those things would happen.

But even if they wouldn't happen for him, they would for the rest of the world. The Alliance would lose more members after this; some mates wouldn't survive, but their children would, and the world would, and that was enough for him.

There was a time when he wouldn't have cared about any of those other people, vampires, or hunters. He would have walked away from this to save himself. Sure, the world would still end, but at least he'd have more time to enjoy it before it went to shit.

However, that time had passed. And he wasn't that man anymore. Saber had chosen to do better when he stopped being a Savage, committed to it when he joined the Alliance, and embraced it when he met Caro.

The second Declan's blade touched theirs, the power vibrating through the swords became so forceful that Saber couldn't control his shaking. Against his side, Caro trembled and rested her head on his shoulder.

The demons' screams reached a fevered, earsplitting shriek that rattled his eardrums until he was sure they would burst. He expected them to break into a frenzy and fight with everything they had, but they turned and raced back toward the doorway.

"Ronan!" Declan yelled to be heard over the demons.

The creatures no longer came at them, the light had scared them away, but some had focused their attack on Ronan while the others attempted to flee. They couldn't let those demons get away.

All the demons needed was for *one* of them to fall, and they'd defeat them all. Because of that, more went after Ronan, who was having an increasingly difficult time holding them back.

CHAPTER FIFTY-ONE

"Ronan!" Kadence's shout of terror was so loud it briefly drowned out the screams of the demons.

"We have to go to him!" Saber shouted.

But before they could move, Ronan turned and sprinted toward them. The red and black color flooding his skin imbued him with power as his strides ate the ground between them.

He was almost to them when two demons pounced on his back. One tore at his back, while the other sank his fangs into Ronan's throat. Ronan's step faltered as his face contorted.

Kadence started toward him, but Nathan seized her wrist and pulled her back. The twins glowered at each other as Kadence thrashed to break free.

"If you leave, we all die!" Nathan shouted at her.

She jerked her arm away but didn't lower her sword as she stretched her hand toward Ronan. Their fingers entwined as Ronan thrust his sword into the air, and their blades clashed against each other.

The screaming demons turned and raced for the doorway. The one with his fangs embedded in Ronan's neck lit up like a firework on the fourth of July as the light from the stones burned so brightly, it became blinding.

Saber pressed Caro's head against his chest to keep her shielded as he turned away from the blinding glow. Rays of different colored light, matching that of their stones, shot around the cavern.

It bathed the walls, demons, and ground in various colors. Beneath the swords, they remained mostly out of its path, but it had trapped the demons.

The power vibrating his body made it difficult to keep his blade connected to theirs. He refused to tear it away as his arm shook and the swords clacked against each other.

He couldn't look at the swords, but he saw the determination etching the features of those around him. This was their final test to prove they were worthy of these stones, and none of them would fail.

Saber had no idea what he'd ever done to be deemed worthy in the first place, but his arm would melt off before he lowered his sword. If one of them broke away now, all would be lost.

He held tighter to Caro as the ground vibrated beneath his feet. The force and noise of it quaked the walls until stones broke free to rain down from above.

The light and swords kept those stones from pelting them, but they created a cacophony of noise that drowned out the demons seeking to flee. They were almost to the doorway, so close to escaping.

It felt like an eternity had passed since Ronan turned to join them, but, at most, it was mere seconds. Maybe no more than two or three.

It wasn't enough for the demons to have gotten away, but they were getting closer. The demons couldn't get away, not now, not when they'd come so close, but though that blinding light continued to fill the cavern, it wasn't doing anything.

Then, the one still feeding on Ronan erupted into ash. It

didn't catch fire first; it simply disintegrated like a sandcastle beneath the relentless waves of the sea.

Saber held Caro closer as her fingers dug into his back. Fear radiated from her, but like the others, she never moved her blade. The light started to burn Saber's irises, but he couldn't look away. He had to know.

Just when he didn't think he could take any more and would have to let go, the light exploded.

He hadn't believed it possible, he'd been clinging to her, determined to remain with her, but the explosion tore her away. It threw them all outward, away from the circle they'd formed.

As a concussion of mixed light raced across the cavern, he saw all the others flying through the air, their mouths agape and their swords still in hand.

He also saw the light tearing into the demons as it shredded their bodies and turned them to ash. Even the one who had made it to the doorway and entered became trapped in the light. Its back bowed before it erupted into dust.

Rocks rained down to seal off the doorway as Saber crashed to the ground. He bounced across the rocks before coming to a stop.

He lay there, trying to catch his breath as he searched for Caro but didn't see her. There were Ronan and Killean, unmoving near the middle of the cavern; he couldn't locate the others.

He was about to rise, but before he could get his arms under him, the cavern collapsed in a rush of creaking, thunderous noise, and the world went black.

CHAPTER FIFTY-TWO

SIMONE'S EYES no longer shed tears; they stopped doing so five days ago. Her sorrow had become a constant, crushing weight on her shoulders, but she'd stopped crying. She didn't have any tears left in her to shed.

Instead, she remained focused on the dauntless task before them. Days ago, she stopped feeling the pain in her shoulders and hands. Her nails had grown back from being torn away, but she'd lost more of them today, and blood dripped from the ends of her fingers.

Her fingers were scraped raw and also bleeding. She'd dug away so many rocks and dirt over the past week that the wounds wouldn't heal anymore because they were repeatedly and constantly inflicted.

She didn't care if they ever healed again. She could lose an arm down here; the pain still wouldn't compare to the raw anguish crushing her chest.

It had been a week since she last saw and held Killean. She never got a chance to tell him about the baby. That life was still so new, she hadn't realized it was growing inside her until three days ago.

The realization her increased thirst for blood and bouts of queasiness could be for something other than the physical labor of trying to dig out her loved ones was slow in coming. But once it did, she *knew* she was right.

Killean's baby was growing inside her, and it might never get a chance to meet its father. She could feel him out there, beneath this endless mound of rubble, growing weaker with every passing day.

His life at the end of their bond was barely more than a spark. The cave-in had crushed him, and she had no idea what other injuries he'd sustained.

Something major had happened here; the ceiling wouldn't have given way if it hadn't. She had no idea what was done to him before these rocks entombed him.

Is he bleeding out? Broken? Searching for me?

She'd tried to connect with him, to talk to him, and ask him these questions, but he'd shut her out. He wasn't communicating, probably because he was in severe pain and didn't want her to know.

That didn't help keep her calm, but at least the connection remained, though she feared it was growing weaker. She didn't know if it was true or just her increasing dread that the more time it took to find him, the less likely it would be alive.

Even if she lost him, she would make it until she had this baby. It would devastate her to lose Killean, and she didn't know how long she could hold on after their child was born, but she would do whatever it took to ensure their baby entered this world.

She couldn't think about the possibility she might not be the one to raise their child; she remained focused on finding Killean and *any* of the others instead of traveling that dark road.

Since they already knew they were all somewhere in this cavern, Brian wasn't much help. Now that they'd removed the debris blocking the entrance and part of the tunnel, he might be a bigger help in locating where each member of the Alliance was, but so far, the amount of remaining debris was proving to be a hindrance.

It was taking a long time to remove the tons of debris that had fallen from the ceiling and do it carefully enough not to further crush anyone who lay beneath. Once they got a Bobcat down here from another entrance they discovered in the woods on the outskirts of White Bridge, things started going faster, but they still had to be careful.

Simone lifted a large rock and tossed it behind her. A hunter from Arizona threw it onto the Bobcat Saxon had steered back into the cavern. Now that they had some more room, they were bringing more machines down today, but they couldn't get anything bigger into the tunnels and cavern.

She wished they would find *someone*. It would boost the morale of everyone in this place. Even with all the lanterns they'd brought down and set out around the cavern and tunnels, the area was dark and dreary.

No hope hung in the air, and no one spoke as they worked relentlessly onward. She couldn't recall the last time she slept, and neither could anyone here.

When they were about to drop, they stopped to rest, but none stopped for long. She was starting to near the point of collapsing but pushed herself onward.

She would have to feed soon. They'd brought blood down and stored it in the tunnel. However, she wasn't ready to pull herself away yet.

I want to find just one alive.

Not only was her mate buried here, but so were others who had become her family. At one time, she was supposed to marry Nathan. Kadence had been her best friend since they were old enough to walk.

Whenever she thought about her best friend, her heart ached more, so she tried not to focus on her lost mate and friend.

Instead, she focused on using her shovel and hands to clear away the debris from the cavern's collapse.

The constant beeps of the Bobcats Saxon, Logan, and Asher used and the rattle and clatter of rocks were the only sounds. It was rare when anyone spoke.

Thankfully, the collapse hadn't alerted the humans to these tunnels and caverns beneath the earth. The cavern was too far below the ground, and the tunnels twisted deep into the woods. They were convenient for hunting but not where the demons had centered themselves.

At least fifty of the Alliance members from their compound remained, and all of Willow and Vicky's family had survived. They remained to search for Willow and Nathan. A handful of the hunters from the Arizona compound had survived and stayed to help.

So far, everyone said they still had some connections to their mates. Logan was the only one who had briefly talked with Elena before she shut him out. The rest were closed down, but the bonds remained... for now.

They'd all been left here to work to free those they felt guilty about leaving. There was nothing they could have done, and though she didn't know exactly what happened, she suspected they wouldn't have survived if they had remained.

They were ordered away by those chosen to fight, but that didn't make it any easier. She should have been with her mate, even if it meant her death because mates stood by each other no matter what.

The second she thought it, she realized how wrong it was. She would always stand by Killean's side, but for some reason, this part of the war wasn't hers to fight. And if she had died, then their child would have ceased to exist.

The knowledge of their child's existence was new, but she loved it already. It was the most difficult thing she'd ever done, but walking away was her only choice.

With a sigh, she sat back and stretched her aching back. It was time to feed. She wasn't ready to rest, but she wouldn't make it much longer if she didn't drink some blood soon.

She was rising to her feet when an excited cry came from somewhere on her left. From a few feet away, Vicky jumped up and staggered toward where Lucien, Callie, and Cabo were kneeling on the ground and using their hands to rapidly tear the rocks away.

"We have someone!" Callie cried.

CHAPTER FIFTY-THREE

VICKY STUMBLED and nearly went down when rocks and debris rolled out from underfoot. Her heart hammered with excitement, and her soul yearned for her mate.

Please be Nathan. Please be Nathan. Or Willow. Please be Nathan or Willow.

A part of her was missing without her mate, but she also missed her wiseass, annoying sister and hated the heartbreak on her parents' faces. They both stopped what they were doing and clambered over the rocks to her.

Her mom hugged her, and they clung to each other as her dad and uncles, Mike and Jack, fell to help the others dig out whoever they'd discovered. Vicky chewed on her lip as she anxiously awaited news of the discovery.

But as they carefully pulled away the debris to reveal the hand sticking out from the rubble, she realized it wasn't a man's hand.

Willow!

Hope surged through her, and her mom's arms constricted more as their gazes remained latched on the delicate fingers curling up from the debris. They were covered with dirt, broken and bloody, but they twitched when the air hit them.

The tips of her fingers were raw as whoever they belonged to had been digging her way out. When they removed more rocks, Vicky and her mom crept closer.

There was no room for them to help dig, but they had a good view over the shoulders of the workers. When she lifted her head, she caught the eyes of her identical twin, Abby, standing beside Brian, before Abby's attention shifted back to the woman.

Simone came to stand beside her. Without thinking, Vicky clasped the other woman's hand. Simone's fingers tightened around hers. It wasn't Killean either but whoever was beneath that debris was someone they both loved.

As they carefully pulled away more rocks and everyone else in the cavern gathered closer to see who it was, Elena's dark hair and beautiful face came into view. A murmur of excitement ran through the hunters from Arizona. Vicky didn't understand what they said, but they moved closer as Logan shoved through the crowd.

Tears streamed down his face as he clasped Elena's hand and brushed away the dirt on her cheeks. Her eyes remained closed, and her lips parted, but her eyelids fluttered when Logan pressed her hand to his chest and bent to kiss her.

He pulled away and bit into his wrist. As the others continued to uncover her, he placed his wrist against her mouth to let her feed.

When they succeeded in exposing her chest, they revealed how crushed she was by the debris. Her ribs all appeared broken, and her breaths came in shallow pants that rattled in and out, but she was *alive* and *free!*

For the first time in days, renewed hope filled Vicky when they pulled Elena free and carried her away. It wasn't Willow or Nathan, but they'd found someone! They *would* find the others.

Elyse pulled Elena's sword from the debris and handed it to

Asher, who turned to follow his friend down the pile and into the tunnel.

Vicky hugged her mom and kissed her cheek as her dad walked over to take her mom's hand. Determined to find her mate and sister, Vicky held Simone's hand as they gazed over the vast rubble beneath their feet.

It was a daunting task, but she wasn't giving up.

CHAPTER FIFTY-FOUR

It took two more days before they pulled someone else out. When they removed Kadence from the rubble, she was thin and broken, and every time they had to move her, she flinched, but no sound issued from her, and she didn't wake.

Saxon was almost afraid to touch her as he carried her from the rubble with Simone hovering by his side, but she couldn't stay in the cavern with its dust-filled, dirty air. The cheers of the others died away as they left the cavern behind.

Outside the cavern, the tunnel wasn't a much better environment, but at least he could set her down on something other than loose rocks. He set her on the ground near the blood supply they'd brought down.

He took the blood bag Elyse offered him and tore off the top. Simone carefully pried Kadence's mouth open, and he held the bag to her lips as Elena joined them. She rested Kadence's sword against the wall and leaned against it as Logan arrived.

Blood filled Kadence's mouth, and eventually, she swallowed. It would take time for her to heal, and blood straight from the vein of her mate would have been better, but they hadn't found Ronan.

Saxon lifted his head to stare back down the tunnel as the beeps of the Bobcats started up again. They'd worked nonstop these past nine days to clear away the debris, but they were little more than a quarter of the way through it.

Will the others survive much longer?

He didn't know the answer to that question, but he sure hoped so. He looked at his mate and smiled when their eyes met.

She'd healed well, but the fight had taken a toll on her. She was thinner, with shadows under her eyes and a sadness that wouldn't leave them.

That sadness came from more than the knowledge their friends were buried and suffering. It also came from finding her mother's body amongst those who died in the battle far from this cavern.

Their relationship was awful, but it was still difficult for her to have lost the woman who was supposed to love her unconditionally... and didn't. She also missed their daughter, as did he, but neither of them was willing to leave this place until they found everyone... dead or alive.

His attention shifted to Elena as Logan joined her in the hall. "How are you doing?"

"I'm good," she replied. "My ribs still ache, but they've mostly healed."

He sensed more as she seemed sad and withdrawn, but being trapped beneath thousands of pounds of rubble and unable to escape had to take a toll on someone. "Good."

A rattling clang came from the cavern, and another shout of joy went through the crowd. He didn't have to see them to know they'd found another!

It had taken so many days to find the two of them; now, they'd already uncovered another. Maybe it would get easier from here on out.

Simone turned and ran toward the commotion in the cavern

beyond. He almost leapt to his feet and chased after her, but he couldn't leave Kadence.

Elyse knelt at his side and took the blood from him. "Go."

"But—"

"Go, I have this."

He looked to Kadence again, but he had to know who they'd found. If it was Ronan, then the best thing for Kadence was to reunite them.

Saxon rested his hand against Elyse's cheek and kissed her before rising. He ran back down the tunnel as the beeps from the Bobcats stopped. Rocks rattled and clanged as they were tossed away from where a dozen members of the Alliance knelt. The rest of the survivors pressed close to them.

Saxon leapt up the pile of rubble. His ankle twisted a couple of times, but he didn't let it slow him as he rushed to see who it was.

He was almost to the top when Vicky let out a cry of sorrow and joy. She pulled away from her sister as she rushed forward.

"Nathan," he whispered.

It made sense. If they didn't find Ronan near Kadence, then they would find her brother.

By the time he made it to them, Vicky was already holding her wrist to Nathan's lips as the others worked to free him from the remaining debris. Nathan was so broken and battered by the crushing pile he appeared more like a pancake than a vampire.

But if Vicky was trying to feed him, then he was still alive... or at least Saxon hoped he was.

It wouldn't be too far-fetched to have a mate completely lose it and try to bring the other half of their soul back to life by giving them blood, even if it was hopeless. His eyes darted around the rest of the crowd as he sought some answer from one of them.

Did they see something from Nathan before I got here?

He didn't see any answers on their faces, but no one was trying to stop Vicky, so that had to be a good sign, didn't it?

Saxon's gaze settled on Lucien as he rested his hand on Callie's shoulder and pulled his mate closer to his side. Then, Lucien's eyes flicked up to meet his.

Holding his breath, Saxon waited for some sign from Lucien that everything would be okay here. Lucien must have seen the question he wanted to ask written all over his face as he nodded.

Saxon smiled before turning and heading back to Kadence and Elyse. Vicky would need blood to keep supplying Nathan, which meant the twins would be reunited soon.

CHAPTER FIFTY-FIVE

Everything hurt. There was no avoiding the pain, darkness, or hunger clawing at Caro's insides. It tore at her throat and burned through her veins; her body was beyond parched and broken.

Her mouth was so dry she couldn't swallow; her lips were chapped and split open. They bled in the beginning, and she eagerly licked away the blood though it did nothing to sate her increasingly ravenous appetite.

But the bleeding had stopped. She was too starved to bleed and too dehydrated to shed the tears that fell in the beginning.

Is this it? Am I going to remain trapped in this prison forever?

She was a vampire; eventually, her body would shut down from lack of blood. She'd heard of it happening before. Her father told her about it once, but she'd half figured it was a story he told her to scare her one night.

Now, she knew the truth. She would become one of those dried-up husks if she remained here. She would be too weak to move, too weak to feed, and broken in more ways than the bones smashed beneath the impact of the cave-in.

Despite her lack of blood, the wounds she sustained during

the battle had healed, but having them do so had taken a toll on her and depleted her further. Pushing her closer to starvation and... and... and she didn't know the answer to what would become of her.

And if she didn't become a withered, dried-up husk, would she die from the insanity sure to come if she remained entombed here, alone and starving for centuries?

That possibility already had her teetering on the edge of madness.

She wanted to scream and *did* scream in the beginning, but her vocal cords were too dry, raw, and torn to make any noise anymore. So, she lay there, scraping away at the rocks of the small hole the rubble created when it fell around her.

She pushed away the stone and funneled it behind her. It had taken time, but she'd started making her way out of the hole, or so she hoped. For all she knew, she was digging herself deeper.

She couldn't think about that; it would only make the looming insanity worse. Lying there and doing nothing made everything worse. She had to do something.

But her energy was waning, and her body was growing weaker with every passing day and the exertion she used to dig. It was getting harder to make her way out.

So she stopped and rested as she tried to breathe through the constriction in her chest. She'd wiggled her way into tighter confines, making breathing more difficult.

Closing her eyes, Caro resisted the panic trying to rise. If she lost it in here, if she went mad from all the rock and uncertainty surrounding her, she'd never get out.

Instead of focusing on her inability to break free, she used her finger, which didn't have a nail, to etch Saber's face onto the rock before her. She longed to hold him again as badly as she did for fresh air and blood.

Saber was out there, somewhere. She still felt him through

their bond but didn't try to connect with him. She didn't have the strength, and she couldn't bear to find him closed off to her still.

Gathering what remained of her dwindling strength, Caro gripped the sword by her side and worked to bring it up toward her head. Finally, she managed to get it beside her in the hole and, using the tip of the blade, she worked to break and move more of the stones out of her way.

As she worked, she recalled what she saw before the cavern caved in. They'd destroyed the demons, she saw them die, but a different kind of demon haunted her here.

Every waking second was a never-ending nightmare, and most of her sleeping moments brought her more of them. Sometimes, dreams of Saber holding and kissing her broke through the nightmares.

During those dreams, she got lost in his arms. His peppermint smell filled her nostrils, and she lost herself to the joy he brought… only to wake to misery.

Caro tried to retain hope she would survive this. She would either be rescued or escape, but her hope faded as sleep continuously blended into waking.

She didn't know how long she'd been down here, how much time had passed, or what day it was. It felt like an eternity.

Caro twisted her hands and sword before her, but she couldn't see anything, not even the rocks keeping her trapped here. Blind and trapped, she barely cleaved to her sanity as she chipped away at more of the stones.

Please don't let me be digging down. Please.

But she didn't think that was possible. She'd landed on the ground, after all. There was no way for her to go down. It was impossible.

Wasn't it?

She *really* hoped so.

Caro tilted her head back to take in the stones over her head.

She'd give anything to see them, to see *anything* in this fucking place.

Her chest became more constricted as breathing became a difficult endeavor and anxiety clawed at her. *Stop it! You'll die down here if you don't get control of yourself!*

Her boots scratched against rock when she wiggled them to push herself forward. And then she heard something.

At first, she thought she imagined it, but there it was again… a scrape, a rattle, and then another scrape that had nothing to do with *her*. Caro held her breath while waiting for the rocks to collapse.

And then, miraculously, a pinprick of light flooded her prison. Caro gasped, and her fingers stretched toward the glow as she sought to break free.

She opened her mouth to cry for help, but only a tiny croak emerged. If there was someone out there, they'd never hear her.

Determined not to die here, Caro dug her toes into the rocks and pushed herself toward that light. It was there, just beyond her reach. A hope she didn't have seconds ago but it taunted her as she remained unable to break free.

But as her hand stretched toward it, it moved further away from her. *No!*

The scream reverberated through her head as madness clawed at her mind until she was sure it would fracture and break apart. Was she dreaming again? Was this a new nightmare and she would wake to discover herself still locked in her prison?

She closed her eyes as she tried to contain the madness screeching like banshees across her mind. Trapped, starving, and denied this hope, everything was falling apart around her.

Saber!

His name blazed across her mind as something fell over the light, and she was thrown back into complete darkness.

Noooooooo!

She tried to push herself higher so she could get a better position to reach for the light, but it was nearly impossible as she was wedged firmly between the rocks. All she could do was fist her hand and beat against the wall.

She wanted *out!* She couldn't take one more second of being trapped beneath this debris. It was too much. It was all too much!

The screams rebounded in her head as she begged to be able to move again. She couldn't stay here anymore. She'd been buried alive.

But at least I'm still alive.

Are you?

Maybe you're dead and this is Hell.

It wasn't the first time the insidious possibility occurred to her, and it only made her mind creep a little closer to the edge of fracturing. She had no idea what she could have done to be trapped in Hell; maybe killing demons was a sin, and if so, she still would have done it.

Was she dead? Was any of this real?

She closed her eyes, or at least she believed she shut them. It was just as dark whether they were opened or closed. Caro tried to breathe through the impending insanity, but her heart hammered her ribs as adrenaline coursed through her starved body.

If you were dead, you wouldn't still feel Saber.

She didn't know if that was true or not; maybe it was some other torment of Hell. But, if it was true, she couldn't lie here and give up. She had to do everything she could to get back to him.

Shoving forward, she finally managed to push beyond the rocks she'd wedged herself between. Her fingers stretched for the light again, but she found only solid rock.

It had been a figment of her rapidly fracturing mind, but it wouldn't stop her. Tearing at the rocks, she clawed her way forward with renewed intensity.

Real or not, that light had given her hope, and she would feel the sun's rays on her face again. She *would* find Saber.

A creaking sound came from all around her a second before the rocks collapsed on top of her. Something in an arm and leg broke. Their weight crushed the air from her chest as her ribs shattered.

A scream resonated through her head as agony blistered across her nerve endings. Before she lost consciousness, she knew she didn't have enough blood or strength left to heal from this.

There would be no escaping her tomb.

CHAPTER FIFTY-SIX

Saber had been furious many times in his life, but now it boiled inside him like lava in a volcano getting ready to blow. It rose higher and higher toward the surface as he clawed at the rocks and battered his prison until his blood ran freely and his bones broke.

He couldn't feel his hands anymore as he tore away rocks, but every time he pulled one out, another fell into its place. With a roar muffled by the tons of rock and dirt surrounding him, he smashed at the stones again.

He couldn't sense Caro through their bond. In the beginning, and for a while afterward, he felt her out there, but now she was gone.

It was as if their connection had completely severed as if she didn't exist anymore. As if she was... dead.

But that couldn't be. He couldn't have lost her! Not after he finally found her; not after he finally realized how much she meant to him.

He never got to tell her he loved her; they never got to fully share their lives. Life was unfair; he'd always known it, but this was the cruelest joke it had ever pulled on him, and he wanted to kill *everything* he could to get to her.

But there were only rocks to kill here, and they were nowhere near as satisfying as ripping into flesh.

He pummeled the walls and tore away rocks and stone. The sounds coming from him were more than animal; they were the sounds of a demon, a man on the edge, and someone who would burn this world if they got the chance.

WHERE THE FUCK IS SHE?

The question reverberated through his head as bloodlust threatened to splinter him apart. He knew this bloodlust; it had ruled him for far too many years.

He'd sworn he'd never return to his old ways, never be that man again, but the man he'd become was fading away beneath the gaping hole the loss of his mate had created. Something was missing from his soul; a large piece had been ripped out to leave him exposed and suffering.

And the fury was the only thing loud enough to almost drown out the melancholy. It couldn't completely ease it, but it was better than curling into a ball and giving up.

He wouldn't give up until he saw her again and knew she was gone. But a part of him, the best part and maybe the only good part left, already knew the truth.

Saber pummeled at the walls as rocks tore away what remained of his fingernails and bits of his flesh. He had to get to Caro. Even if she was gone, he had to hold her one more time and inhale her ocean, fire, and salty air scent.

He had to feel her silken skin against his hands once more. This time his roar wasn't only one of pure rage but also grief as tears choked his throat.

Burying his grief beneath his anger, he returned to pummeling the rocks as he tried to claw his way out of his coffin. He was so focused on getting free that the banging didn't register until a bead of light pierced through the darkness.

Out of control, he snarled as he surged toward the light. He hooked his fingers into the dirt, tearing away chunks that rained down on his face.

The hole grew bigger, and a face loomed over him. He lunged forward, teeth snapping as he broke free of his tomb, and his fingers encircled a throat.

Shouts followed his attack, hands grabbed at him, pulling him back and prying him away from those he intended to kill. He struggled against their hold until his arms bent back and his shoulder dislocated with a pop.

He didn't feel the pain that normally accompanied such a thing happening. There was no room for physical pain inside him anymore.

"Saber!"

His name came from all around him, but he didn't register who the voices belonged to. They were nothing to him. There was only one who mattered, and her voice and scent weren't amongst those here.

"Saber, calm down!"

"You're okay now!"

"You're out!"

The words were issued in different voices from around him, but the faces were a blur coated in the haze of red clouding his vision. He didn't care who they were or what they said; he'd kill them all.

He bellowed as he threw himself forward. The hands holding him slipped a little as they tried to hold him back.

Something hard crashed into the side of his head. As his ears rang and stars danced across his vision, he shook the blow off before screaming again.

Another blow against his temple brought only darkness as his legs gave out beneath him.

"Shit." Lucien released the sword he'd used to knock Saber out. It had been Saber's sword, and it clattered as it hit the rocks.

"He must think Caro is dead," Kadence murmured.

"But he should feel her through the bond," Elyse said.

"Not if she's dead," Killean replied.

It had taken them three more days, but they'd finally managed to locate everyone except Saber and Caro in the rubble. Ronan, Declan, Willow, Killean, and Brie were all in really rough shape when they emerged, but they'd all started healing. Blood and being reunited with their mates had sped up the process.

Now, on the thirteenth day, Saber was finally located. However, unlike the others, who hadn't emerged looking to fight, he was primed to kill.

Most of the others were unconscious when they found them. Only Ronan and Willow emerged with their eyes open.

Lucien ran a hand through his hair as he studied Saber before shifting his attention to the mound of rock before them. They'd already spent thirteen days in this hellhole. They were all filthy, exhausted, and stunk almost as bad as the demons.

It was time to return to the world and their duties, but they couldn't leave Caro behind, even if she was dead. He wasn't that much of a prick.

"Shit," he muttered again.

"If she's dead, we'll have to destroy him," Saxon said.

Ronan returned to digging into the pile. "We don't know anything for sure yet. Keep digging."

Lucien glanced back at Saber before looking to Callie and Elena; Brie knelt at her brother's side and brushed away his filthy hair to reveal the lump already forming at his temple. Asher knelt beside her.

"Let me know if he moves," Lucien said.

"Should we tie him up?" Callie asked.

"Do you have any chains?"

"No."

"That's the only thing that will hold him, and probably not even them if she is dead. If he so much as twitches, let one of us know."

"I'll watch over him," Brie vowed as she rested a hand on her brother's arm. "He's not going anywhere without me."

Lucien exchanged a look with Asher, who looked anything but pleased with this, but Asher gestured toward the pile before resting his hand on Brie's shoulder. Lucien hesitated as he studied them.

Asher probably shouldn't be down here. The demons were gone; this open Hell dimension was closed, but Brie had seen Asher's demise down here, and the demons being gone didn't necessarily mean he was out of the woods.

Could Saber, not the demons, cause Asher's and, therefore, his sister's demise?

Lucien started to say something about it but decided against it. Asher was a grown man who wouldn't leave Brie's side no matter what Lucien told him.

"Be careful," he said.

Brie glanced nervously between them before focusing on her mate.

"I'm not leaving," Asher stated.

Brie sighed before shifting her attention to her brother. She studied him with the intensity of a surgeon getting ready to cut. Lucien had no doubt she'd let them know if Saber moved again.

He turned to Callie before he started digging again. "Stay near me and away from him."

Her fingers brushed his. "I will."

CHAPTER FIFTY-SEVEN

Sweat dripped off Ronan as he tossed another rock down to where the Bobcats had resumed their beeping and removal of the stones. The clatter of rocks and the grunts of strenuous work were the only sounds filling the air for the past two hours.

No one dared to speak as they worked to uncover Caro. Saber had stirred a few times since then; Lucien, Asher, and Killean had knocked him out again.

He would wake with a headache and concussion, but they would be the least of Saber's problems if Caro was dead.

Ronan lifted another rock and discovered an upturned hand with its delicate, bloody fingers curled inward. No fingernails remained, and a jagged slice ran down the palm.

Ronan barely knew the woman who forged the swords for them, but he stroked her fingers and palm as his heart sank. She was cool to the touch, not deathly cold, but she could easily be heading that way.

Fuck.

"She's here," he said.

Stones and dirt crunched as the others stopped working and

started toward him. Someone must have signaled the Bobcat operators as the machines went silent.

Ronan lifted another rock and another. Nathan, Logan, Lucien, and Kadence bent to help dig her free. Unable to get any closer, the others hovered nearby as they waited.

When he pulled a few more rocks away, Ronan exposed Caro's bruised and bloodied back. The original position of her hand made him think she was lying face up, but he'd been wrong.

He carefully removed the rocks from her spine before gently rolling her over. The large gash across her middle exposed some of her ribs. No blood issued from her; she had no blood left to spill, which meant she could be dead.

However, he'd seen vamps like this before, ones who bled out so much they went into a hibernation-like state. All their functions ceased, but they sometimes returned to life once they received enough blood.

Caro didn't have a stake in her heart, and her head remained attached, but she'd lost enough to bleed out completely. He felt for her pulse but found none, which would explain Saber's reaction. Their bond would break if she wasn't breathing and didn't have a pulse.

Shit!

It doesn't mean she's dead. Her heart and head are still intact.

Caro's face was a bloody, bruised mess. Her cheeks were so swollen he could barely see her eyes, and the color of her lips was comparable to a blueberry.

There was no rise and fall of her chest, and though her face was too bruised and dirty to be pale, an unmarked section of her arm was far too white. He didn't say anything as he carefully lifted her from the rubble and settled her beside Saber.

The second he set her down, Saber started twitching. Lucien

lifted a sword to knock him out again, but Ronan stayed his hand.

"If anything's going to save her, it will be his blood."

"And if it's too late?" Lucien asked.

"Then a stake is a better option than a sword. Let's leave his head intact."

Lucien debated this for a second before nodding.

"No," Brie whispered.

Ronan didn't bother looking at her; he didn't have time to coddle anyone. She had to know her brother was as close to death as his mate. If Saber didn't willingly choose to die, Ronan *would* decide for him.

He liked the man, he'd come to trust and respect Saber, but they couldn't allow a vampire as powerful as him to turn Savage again. The demons may not be a threat anymore, but they'd never eradicate all the Savages, and if Saber decided to lead them, it would only lead to another bloodbath and brutal war.

Ronan would never allow such a thing to happen.

When Saber's fingers twitched again and inched toward Caro, Ronan stepped protectively in between him and Kadence as Saber's eyes cracked open.

"Easy," Ronan coaxed. "I've seen vamps like this before, Saber. They go into a state of hibernation to survive. Let's hope that's what her body did, but she needs your blood if she's going to survive, and you have to remain calm enough to give it to her."

Saber had to be starved and didn't have a whole lot of blood to give her, but there was no way Ronan was going to provide him with more. They couldn't make him stronger when he was such a threat.

Saber's red eyes met Ronan's. Unlike the rest of them, red and black color continued to swirl throughout Saber's skin as his attention shifted to Caro.

Ronan knew when a powerful being was on the verge of

losing it, and because of that, his fingers tensed around his sword's hilt. He waved Kadence back with his free hand.

She planted her feet as she stood her ground. She'd faced off against demons with him but had to be there for that; she didn't have to be here for this.

They'd faced enough danger lately, and he *would* protect her when he could. Unfortunately, she didn't seem to agree as she refused to leave him. It was one of the reasons he loved her and also why, if he were human, he'd have a full head of gray hair by now.

They glared at each other before a shifting of rocks drew his attention back to Saber.

CHAPTER FIFTY-EIGHT

Saber didn't know how to explain his emotions. They'd become such a roller coaster of turmoil that he couldn't begin to think. Everything in him was a mass of wrath and melancholy, the likes of which he'd never known.

He never would have believed anything could top the loss of his mother, father, and sister so many years ago. But every beat of his heart sent shards of agony through his bloodstream until it felt like his veins were nothing but shredded remnants of what they once were.

And it wasn't because he was ravenous for blood. It had nothing to do with his hunger and everything to do with his breaking heart.

Did he have a heart anymore? It continued to pump; he felt it smashing against his ribs and pulsing sorrow through him, but it felt like a dead weight as it hung in his chest.

"Saber...?"

He heard the yearning in his sister's voice but couldn't look at her. He'd vowed not to let *her* close so he didn't break her heart, and he'd failed.

Now, Brie would be the one to pay for it. His lips skimmed

back when she tried to touch him as he bared his teeth. She didn't seem fazed as her hand grazed his shoulder, but her mate was not so unshaken.

"Hey!" Asher shouted as he ripped Brie away and jumped between them.

Brie leapt to her feet and planted a hand on her mate's chest. "Don't!"

"You have to leave," Ronan said as he stepped between them.

"But—" Brie started to protest.

"No, no matter what, it's best if you're not here. *Go.*"

Brie continued to try to protest, but Asher rested his hand on her shoulder and pulled her away. Nathan, Vicky, and Logan fell in behind them to ensure Brie didn't try to return as Asher led her down the pile of rubble and toward the tunnel.

∽

ONCE THEY REACHED the bottom of the pile, Brie planted her feet and refused to go further. She would not leave her brother behind to face this alone.

Being near him right now wasn't a good idea; it would only cause problems between him and Asher, but she had to see him and offer her support. He'd run into a fire to try to save her, and now that he was burning in misery, she wouldn't abandon him.

She may not have been in that fire anymore to save, but he'd still done it because he wasn't going to leave her alone at the end. She wouldn't leave him alone either.

"Stop it!" she snapped and pushed back against the others. "He's my brother, and I'm not leaving him."

"Brie—"

"I'm not leaving him, Asher."

His face hardened for a minute before softening. He clasped her elbow and stepped aside so she could see Saber again. What she saw of him terrified her, but she didn't look away.

CHAPTER FIFTY-NINE

SABER COULDN'T BREATHE AS he lifted Caro's head and settled it in his lap. Her ribs were crushed and ground together when he moved her, an arm flapped uselessly at her side, and one leg twisted at an unnatural angle.

His fingers trembled as he brushed her mahogany hair back from her face. She was so unmoving and so cold. Her lips were that awful, hideous blue color, and when he whispered her name, he didn't get any response.

When they first met, when he spoke, she always showed some reaction, even if it was anger or disgust, it was *something*. And many times since they first met, she looked at him with annoyance, disbelief, and love.

He could easily recall each of those looks, but he never would have guessed they would lead to this... *nothing*. It should have been him lying here like this, not her.

She told him she loved him before the demons brought them here. He'd seen the truth of that love reflecting in her eyes and heard it in her voice. She'd loved him; there was no doubt.

And he was such a cold asshole, he hadn't said anything in

return. She loved him, he had no idea why, but she did. In return, he'd given her no such assurances.

This strong woman with a heart of gold and the courage of a lion was his mate, and he'd failed her on *every* level. She loved him, and he was too broken to tell her that he loved her too, and he did.

He really did.

He didn't know when it happened or how she managed to break through all his barriers, but he loved her so much, it fucking hurt.

While trying to dig his way out of the rubble, he'd been determined to destroy everything. Now, all he wanted was to see her eyes, hear her voice, and tell her that he loved her. Instead, her battered body lay limply in his arms.

He would have sold his soul or torn out his heart for those things.

"Caro."

Still, there was no reaction, even when he bit his wrist and his blood welled up. The scent of blood was enough to attract any vampire's attention; the smell of a mate's blood could drive a vamp insane.

Not so much as a flicker crossed her face.

"Caro," he breathed again.

He didn't care that the others gathered around to watch them. He'd never been more vulnerable in his life, they were watching him lose his mind, would kill him if this failed, and none of it mattered.

Gently pulling her blue lips apart, he pressed his wrist to her mouth. He was starved and beaten, but he'd give her every last drop of his blood if it could save her.

Some of his blood trickled down her chin, but some got into her mouth.

Please, he pleaded as his blood filled her mouth, and she remained unmoving.

Ronan shifted his grip on his sword as he looked at the others. He nodded his head for them to leave.

If Saber had to die, he would do it, but it didn't have to be in front of everyone. Saber deserved for this to be handled privately, and Ronan would ensure it.

The others all hesitated before moving away to funnel down the tunnel. Brie remained unmoving at the entrance, her chin raised and her eyes defiant as they held his. She didn't have to say it; he knew she wouldn't leave. Asher stayed with her, but the others left.

Kadence also remained, standing slightly behind him with her hand on his arm as she watched Saber and Caro with tears in her eyes. He almost told her to leave too, she didn't need to see this, but the words stuck in his throat. She wouldn't go, and was this any worse than what she'd already witnessed?

All he'd ever wanted was to keep her safe, but she was determined to do the same for him. Because of that, his queen would always be in the thick of things.

When his attention returned to Saber, with Caro cradled in his arms, he stretched his hand out to Kadence. Their fingers brushed against each other before falling away.

Ronan didn't know what he would do without her, and he hoped never to find out. He couldn't imagine losing her without pain stabbing through his chest, so he never dared to venture into such treacherous territories.

Now, Saber was experiencing the loss no mate should ever endure as he held his bleeding wrist against his mate's mouth, kissed her forehead, and pleaded with her to return. Ronan silently begged for her to return too.

There was a chance, however small, she would somehow survive this *if* she was one of those vampires who had shut down to go into a hibernation state. And if she was, a mate's blood would be the thing to save her.

The problem was he didn't know how much blood Saber had to give her. He didn't want to lose Saber or Caro, but he couldn't have Saber attacking what remained of the Alliance.

If worst came to worst, he would give Caro some of his blood. Saber wouldn't want to witness it, but he might not have a choice.

CHAPTER SIXTY

Brie held her breath and bit her lip while she watched her brother. She'd *just* gotten him back into her life, they were making steady progress on their relationship, and she couldn't stand the idea of losing him again.

And *no* one should ever die this way. Her heart clenched as she looked at Asher. A vampire should never lose their mate, the other half of their soul, and the one they loved.

She closed her eyes against the anguish that washed over her at the idea of losing Asher. She'd seen his death in her visions, and it devastated her. To actually *witness* it unfolding before her, like her brother, was a nightmare she couldn't imagine.

But as she silently implored Caro to wake up, the woman remained unmoving. Her body was so broken, and her clothes so soaked with blood, Brie didn't see how Saber could save her.

However, if anyone could bring Caro back, it was her brother. She recalled Milo, the little mouse, nestled in Saber's pocket and the way its head would pop up in search of food or some other treat he had to offer.

He hadn't been Saber then, but Gabriel—a kind man with a

heart of gold and an uncanny knack for rescuing things on the verge of death.

The smile on her brother's face while he fed the mouse was impossible to forget. It lit the room with its warmth, and his eyes twinkled when the little mouse nibbled bits of food from his fingers. But before then, Milo was a tiny, barely alive creature she didn't think could be saved.

How did someone save a creature who required its mother's milk and was maybe a day old? But somehow, her brother did it on little more than goat's milk and love.

If anyone could save Caro, it was him. Beneath his far gruffer, exceptionally more cynical, and often callous exterior, Brie *knew* that big heart still existed. She saw it every time he looked at Caro and how he held her so tenderly now.

When they were younger and he was saving countless wounded animals with his unique ability to heal, she would sometimes ponder if her brother had received a gift too. But, unlike her gift, his wasn't so blatantly obvious or something that would get their family killed.

The fact Saber managed to save Milo, when the mouse was so young and tiny, had been a miracle to her. Even after all her years on this planet, she didn't know anyone else who could have saved Milo, especially not back in the days when they didn't know as much about the world and had far less to work with.

Someone could probably do it now, but it wouldn't be easy, and she didn't know many who would bother to try. If she had to choose anyone to save Caro, it was Saber.

And not because he was her mate and their bond was so strong, but because if anyone could bring someone back from the brink of death, it was *him*.

In the years since he'd become a Savage, she doubted Saber had tried to rescue or save anything, but would the creature have survived if he had? Could he still save someone or something when death ruled his soul?

She believed he could have, and she had to believe he could still do it now.

Her hands twisted together as she willed him to perform another miracle. But though she saw many things others never would, she couldn't will things into existence.

She hoped Saber could.

Her brother caressed his mate's cheek with a tenderness Brie wouldn't have considered possible from the cruel, distant man he'd become. His care was so similar to the man who existed before the horrible events that shattered their family. For a second, it flung her into the past, their home, and the love once enveloping them.

Blinking away tears, she focused on the present as the past tried to blend with it. Those times were gone, but they could build a future together if he could save Caro.

He *had* to save her because Brie wasn't ready to lose her brother again.

She should have seen this coming, maybe she could have done something to help prevent it, but like so many other things in her life, this blindsided her. She and Saber were so worried about keeping Asher safe, they hadn't seen his possible demise looming on the horizon.

Why had her ability, which she'd often cursed and was cursing again, failed her once more?

But she couldn't have stopped it if she had seen Caro's death. One of the stones had chosen Caro; she was selected to march into this war and, because of her help in defeating the demons, they'd blocked this doorway into Hell, the demons were dead, and any surviving ones were confined back in the pit where they belonged.

Because of this, millions, if not *billions*, of lives, had been saved. Maybe her ability was protecting her from the cruelty of seeing Caro's death and not being able to do anything about it. Living with that knowledge, and being unable to stop it, was far worse than the not knowing.

She couldn't have stopped this, but she *loathed* everything about it.

Brie didn't realize she was crying until a tear dripped onto her hand. She looked down at the single bead of liquid on her filthy hand before shaking it away.

Asher wrapped his arm around her waist and pulled her close. She rested her head on his chest as she wiped away the rest of her tears.

There was plenty of time to cry later; they'd all lost so much down here, but she had to be strong for her brother now.

CHAPTER SIXTY-ONE

SABER WILLED Caro to open her eyes; he'd give anything to see their beautiful, turquoise depths again. But they remained shut, and her skin was still cold as he pulled his wrist from her mouth.

When he bit into it again, fresh blood welled forth, and he placed it against her lips once more. She wasn't swallowing, but his blood still seeped down her throat and into her system. If the *smallest* piece of her remained alive, his blood would help bring her back.

Willing her to live, he rested his lips against her ear and pleaded with her to stay with him. He couldn't go on without her.

She was the one who brought love and hope back to his life; he'd lived without them for centuries and couldn't go back to that bleak existence. He couldn't live in a world that didn't know her laughter, the fire in her eyes, or her absolute refusal to bend to his will.

She infuriated as much as she fascinated him; there was no life without her. He whispered this as he fed her.

He sensed the uneasiness of the others as they shifted in the small space; Ronan believed there might be a fight from him, but he was wrong. Saber would gladly meet his end if it meant escaping from this world and moving on to one where Caro might exist.

But who was he kidding?

If something existed beyond this, and it most likely did considering they just defeated *demons*, he and Caro were going to two *very* different places. He'd never see her again.

He would burn in Hell for eternity, but at least he wouldn't have to live in a world without her. That was a far crueler fate.

He had no idea how much time passed as they stood and waited for something to happen… nothing did. He wasn't sure how often he bit into his wrist, but it was sore and chewed up, and his bites had stopped healing and now continuously oozed blood that he fed into Caro.

Though blood only seeped from the small punctures in his wrist, he'd bit into them so often that an increasing weakness spread through his body. He'd been exhausted and starved before they pulled him from the rubble, but adrenaline and his desperation to save Caro had tempered that.

It was coming back with relentless determination. It had been too long since he last fed, and he'd been battered by the rocks trapping him beneath the rubble.

He had no idea how many days they spent trapped, and when he tried asking, he didn't have the strength to do so. Saber was weakening from blood loss, but he couldn't stop giving her more blood. He'd kill himself to save her.

CHAPTER SIXTY-TWO

"How long do you plan to let this continue?" Kadence whispered into Ronan's mind.

Her sorrow emanated across their bond. She couldn't look at Saber and Caro anymore as she kept her head bowed and her eyes closed against Saber's grief.

"You don't have to stay," he told her.

"Yes, I do."

"I'm okay," he assured her.

Though, he wasn't so sure. He'd never become exceptionally close with Saber, but he liked the vamp and was amazed at how far the ex-Savage had come over the years. Not only was he a powerful fighter, but he'd overcome his Savage nature, something most couldn't fight once it consumed them.

A man that strong-willed deserved better than this.

But there was nothing he could do to change it. He could only stand here, wait for Saber to accept his fate, and protect the others if Saber turned violent again.

"I know," Kadence whispered.

"Go."

"He deserves as much comfort as he can get right now."

"*I doubt he knows we're here.*"

"*He knows.*"

Ronan sighed over his mate's stubborn nature. "*It will go on until he's had enough.*"

He was beginning to think Saber might kill himself trying to save his mate, and maybe that was for the best. He would have done the same if it were him and Kadence sitting on this pile of rocks.

Ronan glanced toward the mounds of rocks still between them and the doorway. There was no sign of the entrance to Hell, and he would ensure it remained blocked off.

As Saber grew weaker, Brie stepped forward. Asher reached out to stop her, but she shook her head and stepped around the hand he held toward her as she cautiously approached her brother.

When she stopped behind Saber, she went to rest a hand on his shoulder but dropped it before connecting with him. "I can give her some of my blood."

Saber cradled Caro closer.

"You're weakening. You've lost too much blood and haven't fed in a while. Let me give her some of mine," Brie insisted.

When Saber lifted his head to meet her eyes, their red color was brighter than a stoplight. Despite his blood loss, the red and black swirling through his flesh became deeper and more vibrant.

The blood he'd lost had weakened him, as was evidenced in the slump of his shoulders and the growing circles under his eyes, but he was still incredibly volatile and capable of destroying anyone who got in his way. When Asher stepped toward his mate, Ronan seized his arm.

Brie had received a vision of Asher dying down here; they'd all assumed it would be because of the demons and Savages, but while they remained anywhere near Saber, Asher was in danger. And his brother-in-law could be the one to unleash his death.

From the looks of Saber, he might go after Brie too, but it was less likely. However, another male near his dead mate could be the thing that set him off. And in this state of mind, Saber might not know who he was attacking.

The look Asher gave him would have terrified many vampires; Ronan didn't acknowledge it. He understood Asher's need to go to his mate, but he wouldn't do Brie any good if he ended up in a fight with her brother. And he wouldn't do *any* of them any good if he was dead.

Ronan didn't want to fight the hunter-turned-vamp, but he would if it meant keeping Brie and Kadence safe. Asher's interference wouldn't help with that.

"Brie," Asher said in an irritated voice.

"Go back to your mate," Saber growled at his sister.

"I can help you," Brie insisted.

"No one can help me."

Brie paled, and Ronan released Asher to step in front of Kadence. He adjusted his hold on his sword as, with those words, Saber confirmed what Ronan had already suspected… there was no saving his mate.

Now, it was a matter of how Saber would choose to go: at the end of Ronan's sword or by his hand. Saber seemed to confirm which it would be when he stopped stroking Caro's face and rested his hand on his sword's hilt.

"Brie," Asher said more sharply.

Now that Ronan was out of his way, Asher stepped forward again. When he did, Brie rested her hand on Saber's shoulder and squeezed.

Ronan held his breath as he waited to see what would happen. If Saber reacted violently to the touch, a battle would ensue. Saber was weakened, but rage and despair over losing his mate would propel him to strengths and feats most couldn't accomplish in his weakened state.

Instead of erupting into a fury and looking to slaughter

everyone, Saber's shoulders slumped a little, and he released his sword to rest his hand over Brie's. "Go on now, little sister. Return to your mate."

"I love you, Gabriel," she whispered.

He stiffened at the name before relaxing again. "And I you."

With tears streaming down her face, Brie retreated to stand beside Asher again. Kadence's shoulders shook, and she wiped her eyes before lifting her chin and staring stoically ahead.

This would be over soon. Of that, Ronan was sure.

CHAPTER SIXTY-THREE

Saber caressed Caro's cool cheek before bending to kiss her brow. He bit into his wrist again and returned it to her mouth; his blood flow had slowed considerably, but at least she was still getting a little.

He'd given up hope his blood would help. However, he'd drain himself dry before giving up completely. It may not be healing her, but he couldn't stop until he put a blade through his heart and ended his despair.

First, he had to take her from this dirty, cold, desolate place. He'd never let Caro's final resting place be in this literal hellhole.

She should be in the sun and by the sea, which had become an integral part of her scent. She deserved salty air and a place of warmth that matched the beauty of her soul.

Caro may already be gone, but he hoped her soul remained until it could be set free in a place of beauty like it deserved. No matter what, her body wouldn't stay here.

If he chose to die here too, the others would carry her above and take him. But *he* would bring her into the light and hold her while his existence ended.

He'd like to walk into the sun and catch fire with her, so they could burn together, but he'd have to start killing again for the sun to burn him. While earlier he would have given anything to destroy everything in his path, he wouldn't leave this earth a monster.

Caro would never want that, and she especially wouldn't approve of it happening because of *her*. Despite the rage and anguish tearing at his soul, he couldn't return to being a Savage.

Besides, maybe purgatory existed too. And maybe, by some miracle of a chance, he might end up there to pay for his countless sins before being deemed worthy enough to be set free to find her soul again.

He cleaved to that small chance as he clung to what little remained of his shredding sanity. The malevolence creeping through him again whispered of death and destruction. It begged him to kill again and make all those who had done this pay.

The demons were dead or buried back in Hell where they belonged, but Savages remained. He could hunt and ruthlessly slaughter *all* of them. It might be impossible, but he'd give it his best shot.

As he considered it, his hands tightened on Caro, and his fangs lengthened. Veins throbbed in his neck and arms as he restrained himself from rising to hunt.

If he left here, he wouldn't only kill Savages. He could try telling himself he would, but he knew the truth.

Saber could never control this long enough to keep himself from killing everyone he encountered. He'd destroy anyone in his way, innocent or not, and once he started killing, he wouldn't stop.

He'd carve a path of wrath across this world, leaving only the dead in his wake. It was all so tempting he could taste their warm blood filling his mouth, feel the flesh tearing apart beneath his hands, and hear the snap of bones.

For a second, his vision blurred, and he lost himself to the insanity before Caro's scent wafted up to calm him. It helped pacify the madness enough that he could think rationally again.

Caro would hate it if he killed any innocents because of her. And if there was a purgatory and he had any chance of going there, he would blow it by murdering everyone in his path, even if he craved it more than the blood his starved body required to survive.

He could spend a thousand years being tortured and tormented in Purgatory, or whatever happened there, if it meant having a chance of seeing her again. He could spend a million years in that state for only a *glimpse* of her again.

Shifting his hold on her, he settled Caro down before sliding his sword into the sheath that had remained on his back. If he couldn't walk into the sun with her, he could plunge it through his heart, and hopefully, his stone would have the same effect on him as it did on others. If he was still holding her, they could burn together.

If his sword didn't kill him, there was always Caro's or someone else's to do the job, but she would be in his arms when he died. And he would ensure she was beneath the sun and on the seashore she loved so much when it happened.

Caro was once life, everything exciting, and the promise of a new start that he'd resisted. Now, his fresh start was gone, and though he'd never believed it possible, he was more broken than ever.

He was also a fool.

Resting his hand against the rocky ground, he pushed himself up. His legs shook as he rose and nearly went down, but he locked his knees in place to keep from doing so.

He bent and lifted her when he was stable enough to remain standing. Her head fell to rest against his chest as he held her against him.

A memory of her, with her head on his chest and her hand on his stomach, swam to the forefront. She'd been so warm, loving, strong-willed, and free-spirited.

She'd been everything he never wanted and all he'd always needed. And now she was gone.

Tears burned his eyes as his heart tore and a bellow rose in his throat. This time, he didn't resist it as he tipped his head back and all his sorrow and fury poured out. His roar rebounded off the rocks and echoed around them until it became a cacophony of misery.

It should have been him. She couldn't have survived without him, but she shouldn't have died down here, in the dark and all *alone*. She should have walked back into the sun, felt its warmth one more time, and breathed fresh air.

She'd deserved so much better than the death he delivered to her the day he showed up at her parents' store. If he had it all to do over again, he would have taken her away and let the world burn, or he would have taken her home, left her there, and never returned.

It probably would have been impossible for him to stay away, even then, when they barely knew each other, but he never would have entangled her in this mess. He was so selfish he would have said fuck everyone else, but Caro wasn't.

She would have fought anyway.

When his scream cut off, he bent his head to nuzzle her temple as his tears fell onto the dirt coating her striking features. Every part of him was shattered; if anyone deserved it, it was him. He'd probably left many people and families feeling like this over the years when he was a Savage.

But Caro didn't deserve this. She was just one more innocent victim of *him*.

Wiping his tears and some of the dirt they smeared from her face, he straightened his shoulders and started down the rocky pile of debris. He carefully placed one foot in front of another to avoid having them roll out from under him.

If he went down, he wasn't sure he was strong enough to get up again. He didn't want help, and no one else would take her from here.

He should have told her he loved her. It was true; he did love her, but he'd been too stubborn to realize it until it was too late, and she'd died without ever knowing it. He *loathed* himself for it.

"What are you doing?" Ronan inquired.

"She's not staying down here," Saber managed to choke out in a voice barely above a whisper. "It will be one of the last things I do, but I'm carrying her from this place. She deserves better."

"I can help," Brie offered.

"No." Saber nodded toward Caro's sword. "Can someone please get that?"

Kadence crept sideways toward the sword and lifted it from the ground. Ronan kept his body between them, but Saber had no intention of harming anyone... other than himself. He didn't tell them that; he didn't feel like talking.

When he got to the bottom of the pile and entered the tunnel, he kept his shoulder against the wall and used it to help support himself as he carried Caro through the long journey to the surface. Before they arrived at the exit, he encountered what remained of the Alliance as they waited for them in the tunnel.

As he carried Caro out of the darkness and into the light, no one spoke. Stepping into the fresh air, Saber discovered himself surrounded by trees. He had no idea where they were, but they weren't beneath the city.

Tipping his head back, he closed his eyes as the sun beat down on him. He'd worked for centuries to walk beneath its rays once again; at one time, its warmth meant so much to him, but it meant nothing now.

Breathing in, he discovered it was an especially cruel knife to his heart that the world smelled so much like his Caro.

"I'm going to take her to the ocean," he said.

"Then we'll take you there," Ronan stated.

CHAPTER SIXTY-FOUR

SABER RESTED Caro carefully across his lap as he settled into the middle row of the SUV. The vehicles had been driven as far into the forest as they could go.

Ronan sat behind the wheel, and Killean settled beside him while Lucien and Saxon climbed into the seats behind him. They'd left some members of the Alliance behind to make sure nothing broke free of the rocks before they could seal off the tunnels and establish a security system.

Normally, Saber would make the bombs to ensure nothing left those tunnels. They'd have to find someone else to do that.

Saber didn't look at any of them as his attention remained on Caro. The sun beating down on her pale complexion had warmed her skin, but she remained unmoving.

Some of his bites had healed, and no blood seeped from them, but others still oozed what little blood remained in his system. Wanting fresher blood for her, he bit into his wrist before forcing it between her lips.

She was bloody, bruised, and dirty, but even in death, she was beautiful. He wiped more dirt and blood from her face as he kissed her forehead. He would take her into the sea and clean her before his time on this earth ended.

He rested his forehead against hers as he closed his eyes and waited to meet the death he'd welcome with open arms. His suffering would end soon.

He'd never considered death at his worst moments or during the cruelest times of his life. Part of it was he'd been too self-centered to destroy himself to save others, but it was mostly because he enjoyed life even when he was killing and filled with rage.

He'd never deny that he loved to kill. Becoming a Savage brought him happiness and allowed him to thrive in his bloodlust, but love was not a part of his life then.

Most sane, living beings couldn't find much joy in a life like that, but he'd happily lived it until the day it all changed. And then, he stopped being content with his life of death.

After forsaking his life as a Savage, and throughout the withdrawal and misery following his conversion from a Savage back to a regular vamp, he enjoyed his life—mostly because he still killed afterward; he just focused his murderous rampage on Savages.

Now, he'd happily see his existence come to an end.

He was sorry Brie would end up hurt by this. He should have maintained his distance, but Caro had hammered away at the wall he kept around himself, and Brie dug her way into the cracks.

He'd known better than to have any relationship with her, and his sister would be the one to suffer for his stupidity, but at least she had Asher to help her through it. He was a good mate, and Saber was glad they'd found each other.

As weakness seeped through him, he closed his eyes and slumped against Caro. He could only hope that they might be reunited one day.

I love you, he whispered in his mind, but there was no bond connecting them for her to hear it, and he'd been too cowardly to speak the words she'd deserved to hear.

When Ronan stopped the vehicle, Saber lifted his head. Too weak from blood loss, he couldn't hold it up; his head bobbed forward before falling back.

Blackness seeped around the edges of his mind. He didn't know what happened, but when he regained consciousness, the SUV was moving again.

Saber jerked his head upright as he fought to stay awake. He had only a few minutes left to hold Caro in his arms; he wouldn't spend them blacked out.

His eyes cracked open, and when they did, he thought he saw movement beneath Caro's pale lids with fine blue veins visible through them. But it was visible for only a fraction of a second before it vanished.

Saber frowned, closed his eyes, and squinted them open again. His vision blurred; he couldn't see anything as his head swam and darkness tried to take him under again.

Fisting his hand, he tried to stay alert as his muscles shook and his heart stuttered from the lack of blood required to keep it pumping. Words formed on his tongue, but it had become so thick and sluggish that he couldn't get it to move correctly.

He had to get the attention of the others and learn if they could see it too. Was he hallucinating, or was she coming back to him?

His heart clenched, but he didn't know if it was from a lack of blood or the bubble of hope in his chest. He shouldn't have hope; she was still cold, her lips remained blue, and he was so close to the end.

He was still trying to speak when his head rolled forward before snapping up. His tongue moved in his mouth, but only a weird, gurgled sound came out.

And then fangs sank into his flesh. A strangled cry issued from him, and he almost jerked his wrist away in shock. Still unable to speak, he kicked the back of Killean's seat, knocking him forward a little.

Spinning around, Killean started to say something, but his jaw dropped. "Shit!"

"What is it?" Ronan demanded.

"Pull over," Killean commanded.

Lucien and Saxon leaned over his shoulder, but he couldn't focus on them. He couldn't concentrate on anything other than Caro draining him of the little blood remaining in his system.

He opened his eyes to look at Caro again but couldn't see anything. His vision had failed him; the world was only blackness and sound, though that sound was growing muffled.

"What is it?" Ronan demanded again as gravel crunched beneath the tires and the vehicle slowed.

"She's alive."

"Fuck," Lucien breathed.

Blinking, Saber was able to bring the world back into view as the SUV screeched to a halt. Ronan had pulled over so fast that another Alliance SUV blew past them before screeching to a stop.

Declan and Logan jumped out of the vehicle in front of them. Doors opened and slammed closed from another car. Another vehicle screeched to a halt from somewhere behind them.

When they first left the tunnel, Ronan sent most of what remained of the Alliance back to the prison. They didn't need everyone there to witness Saber's death, and they no longer required large numbers to stand against the demons.

Some remained in the tunnel, and Vicky and Nathan had left with her family to retrieve their son. They would also bring back those who sought shelter on her family's compound. Saber didn't know how many vehicles remained with them, but it wasn't many.

The SUV creaked as one of the guys behind him turned and

started rummaging through something. A few seconds later, a blood bag appeared in front of his face.

Even through the plastic, he detected the coppery tang of the blood inside. Starved and weakened, that scent caused saliva to fill his mouth. He tried to lift a hand to take the bag from Lucien but was too weak to move.

Lucien tore the top off and put the bag to Saber's mouth. "Drink."

It didn't surprise Saber that they had blood in this vehicle the whole time and hadn't given him any. It was safer for them and their mates if he was weaker.

He didn't blame them for keeping him hungry; he would have done the same thing to protect Caro. Now, he drank the bag in two gulps. When Lucien moved the empty bag away, Saxon held another open one before him.

While the others hovered around him, Saber drank more and more bags until Lucien put down his window and called out, "Get us more blood!"

The whole time he drank, Caro fed from him. Almost as soon as he got blood into his system, she took it out again, leaving him weak and barely able to see but so happy.

Saber didn't care how weak he was, he'd do anything to save her as he cuddled her closer. This time, the tears sliding down his face were ones of joy.

CHAPTER SIXTY-FIVE

It was nightfall by the time they returned to Caro's home. She still hadn't regained consciousness, but the color had returned to her face, and her injuries were healing.

She continued to feed from him every few minutes, but it had slowed enough that he could keep some blood for himself. He was weaker than he liked, but at least he could see again and wasn't on the verge of passing out.

Her heart beat a steady rhythm, and her shallow breaths moved her chest. He rested his hand over her heart and smiled at its reassuring pulse.

Ronan pulled up in front of the house and parked the SUV. They'd already discussed that Saber would remain with Caro while Ronan and the others returned to secure the tunnels.

Ronan offered to leave men with them to ensure their safety, but Saber preferred to be alone with her. They needed this time together and would be safe. They had security and plenty of traps to ensure that.

Besides, Ronan and the others needed as many with them as they could get while they worked to reestablish some normalcy to their lives and secured the tunnels. The surviving hunters from the Arizona compound would also return home soon.

From the Alliance members they left behind to guard the injected, they'd learned all those infected with the demon blood had returned to their old selves. At least they would add to their numbers, but not much.

The demons were gone, but there was still a home to rebuild and Savages to keep in check. After the drastic hit their numbers had taken against the demons, the Alliance couldn't afford to leave anyone here with them.

Saber opened his door and stepped out of the vehicle with Caro in his arms. Earlier, he believed neither of them would live to see this night, yet they now stood within its embrace. The air was crisp and clear; as he inhaled it deeply, he appreciated it more.

"We'll return to the prison while you and your mate heal," Ronan said. "You know where to find us; call if you need anything, and we'll be here."

"Thank you," Saber replied. "I'll let you know when I can set the explosives in those tunnels."

"We'll dig up the city plans to ensure we don't disturb anything the humans have done and get them ready for you. We'll also have a map of the tunnels the demons and Savages created by then."

It would be some time before they were ready for him to set the explosives, and Saber would gladly take all of it to spend with his mate. Saber started to turn away from the vehicle, but Ronan's next words stopped him.

"Saber." He looked back at his king. "You *do* deserve her."

Before Saber could reply, Ronan put up his window and shifted the SUV into drive. A couple more vehicles drove past as they headed for the gate, but the third one stopped beside him.

From the passenger side, Brie leaned across Asher's lap to talk to him out the window. "We can stay if you'd like."

"No. I appreciate the offer, but I want to be alone with her." When hurt flashed across Brie's face, Saber rushed to continue. "I'll call and see you soon, but I need time alone with her."

"Understandable," Asher said.

"Do you have enough blood here?" Brie asked.

"There's plenty," Saber assured her before meeting his brother-in-law's eyes. "Take care of her."

"Always," Asher vowed.

Saber looked at his sister again. "I'll be in touch soon, I promise."

Brie smiled wanly. "I love you."

Saber didn't say anything; the words were foreign as they lodged in his throat. He tried to force them out, but they refused.

When he was younger, those three words always flowed freely in his home. Their father wasn't the most expressive man, but from his warm hugs and laughter, as he slung his arm around their shoulders, his love was evident. The words came from him but not as often as his mother, who was free with her hugs, kisses, and love.

At the time, Saber was freer with the words too. Not a day went by without him telling his parents and Brie how much he loved them, but those days were centuries ago and the last time he uttered the words.

After his parents died, he'd believed love was a thing of his past and gone from his life. And it was gone until Brie walked back into it and he discovered Caro. Now, he loved again but was still too broken to express it.

"And I you," he said as he smiled again and strode toward the barn.

Tires crunched over the drive as they left him and Caro behind. He climbed the steps to her apartment and slid the glass door open before carrying her inside.

Carefully, he set her on the bed and kissed her forehead. He checked to make sure she was comfortable before leaving the apartment. He sprinted down the driveway to ensure the gate had closed after the Alliance left and they were securely locked in.

When he reached the end, he stopped to stare at the steel gates blocking his way. A sense of loss and regret filled him; he should have told Brie what she needed to hear.

He did love her. He'd tried not to, but, like Caro, she'd worked her way into his heart and lodged herself there.

When he saw her again, he would say it. But as he vowed this to himself, he felt the words sticking in his throat. He wondered if he'd ever get them out again.

Cursing his inability, he turned away from the gates and raced back to the house. A few seconds later, he returned to Caro's side.

She was still too pale, but her lips were no longer blue. He went to the fridge and removed some blood before sitting on the bed. He settled her head on his lap and cradled her there as he opened another blood bag and drank while offering her his wrist.

∼

THREE DAYS LATER, Caro finally opened her eyes, and their beautiful, turquoise depths met his once more. He almost cried at the sight of them as he kissed her.

"You're awake," he breathed.

She smiled before closing her eyes again.

On the fifth day, she could stay awake for an hour at a time. He carried her into the bathroom and helped her bathe.

He'd cleaned her the best he could while she was healing, but a sponge bath was nothing compared to the one he made for her. She moaned as she sank into the warm water full of the eucalyptus-scented bubble bath he'd found beneath her sink.

When she finished, he carried her back to bed, where she passed out again. On the seventh day, he brought her outside to watch the sunset.

She wore only a knee-length T-shirt, but he swathed her in a warm blanket as he held her in his lap and watched the colors dance across the sky. With her head resting on his chest and her warm body cuddled against his, he'd never felt more content.

Ronan had said he deserved her, and while Saber wasn't sure about that, it didn't matter because he would never let her go. He'd almost lost her, and he would spend the rest of his days working to become the man she deserved.

Caro closed her eyes as she listened to Saber's heartbeat. Her chest still ached as her now bruised ribs continued to heal, but she was alive, a miracle she never could have expected. And she was incredibly grateful for that miracle and the man who saved her.

It had taken her a while to heal and absorb her surroundings again. When she did, she saw the toll her near demise had taken on Saber.

Upon first waking, she discovered that he'd lost twenty pounds since the last time she could clearly recall seeing him. Thick stubble, almost full enough to be considered a beard, lined his normally clean-shaven face.

His hair, which had grown longer while she worked to forge the swords, now fell below his shoulders. She twirled the soft strands between her fingers as she savored his warmth.

She liked the longer hair on him. It wasn't like he needed it, but it made him appear more menacing. It was sexy as hell.

This man has completely made me lose my mind. And she loved it.

Circles shadowed his cobalt-colored eyes. She'd never seen the haunted look that remained in them and hoped it would go away soon.

Even before Saber told her what happened, how he believed he lost her, and what he'd done to save her, she saw the effects his suffering had on him. He'd also told her about his plan to die with her.

His revelation rattled her; they'd both come so close to death, but she understood his decision. She would have made the same one if their roles were reversed. A vampire couldn't live without their mate.

She was glad he hadn't gone the other way and started killing again. Without being told, she knew this man still doubted the goodness of his heart, but she never would.

He'd given everything to save her, and while he couldn't say it, those actions showed her, more than three little words ever could, how much he loved her.

And she was content with that knowledge as she rested her hand on his stomach. Over the past two days, since she first woke, he'd regained much of the weight he had lost and shaved his beard, but his eyes remained haunted.

Her near death had rattled him, and it would take time for him to recover, but he was getting there. And so was she. She'd spent most of this day awake, and while she was still tired and healing, she felt a lot better.

Which meant it was time to get back to reality.

CHAPTER SIXTY-SIX

"Have you talked to Brie lately?" she asked.

"I called her this morning."

"How is she?"

"Good. Things are quiet there, the injected are adjusting, and she hasn't had any more visions about the world burning."

"Have you?"

"No."

"That's great," Caro murmured. "I bet you received that one so you would reach out to her and start to reconnect."

"Maybe."

She lifted her head to meet his eyes. "Really? Do you think it could have been that? I expected you to argue with me."

He smiled as he ran his fingers through her hair. "I'm sure I'll argue with you about *many* things in the future, but I'll agree with this one."

"Oh, I'm sure we'll argue plenty in the future too."

He kissed her nose. Caro waited for something more, but it didn't come. He'd treated her like she was breakable since she woke and did little more than give her quick pecks.

She understood why, but her ribs had healed, her heart had

stopped stuttering when it beat, and she could breathe without experiencing stabbing pains. The broken bone in her leg had fused back together, as had the one in her arm.

And she wanted more than a small kiss. She *needed* to reestablish the bond they'd lost.

She didn't think she'd been officially *dead*; it would have been impossible to bring her back from that, wouldn't it? She frowned as she pondered this, but it would have to be impossible.

No one rose from the dead.

But there was that time in her memory when there was nothing. Just absolutely *nothing*.

She remembered digging through the rocks before they collapsed on her and then biting him in the SUV. There was nothing in between.

And after biting him, her memories were foggy as she drifted in and out while her body healed from the vast damage it sustained. But even then, she'd floated in and out of some awareness and known she was alive. After that cave-in, there was *nothing*.

She shuddered at the memory. *You lost a lot of blood and were flattened; of course you don't remember anything.*

Still, that complete unknowing scared her. She didn't like thinking about it. And she *really* disliked that she'd been so far gone from life it severed their bond; she missed their connection.

Caro ran her fingers up his chest and across his shirt; her skin prickled as it craved his touch, kiss, and the way he felt inside her while they fed from each other. Leaning closer, she breathed in his peppermint scent as she pressed her lips to his throat.

His hands tightened on her, and he shifted away. "You have to heal."

"I am healed," she murmured while kissing him again.

He remained rigid against her, but not for long, as she sensed the desire vibrating through him. She leisurely pushed apart the buttons of his shirt until her hand rested against the warm skin of his chest.

When it did, tears pricked her eyes. If it weren't for him, his determination, and willingness to push his body beyond the blood loss it shouldn't have been able to sustain, she wouldn't be feeling the warmth of his skin.

And she couldn't stop touching him. When she kissed his neck, his pulse raced against her lips.

Her fangs tingled, but she resisted biting into him; she would feed on him when he was inside her. Turning in the chair, the blanket fell away from her shoulders a little, but the fire his kiss created as it sparked through her cells and brought her nerve endings to life didn't allow the cold to creep in.

Saber's fingers dug into the ends of the Adirondack chair. Wood bit into his flesh, but he didn't let the arms go. If he did, he couldn't stop this because the second he touched her, his fight to keep himself restrained would end.

He couldn't take her now, not when she'd been so close to death's door. She was feeling better, but she wasn't ready for this.

"Caro," he bit out from between his teeth.

"I feel better, and I'm alive; I'm going to celebrate that, and us, and renew our bond. I miss fucking you."

He was the snake, lost to the charmer's spell, and she was the one playing the punji. She knew it too, as her fingers slid over his skin and she nibbled his bottom lip.

That she held so much power over him should infuriate him. There was a time in his life when this knowledge, combined with the loss of control she so easily evoked, would have sent him into a frenzy.

But instead of being infuriated or lashing out to drive her away, he relaxed as she pushed his shirt further open. When their eyes met, love filled her striking, turquoise depths.

Who was he kidding by trying to fight this? He could never deny her anything she needed.

Placing his palm against her cheek, he cupped it as he relished her warmth before running his fingers through her silken hair. He pulled her closer to claim her mouth. Her fingers curled into his shirt while their tongues entwined.

Caro was eager to be with him again. She sensed his need too, but she lost herself in his kiss as her arms slid around his neck and they simply enjoyed the taste of each other.

It had been so long since they shared this, that she'd forgotten how it felt when his touch and kiss awakened *every* part of her. How it felt to have his muscles bunching and flexing around her while he stroked her.

When she shifted in the chair, her legs fell between the armholes as she straddled him. His cock rubbing against her intensified her hunger for him; she ached so badly that it was borderline painful. He was hard and thick beneath her, and his jeans had to be uncomfortable, but he didn't protest as she slowly rode him.

Her hands slid down his chest to the button of his jeans, and he breathed a sigh of relief when she released his dick. When he carried her out here to enjoy the sunset, in nothing more than a T-shirt and blanket, he had no intention of this happening. Now he was grateful for it as his shaft rubbed against her entrance, spreading her wetness further.

Shifting a little, Caro drew him inside her as she lifted her hips and slid over him. She moaned as she stretched to fit him.

Once he was nestled deep within her, she broke the kiss to look at him again. Though he hadn't rushed anything and was letting her lead, his red eyes told her he was close to the edge. He never would have asked her for this, but he desperately needed it too.

Smiling, she leaned forward and kissed him again as she rose before sliding down his rigid length. When her mouth traveled to his throat, his hands clenched on her ass as her fangs sank into him.

"Fuck me," he groaned.

Caro stopped feeding on him to reply with a chuckle, "That's what I'm doing."

Saber laughed as his mouth fell to her throat, and he inhaled her beautiful, enticing scent. Her salty air and ocean aroma grew stronger with every rise and fall of her hips.

Unable to resist any longer, he bit down and moaned when her blood rushed into his mouth. She tasted different, but nearly every drop of her blood had been replaced by his and blood bags. Over time, she'd turn it into her own again.

Their minds mingled while their blood and bodies became one, and the mate bond surged between them. Being with her was always a wonder, but after nearly losing her, this joining was more profound and better than ever.

When she came with a muffled cry against his neck, he bit down harder. This time, he didn't pull out as he followed her over the edge.

CHAPTER SIXTY-SEVEN

THE MOON and stars were out, but Caro hadn't moved from his lap as she remained straddling him with her head on his chest. Saber ran his hand up and down her back while savoring the feel of her. His chest swelled with emotion.

I love you formed on the tip of his tongue and lodged in his throat. He tried to say the words, she should hear them, and it was how he felt, but he couldn't get them out.

When she lifted her head and smiled at him, his breath failed as his heart skipped a beat. She was more beautiful than any woman he'd ever seen before, and she was *his*.

How could he go into battle against a demon and still not be able to tell her how he felt? She'd almost died without hearing those words; he'd longed to get the chance to say them to her while he'd desperately willed her back to life.

And now, she was here, smiling at him, and the words were failing him again. He would *not* be a coward; he *would* tell her how he felt.

"I love you," he managed to get out in a voice choked with emotion.

Her radiant smile caused joy to thrum through him. His

hands constricted on her as love swelled in his chest and her eyes danced in the moonlight.

"I know," she said.

He hadn't expected that response. "You do?"

Caro laughed as she rested her palms against his bewildered face. At one time, he'd deeply loved his family, but that was many centuries ago, and now the emotion was more of a mystery than a necessity to him. It was there though; she didn't doubt it.

"Even if you can't say the words, or have trouble with them, your actions show your love." Then she reconsidered her response. "Maybe not *all* your actions; you're often a stubborn, thickheaded, alpha a-hole of a man, but much of what you do reveals your love.

"The way you look at and touch me tells me more than your words how much you love me. But how you fought to bring me back, refused to give up on me, and damn near ruined yourself to save me tells me exactly how you feel about me."

She placed a hand over his heart. "I don't need the words because I *know* what you feel."

At first, he was too stunned to respond as he sat and studied her face. This woman would never cease to amaze him.

"You may not *need* the words," he said, "but you want them."

She lifted a shoulder in a small shrug. "I want *you*, not words. And I have you."

"Yes, you do. Forever."

"I know."

He chuckled as he rested his forehead against hers, closed his eyes, and inhaled their scents as they mingled in the air. Their aromas were as joined as the two of them.

"It's going to take a while, but I'm going to give you those words every day," he vowed.

She kissed his nose and each of his cheeks before finding his mouth again. "And no matter how long it takes, I'll be here to hear them and tell you how much I love you."

His arms tightened around her. "Say it again."

His need radiated in those three words. Love had become foreign to him, but it was still something he craved.

And she would give it to him for eternity. And one day, he would realize how deserving of it he was.

"I love you," she whispered, "but I'm probably going to want to kill you sometimes."

"Right back at you, dear."

When she kissed him again, they forgot about words and lost themselves to each other once more.

CHAPTER SIXTY-EIGHT

A WEEK LATER, Saber opened the door of Caro's car and stepped back to let her exit the passenger side. She was back to full strength and her stubborn old self, but he still liked helping her as much as possible.

Plus, he was a gentleman… sometimes.

When Caro exited the car, they both turned to face the prison that was once a school. The Alliance had transformed it into their base of operations and makeshift home.

Brie and Asher exited the front door of the building and stopped a few feet away from it. A small, hopeful smile tugged at the corners of Brie's mouth. Saber smiled in return and, taking Caro's hand, led her to their family.

When he reached Brie, he hesitated before draping his arm around her shoulder, giving her a quick hug, and releasing her. Over time, he would get better at this too, but his sister had to know he cared about her and was trying.

If he lost her again, he'd deal with the sorrow that would accompany it, and not by becoming a Savage. But regret wouldn't cloud his life should he lose her again. He wouldn't spend an eternity questioning why he was so cold to her.

Instead, he would spend an eternity with fond memories of their time together. He'd survived unimaginable loss before and would again, but he would love until that time came, and he would continue to love after it passed.

Brie covered her astonishment over his brief hug, but happiness and disbelief filled her eyes when she grinned at him. She slid an arm around his waist to hug him back.

Then she turned to Caro and clasped both her hands. "I'm so glad you're okay."

"Thank you," Caro said. "Me too."

Brie kept her hands as her attention shifted back to Saber. "Since you're finally here, I should tell you what I suspect."

Her strange statement surprised Saber. "What you suspect?"

"Yes. I used to wonder about it when we were children and you had Milo, but after witnessing what happened with Caro, I think I'm right."

"About what?" Caro asked.

"I believe Saber has the ability to heal. How strong that ability is, I don't know, but no matter how well you took care of him, there was no reason Milo should have survived after you found him.

"He didn't have his mother's milk. Even now, with everything we know about animals and all the developments in technology, it would be rare for a mouse so young to survive, but somehow, *you* kept him alive on nothing but goat's milk and love.

"Maybe I'm wrong, maybe those things were more than enough to save him, but he wasn't the only one. You brought home dozens of other injured animals, nursed them back to health, and set them free again.

"When they first arrived, I believed many of them were beyond saving, but you fixed their broken legs, tended their wounds, and nourished them until they could go free again. I don't recall you ever losing a single one of them."

"I didn't," Saber said with pride.

Brie raised her eyebrows and gave him a pointed look as she continued. "And somehow, you brought Caro back too."

Saber looked from his sister to Caro and back again. "Ronan told me he'd seen vampires like her before; they went into an almost hibernation-like state when they lost too much blood and didn't wake again until they had enough to nourish them. I'm sure that's all it was with Caro, and Milo and those other animals were pure luck."

"You took good care of them," Caro said. "That's not just *luck*."

"No, it's not," Brie agreed. "I could be wrong, but maybe I'm right. And it might help explain why we shared that vision."

Saber frowned. "How is that?"

"It would make sense if people with gifts could somehow connect, especially if they're siblings."

"Nathan and Kadence do it," Asher said. "He can slow her visions down so she can see them better, and he sees them too."

Brie's mouth parted before she started grinning. "See! Then it really could explain why you shared my vision!"

Saber wasn't completely willing to buy into this, but she did have some good points. "Maybe."

"No matter what, time will tell. As the days pass, you'll have more chances to see if you have an ability because I doubt you tried to heal many animals, vamps, or people while you were a Savage."

Saber issued a small snort of laughter. "The idea of helping anyone, or anything, was the last thing on my mind. Most of those I encountered, I killed."

He heard the familiar defensiveness in his voice and tried to curb it, but he was once a monster, and if they were going to love him, they had to understand that.

"I figured that," Brie said. "But like I said, I think you may have the ability to heal. Maybe one day we'll learn I'm wrong, or maybe we'll learn I'm right. There's no harm in finding out; only good can come from it."

"You never liked admitting when you were wrong."

"She still doesn't," Asher muttered, and Brie playfully slapped his chest.

"Neither did you," Brie said to Saber.

"That's because I was never wrong."

Brie rolled her eyes, and Caro laughed. Saber draped his arm around his sister's shoulders again and turned her toward the building. They'd talked briefly while he was with Caro, but he still had questions.

"Have *all* of the injected returned to normal?" He knew the ones here had, but he didn't know about any others. "Even those in Arizona?"

"Yes," Asher answered. "*All* of them are doing well."

"I guess that means the demons are all dead," Brie said hopefully.

"Maybe," Saber hedged. "But maybe not. I'm sure there are still more in Hell, but I doubt any remain on Earth. I'm pretty sure they all showed up to that fight. But even if they didn't, we still have the swords and decimated their numbers. They'll die if they're stupid enough to try rising against us again."

Caro shuddered at the idea of going up against those hideous things once more, but she'd do whatever was necessary to keep them from destroying the earth.

"Things have been quiet since their defeat," Asher said.

But as the words left his mouth, Ronan, Declan, and Killean strode out the door, armed for battle. Willow, Kadence, and Simone strolled out behind them.

"What's going on?" Saber asked as they stopped walking.

"It sounds like there's been a Savage attack by the waterfront in Boston; we're going to check it out," Ronan said.

"I'll come with you."

"No," Ronan clasped Saber's shoulder. "Stay here and get settled in with your mate."

"Are you sure?"

"Yes. It doesn't sound too bad; if what we've heard turns out to be wrong, we'll call for backup. Besides, we have to finish with the tunnels tomorrow, so get settled in now."

They already had everything mapped out in the tunnels, got cameras they could set up afterward to constantly monitor what would remain of the tunnels, and had gathered the explosives for him.

Tomorrow, they would all head back to Hell, but he'd be happy if he didn't have to leave Caro today. "Okay."

Ronan squeezed his shoulder before releasing it. "It's good to have you back."

"It's good to be back."

And he meant it; returning here was like coming home. He'd always kept the Alliance at a distance, but he belonged here. They'd united against a common enemy and accepted him though he'd tried to keep them at arm's length.

He didn't know when that happened, probably years before he acknowledged it, but they considered him one of them... and he was. He'd sensed their sadness when they believed Caro was dead.

They'd mourned her loss and their perceived loss of him. They were his friends, and somewhere along the way, they became his family too.

But they'd accepted him years ago; he'd just been too closed off to realize it. After everything he'd done, he probably didn't deserve any of this, but he intended to enjoy it. This was his life now, his family, and he'd been granted the miracles of Caro and Brie; he wouldn't waste those miracles.

When Ronan and the others strode away, the four of them walked into the prison to discover Nathan, Logan, and Saxon sitting by the video monitors. The trio waved and smiled before rising and striding over to greet them.

They took turns clasping Saber on his shoulder as they welcomed him back. They greeted Caro with the same warmth and informed her they'd done their best to establish a forge outside, behind the prison, but said it wasn't as nice as hers.

As Caro beamed at them, her happiness came across through their bond. Unlike him, she'd lost *all* her family, but she would find a new one here, amongst friends, as they welcomed her into their lives.

"I'm sure it's great," she told them.

Elena, Callie, and Elyse emerged from one of the hallways; they broke into bright smiles as they hurried over to join them.

"We just finished setting up your room with Vicky," Callie said. "Considering this place was once a school, the walls are concrete, and the rooms don't scream cozy, but we did our best to make it more inviting."

"Thank you," Caro said. "I'm sure we'll love it."

She and Saber had discussed their future before coming here. She was going to keep her family's property, but they'd agreed it was best if, for now, they spent most of their time with the Alliance.

The demons seemed to be gone, but the Savages remained, and the demons had created a fair amount of damage they needed to handle. Once they believed everything was as controlled as possible, they would decide what to do afterward.

He'd promised to take her home at least once a month to visit, and she was happy with that. He hoped to get her home more, but it could be a few months or more before they got away that often.

"We're working on finding another place to build a new compound," Nathan said. "It's going to take some time to find the land we require to rebuild, but we'll eventually have homes, animals, and a place where our children can play freely again."

As if she'd been listening, Vicky emerged from one of the hallways with her and Nathan's son, Wyatt. After the Savages and demons destroyed the compound, Wyatt lived with Vicky's parents while they faced the demons, but now he was home.

Saber was sure most of the other children had returned too; he looked forward to seeing them. No matter how lost in bloodlust and indifference he became, he'd never stopped loving children's laughter.

Vicky smiled and waved to them as she strolled over to stand beside Nathan. Their hands entwined as Wyatt wrapped his arms around his dad's legs.

"Do you want to see the forge or your room first?" Saxon inquired.

"The forge," Caro said as she excitedly rubbed her hands together.

EPILOGUE

SABER CRADLED his infant daughter in his arms while he pushed the rocking chair leisurely back and forth. His tiny bundle of joy slept peacefully with the little fingers of one hand curled around the edge of her blanket. The ones on her other hand clutched his index finger.

Her black lashes shadowed her pink face and hid the turquoise eyes that matched her mother's. She was the most perfect creation he'd ever seen, and his heart was near bursting with the love filling it.

Behind him, Caro slept peacefully while he watched the night beyond the glass doors of her apartment. He'd promised to bring her back here every month, but it had been months since they last returned to her home.

Life, and Savages, had made it more difficult to find a way of escaping the duties binding him. The Savages had proven to be angrier and more united than they expected, but the Alliance was carving up their forces, and things had calmed over the past month.

Things still were far from perfect, but Caro wanted to come home for the birth of their child, and he wouldn't deny her that.

So, two weeks ago, they packed some of their things, and with Brie and Asher, they returned to the property.

A week later, their daughter, Mary Rose Amaral, who shared a name with Caro's mom and had his last name, was born. He'd never thought he'd reclaim his last name or that part of his history, but his parents' legacy should continue, and he couldn't think of anyone more wonderful to carry it on than the precious child in his arms.

He'd reclaimed that part of himself too. He would never again be Gabriel, too much time and shit had happened from then until now for that to occur, but he wouldn't completely shun who he once was anymore.

Saber stroked Mary Rose's cheek as he smiled at the precious life in his arms. He would one day tell her about the choices he made; he wouldn't burden her with them, but he'd never hide them from her, and she should know the perils of life.

For now, he would bask in the miracle of her, and he did it as often as possible. Saber could barely stand to have his daughter out of his arms.

He knew the cruelties of this world too well and had delivered many of them himself. Some nights, he worried his payback for all the death he'd caused would be the loss of his daughter and Caro, but he tried not to dwell on it.

He'd never let them out of his sight if he did, which wasn't a way for any of them to live. But for now, while Mary Rose was still so little, he could shelter her from the brutality lurking beyond these doors.

One day, she would venture out into the world, but that was many years away, and by then, he would have taught her a hundred ways to kill a Savage. She'd know how to protect herself.

As he rocked, he studied the night while humming softly. He'd never believed himself capable of loving anyone again until Caro entered his life.

Then he'd been sure he could *never* love anything as much as her. He was proven wrong again as he swore his heart grew larger the second he set eyes on his child.

When he lifted his head from her perfect face, he studied the forest. Over the past year, he and Caro had worked to remove all the traps they'd set in the woods. They'd cleared them all and filled the holes so the woods would be safe for his children to play in.

They'd also caved in the tunnels the demons had carved near the still-closed doorway to Hell. They'd set up cameras and security systems that they relentlessly monitored.

So far, nothing had stirred, and there were no signs of the demons anywhere. That could all change, but things were calmer than they'd been in years, and he was enjoying it.

Saber blinked as the world changed and blurred before him. His breath caught when the trees, as if years had passed, grew taller and swelled around the trunks. The birds sang, and laughter reverberated across a land that was noiseless only a second ago.

He didn't know how, but he was certain that laughter came from all around the world as it reverberated around him. The sun shone so bright, he could feel its warmth though the sky was dark only a second ago.

And then, like the fire he once saw destroying the world from these doors, the laughter and sun vanished. He was back to staring at the night as the birds stopped singing and the laughter died away. The trees returned to their normal size.

He had no idea what to make of any of it, but it left him with a feeling of peace and a certainty his daughter would grow up in a better world than the fiery one once revealed to him through these doors.

Beside him, his phone vibrated. He lifted it to read Brie's message. *Did you see that?*

Shifting his hold on Mary Rose, he typed out, *I did.*

Do you know what it meant?

He almost said no but decided against it. This vision was as unexpected as the last, and he now understood why he was granted them.

I do.

There were still Savages to battle, and as long as vamps existed, there always would be, but he'd glimpsed a different future than the last one he saw. That future filled with fire was the one ruled by demons and Savages; this future, the one *they* had created, was full of love and laughter.

He'd been granted these visions because of his connection to Brie. This one had assured him the world would go on and his daughter would have the chance to become a beautiful, smart, strong, vibrant woman... like her mom.

With Caro at his side, they would watch their sacrifices come to fruition in a better future. By joining against the demons, they helped change the world.

His phone vibrated again, and he lifted it to read Brie's message. *Good.*

He stared at the screen before typing, *Get some rest. I love you.*

It was still difficult for him to say those words. He had yet to speak them to her, but he'd sent her this message, and it was something.

I love you too, she replied. *I always have and always will. Kiss my beautiful niece for me.*

Saber set down his phone and shifted his attention back to his daughter's perfect face. He gently poked her tiny nose as he breathed in her fresh, baby scent.

"I love you," he whispered.

She didn't react to his words, but he would make sure they never came as a surprise to her. She would hear them from him every day for the rest of his life.

Rising, he returned to the bed and settled her into her

bassinet before lying beside Caro. He drew his mate into his arms and kissed her cheek.

Her labor hadn't been easy; she'd lost more blood than he would have liked, but she'd healed fast, and he'd helped with that. He couldn't heal wounds with a touch, but over the past year, he'd learned Brie wasn't wrong.

It turned out he *did* have a knack for making things heal faster and saving creatures that most couldn't. Like the dove with a broken wing he'd nursed back to health or the snake brutalized by a cat.

He wasn't some miracle worker, but he had some healing ability. Then again, maybe he had performed one miracle as Caro remained with him when he'd been certain she was gone.

Her eyes opened a little. "Hey," she murmured.

He kissed her forehead, nose, and lips before whispering against them, "I love you."

The words still didn't come as easily as he would have liked and sometimes lodged in his throat, but he said them as often as he could. And not a day passed when she didn't tell him how she felt.

Caro smiled as her eyes closed again. "I know."

Saber's attention shifted back to the glass doors. Contentment filled him as he recalled the laughter surrounding him. He was excited to tell Caro about it, but that could wait until tomorrow; she needed to rest now.

Their life would never be free of brutality and death, there would always be Savages to hunt, but it would be a life full of love, laughter, and joy; he would make sure of it.

Saber smiled as he embraced his mate. Feeling blessed, he drifted to sleep, secure in the knowledge they would always be bound by the love they shared. And that love would only grow with their expanding family.

Read on for a note from the author and an excerpt from *Shadows of Fire*. **The first book in the exciting new series by Brenda K. Davies.**

Or download and start reading now:
brendakdavies.com/SFwb

Stay in touch on updates, sales, and new releases by joining to the mailing list: brendakdavies.com/ESBKDNews

Visit the Brenda K. Davies Book Club on Facebook for exclusive giveaways and all things book related. Come join the fun: brendakdavies.com/ESBKDBookClub

AUTHOR'S NOTE

I'm both happy and sad that Bound by Love is the last book in the Alliance Series. I'm happy because I believe it was an exciting, and fitting conclusion to all their stories, but as much as it was time to say goodbye to everyone, it was also incredibly difficult to do so.

Between the Awakenings and Alliance series, I have been writing in this world since I was nineteen years old. Even when I said goodbye to the Awakenings series, I still had the Alliance, and a connection to the old characters, who could drop by for visits.

That's gone now. More than half my life has been spent involved with this world, the characters, and their stories. It was so incredibly hard to say goodbye to them, but it was time.

I hope you all loved reading Bound by Love, and saying goodbye to this world, as much as I loved writing all the books in these two series.

Thank you so much for all your love for these characters and your continued support. Without you, their stories might never have been told.

I will continue to write more stories that I hope you will all enjoy just as much. You can read on for an excerpt from my newest series, *The Shadow Realms*.

Much love to you all.

Turn the page to see a sneak peek for *Shadows of Fire*.

SNEAK PEEK

SHADOWS OF FIRE, THE SHADOW REALMS BOOK 1

Elexiandra tried not to crumple the invitation the crow had delivered as she read it, but her blood pressure rose until it pounded in her ears. The neat, embossed gold lettering was far too cheerful for the words written on the thick parchment.

She'd bet a lot of these invites had gone out through the mortal and Shadow Realms, and that at least a thousand immortals would accept and attend. She didn't reside in the Shadow Realms, but—much to her dismay—King Tove of the dark fae must have decided to include at least some of the immortals who lived in the human realm on his invitation list.

"What is it, Lexi?" Sahira asked as she appeared at Lexi's side.

If Lexi showed her, Sahira would make her go. Her aunt would prattle on about proper etiquette and how exciting it was for them to get the chance to visit the Gloaming, the dark fae realm. But even if Sahira didn't force her to attend, Lexi had no idea how to get out of this.

How did she say no to the king of the dark fae?

She didn't, that was how. But why did he invite *her?*

Sure, her father was a general on the winning side of the war, but he perished in that war, and she was a half vamp, half human who had never entered a Shadow Realm before. The only things separating her from mortals were that she drank blood, as well as ate food, and she was an immortal.

She had no special abilities, no powers, and though she was stronger than a human, she wasn't as strong as a full-blooded vampire. She was a nobody holding an invitation from one of the most powerful immortals in all the realms. And she would prefer to throw it away.

Lifting her head, Lexi pushed back a loose strand of auburn hair as she studied the large manor only fifty feet away from her. At one time, the thirty-room, gray stone building was beautiful and in pristine condition.

Then her father entered the war on the side of the "let's make our existence known to the humans" faction and everything changed.

But then, her father never really had a choice. It was either fight or die, and at least he chose the winning side, even if it wasn't necessarily the right one, but she would *never* voice that opinion out loud.

If he'd chosen the losing side, then the Lord would have most likely taken the manor from them or destroyed it, and she and Sahira would be on the run like all the other rebels.

She was still staring at her home when Sahira snatched the invitation from her hand.

"It's an invitation to a ball!" Sahira gushed.

Lexi winced and braced herself for what was to come. She didn't want to attend some fancy ball, but the sparkle in Sahira's eyes said her aunt was already planning what they would wear.

The invitation specified attending in their finest attire, which meant ball gowns. That was all well and good, but she didn't own anything fancy, and she wasn't in the mood to go shopping.

"It's to celebrate the end of the war," Sahira said, "and the king of the dark fae's sons for helping the Lord win."

Some of Sahira's enthusiasm vanished as she spoke. She may love the idea of a ball and fancy gowns, but they'd both lost a lot during the war and didn't have anything to celebrate.

She'd lost her dad, and Sahira lost her half brother. They'd lost the luxurious life they once lived and most of the humans who once lived at or worked the manor grounds.

But they weren't the only ones who lost a lot. The human realm lost its innocence about the existence of immortals as well as countless lives. Every day, they continued to lose more.

And the dark fae king planned to celebrate those losses. Lexi found this a little strange considering he'd lost more than half his sons in the war.

She bit her tongue as she lifted her head to gaze into the crow's black eyes. When it tilted its head, the sun created a rainbow hue of colors throughout its feathers. The crow was the dark fae's messenger, and it was waiting for her response.

She didn't know what to say. The idea of going to the Gloaming was tempting, she'd love to see how the dark fae lived, but she still didn't understand why *she* was holding this invite.

She'd never met a member of the royal dark fae before. She knew Colburn—or Cole as he was more commonly known—and Brokk were the only sons the king had left on his side. Out of his nine sons, five died in the war, and the other two survivors fought for the rebels.

Like everyone who chose the losing side, they were stripped of their titles, land, and money. They were being hunted throughout the realms.

Many of the rebels ended up in the mortal realm where there was less magic and they were harder to track. Many others hopped through the Shadow Realms to avoid capture and death.

"We need gowns," Sahira continued, and Lexi closed her eyes. "We'll have to go to the marketplace to purchase them. It will be fun."

The two of them had drastically different ideas of fun, but at four hundred and fifty-three years old, Sahira was four hundred and twenty-nine years older than her. Her aunt had grown up and lived through far different times.

Sahira once attended balls held by kings and czars in the human realm while Lexi grew up in jeans and T-shirts. Sahira would sometimes talk about the old days with wistful sadness while Lexi's old days were bowls of cereal in front of her favorite cartoons.

She often missed those days. They were much simpler, and her father was still alive.

This invitation was making Sahira's year and ruining Lexi's day. She dreaded everything about it, but she knew what she had to do.

Opening her eyes, Lexi used her finger to check the yes box for her and Sahira. Created by fae magic, a gold mark materialized on the invite. She lifted the invite into the air, and the crow swooped down to take it from her.

It clasped the invite in its talons, released a loud caw, and soared back toward the clear blue sky before vanishing.

With a sigh, Lexi looked beyond the manor to the smoke in the distance. She couldn't see the ruined remains of the city a hundred miles away, but every day she saw the smoke rising from it.

A week ago, she dared to travel close enough to investigate the devastation the dragons unleashed on the city, but she was still a few miles away when the roar of a dragon caused her to retreat.

She preferred to stay as far from those beasts as possible.

The humans who survived the massacre continued to filter out of the city every day. She'd heard from some that others were choosing to stay behind to rebuild.

Every day, she watched as broken, ragtag groups of survivors fled the city in search of something more, but there wasn't much left out there. Each morning, she walked out to the road to give those survivors food. Some stopped to talk, but most would simply look at her with haunted eyes before taking their bread and walking away.

The dragons unleashed a fair amount of destruction on the world, but most of their larger fires had been extinguished. Some smaller ones still popped up. Lexi had no idea what started them, and she wasn't going into the city to find out, but their smoke filled the sky, and sometimes they burned for days.

The war ended a month ago. It was too soon to accomplish much rebuilding and far too soon to celebrate the destruction unleashed on so many.

Hell, she didn't think what happened to Earth should *ever* be celebrated, but she was sure many other immortals would disagree... including the king of the dark fae.

Time was moving on, and the war was over. The immortals of the Shadow Realms wanted to continue with their lives. It didn't matter that many in the mortal realm still suffered.

The winning side had gotten their way; immortals didn't have to hide from humans anymore. The mortals were aware of their existence now, and that knowledge had ruined their lives.

Despite all that, a small tingle of excitement sparked in her belly. She would soon enter a Shadow Realm for the first time; vampires usually weren't welcome there, not even half vamps.

And while there was a chance she and Sahira might get killed if they tried to cross into the Gloaming, she was excited to see what lay beyond the human realm.

~

TWILIGHT WAS SETTLING across the land as Lexi and Sahira stood before the growing shadows spreading throughout the forest across from them. It had taken them an hour to reach the designated entrance to the Gloaming, and Lexi clutched the invitation that would grant them passage like it was a life preserver in a storm-tossed sea.

Around her, half a dozen other immortals talked excitedly about what was to come, but Lexi couldn't join in their enthusiasm. She was too nervous.

It had been a week since the invitation arrived. In that time, Sahira had managed to barter enough of her potions in the marketplace near their home to purchase two gowns for them.

Her aunt then spent the next couple of days getting those dresses to fit properly and adding special touches to them. They were some of the most beautiful creations Lexi had ever seen, but the exquisite gown only made Lexi feel more out of place. She'd never worn anything like it before.

The other immortals and her aunt were all at ease in their fancy clothes while she felt like an imposter. They were also all excited about traveling to the Gloaming, and she couldn't help wondering if she would be allowed to make the journey.

Maybe the invite was sent to them by accident. Her dad did fight for the Lord, but she and Sahira were both half vampire, and vampires weren't exactly welcome in the Shadow Realms. Neither were humans.

When the time came, would they try to enter the Gloaming only to be bounced back or, worse, destroyed?

She tugged at the collar of her dress as the possibility caused a sheen of sweat to dampen her skin.

Trying to distract herself from the risk of impending death, Lexi studied the two dark fae standing at the edge of the woods. They wore only loose-fitting brown pants; their chests and feet were bare. Like all purebred dark fae, they had black hair, black eyes, pointed ears, and lithe builds.

The shadows swallowed them until they flickered in and out of the spreading darkness created by the setting sun. However, the dark fae were known to be a part of the shadows.

From her distance of ten feet, she sensed their power, yet

their ciphers didn't go past the middle of their biceps. She'd only encountered a couple of dark fae before, but she knew those black markings indicated the amount of power they possessed.

They said the dark fae king and his sons possessed ciphers that extended to their wrists. The oldest supposedly had ciphers to the tips of his fingers, like the king.

Unable to stop herself, Lexi tugged at the collar of her gown again as the sun vanished. There was a moment when the entire world held its breath as the last of the sun's rays stretched across the sky. Then the shimmering, deep purple entrance to the Gloaming came into view.

Sahira clasped Lexi's arm and practically jumped up and down in excitement. Lexi tried not to gawk as the doorway shifted from deep purple to black and back again. The dark fae standing beside it stepped away from the trees and waved their arms toward the portal.

Lexi gulped and grasped Sahira's hand on her arm. Her aunt was stunning in her maroon gown. Twisted into an elaborate coil, her mahogany hair hung against her nape, and black eyeliner emphasized the striking color of her amber eyes.

Most days, Sahira wore jeans and T-shirts like her. She kept her hair in a bun and eschewed makeup until she looked more like a librarian than the half witch, half vampire she was. Now, she'd embraced the roll of ball attendee.

"It's okay," Sahira whispered.

"What if the portal doesn't let us enter? Vampires were banished to the mortal realm centuries ago."

"It will let us enter, and if it doesn't, then I'll be stuck here with you, but we're invited."

"That might have been a mistake."

"It wasn't."

"Vampires aren't welcome in the Shadow Realms."

"We have an invite, and vampires aren't welcome to *stay*.

They can travel through with permission, which we have. Come on, everything is going to be fine."

Lexi wanted to believe her, but her feet remained planted firmly in place.

Sahira tugged at her arm. "Lexi, move!"

Lexi gulped and shuffled forward until she stood at the edge of the portal. Gathering her courage, she closed her eyes and stepped forward. She fully expected to be knocked back on her ass or cut in two, but her feet continued onward.

Her eyes flew open, and she discovered herself surrounded by the dark walls of the portal as she moved toward the Gloaming.

∽

Continue reading *Shadows of Fire now*:
brendakdavies.com/SFwb

FIND THE AUTHOR

Erica Stevens/Brenda K. Davies Mailing List: brendakdavies.com/ESBKDNews

Facebook: brendakdavies.com/BKDfb

Erica Stevens/Brenda K. Davies Book Club: brendakdavies.com/ESBKDBookClub

Instagram: brendakdavies.com/BKDInsta
Twitter: brendakdavies.com/BKDTweet
Website: www.brendakdavies.com

ALSO FROM THE AUTHOR

**Books written under the pen name
Brenda K. Davies**

The Vampire Awakenings Series

Awakened (Book 1)

Destined (Book 2)

Untamed (Book 3)

Enraptured (Book 4)

Undone (Book 5)

Fractured (Book 6)

Ravaged (Book 7)

Consumed (Book 8)

Unforeseen (Book 9)

Forsaken (Book 10)

Relentless (Book 11)

Legacy (Book 12)

The Alliance Series

Eternally Bound (Book 1)

Bound by Vengeance (Book 2)

Bound by Darkness (Book 3)

Bound by Passion (Book 4)

Bound by Torment (Book 5)

Bound by Danger (Book 6)

Bound by Deception (Book 7)

Bound by Fate (Book 8)

Bound by Blood (Book 9)

Bound by Love (Book 10)

The Road to Hell Series

Good Intentions (Book 1)

Carved (Book 2)

The Road (Book 3)

Into Hell (Book 4)

Hell on Earth Series

Hell on Earth (Book 1)

Into the Abyss (Book 2)

Kiss of Death (Book 3)

Edge of the Darkness (Book 4)

The Shadow Realms

Shadows of Fire (Book 1)

Shadows of Discovery (Book 2)

Shadows of Betrayal (Book 3)

Shadows of Fury (Book 4)

Shadows of Destiny (Book 5)

Shadows of Light (Book 6)

Wicked Curses (Book 7)

Coming Spring 2023

Sinful Curses (Book 8)

Coming 2023

Historical Romance
A Stolen Heart

Books written under the pen name Erica Stevens

The Coven Series
Nightmares (Book 1)

The Maze (Book 2)

Dream Walker (Book 3)

The Captive Series
Captured (Book 1)

Renegade (Book 2)

Refugee (Book 3)

Salvation (Book 4)

Redemption (Book 5)

Broken (The Captive Series Prequel)

Vengeance (Book 6)

Unbound (Book 7)

The Kindred Series
Kindred (Book 1)

Ashes (Book 2)

Kindled (Book 3)

Inferno (Book 4)

Phoenix Rising (Book 5)

The Fire & Ice Series

Frost Burn (Book 1)

Arctic Fire (Book 2)

Scorched Ice (Book 3)

The Ravening Series

The Ravening (Book 1)

Taken Over (Book 2)

Reclamation (Book 3)

The Survivor Chronicles

The Upheaval (Book 1)

The Divide (Book 2)

The Forsaken (Book 3)

The Risen (Book 4)

ABOUT THE AUTHOR

Brenda K. Davies is the USA Today Bestselling author of the Vampire Awakening Series, Alliance Series, Road to Hell Series, Hell on Earth Series, Shadow Realms Series, and historical romantic fiction. She also writes under the pen name, Erica Stevens. When not out with friends and family, she can be found at home with her husband, son, dog, cat, and horse.

Printed in Great Britain
by Amazon